W9-BWF-001

The Crystal Nights

ALSO BY MICHELE MURRAY

Nellie Cameron

THE CRYSTAL NIGHTS

a novel by

Michele Murray

The Seabury Press New York

LIBRARY OF CONGRESS CATALOG CARD NUMBER: 72-93807
ISBN: 0-8164-3098-5

DESIGNED BY JUDITH LERNER
PRINTED IN THE UNITED STATES OF AMERICA

TO

My Mother

My Daughter

Myself when young

PART ONE

The Crystal Nights

1

STANDING ON THE stairs behind the half-open kitchen door, Elly was between two worlds. On the other side was the bright, warm kitchen, filled with the noise of her parents, her grandmother, and her older brother Phil and rich with the smells of the dinner to come. Upstairs her room was bleak and cold in the swiftly-settling November night, but it was hers alone. Only the cold had driven her down from her books and movie magazines and dreams, and she was wild with frustration and the need to be pleasant. "Put a smile on your face, please," was Mama's insistent note.

"Why?" was Elly's.

"Why not?" was Mama's reply. They did not always agree.

She straightened up, pushed open the door, and closed it behind her to keep the crackling cold of the back hall out of the kitchen.

"Why, Greta Garbo, so pleased you could come to dinner in our humble abode," Phil said, grinning.

Elly sat down heavily at the table. "Anything I can do?" she mumbled.

"Not a thing, darling," Baba said. "So sit. Soon we eat."

Mama turned around from the stove, her cheeks glowing red. "Mamushka, Elly doesn't need to be spoiled so much. I thought you were supposed to set the table. Why weren't you down? What's so fascinating in your room that you stay there all day in the cold?"

"The table got set without me, didn't it?" Elly asked roughly. "I was busy."

Phil nudged her. "Guess who did it, though?"

"Wasn't you, that's for certain. So why don't you mind your own business?"

"Hey, what's gotten into you, Elly? You in the running for sourpuss of the year? You and Mussolini?" Phil thrust out his lower jaw and postured.

"Ho, ho, ho, very funny," Elly said. Pop looked at her over the top edge of his newspaper, and then she was ashamed. "It's so dreary here, there's nothing to do, like today. Armistice Day. Who cares? If we lived in town at least . . ."

"So come. Here's the soup ready," Baba said. The smell of cabbage drifted through the kitchen.

"Nothing to do?" Mama said. "Fix your room for a start, maybe, eh? Then you could collect the eggs—once more your Baba brings them in for you—and cookies you could make."

Elly bit back a sharp answer because Mama was already making the sign for prayers. Pop, who said he was "Jewish only because others say so, and then I would never deny," did not believe in anything. Mama and Baba, who were followers of the Gospel as interpreted by Count Leo Tolstoy, believed in a lot of things, beginning with God and including working the land, living simply, and praying. Elly peeked at Phil over her clasped hands, and he raised his eyebrows at her. All was well between them again.

"Creator of the Universe," Mama murmured, "from whom all life comes and to whom all goodness belongs, sanctify this food which belongs to you and those who eat it, who also belong to you and only to you. Amen."

The soup was delicious.

"What time is it?" Pop asked anxiously. "Good! Fifteen minutes until the news comes on." The radio was on a shelf over the table, like a sentinel waiting to be summoned. "Meanwhile, I can tell you that I got today a letter from Anna. She has a passport . . ."

"Praise God!" Mama said.

". . . but for sixty days only," Pop continued, "and now she gets cold feet and thinks of her furniture, her linens." Pop unfolded the letter written on thin, crinkly airmail paper. "She writes this way, a foolish woman. She says maybe they would be in England more comfortable, more civilized."

Mama's mouth was grim. "She is under great stress, of course. Does she say nothing about Michael, about Margot?"

"But imagine!" Elly cried out. "To leave it all behind, your language, your *home!*" Of course, her parents and grandmother had done just that, perhaps they saw it differently, but she shuddered at the possibility.

No one answered her. Pop reread the letter. "Michael has no work now, he goes out for the shopping, Anna is afraid, and Margot, now that she cannot attend school, sits in her room all day."

Baba crossed herself. "This is so terrible, it cannot be. Elly, eat, eat. So thin you are, darling, I don't like to see on a healthy girl."

Elly hooted. "Baba, I'm entirely too fat as it is. Mrs. Wilbur won't let me act in her plays if I don't do something about it. Is Bette Davis fat? Good lord!"

Any other time Baba and Mama together would have answered her, but now they were thinking about the letter. Aunt Anna was Pop's youngest sister, who had stayed in Germany and married a doctor, Uncle Michael, and lived in Berlin with him and their daughter, Margot, who was fifteen, the same age as Elly. Pop had been trying to bring them to America for five years, since Hitler had come to power in 1933, rabid with hatred of the Jews. In the beginning Aunt Anna and Uncle Michael said that was all talk to gain power, Germany couldn't manage without the Jews, and Hitler would change once he was in office. World opinion would force him to recant. And for a while nothing *had* happened. Aunt Anna's letters were as smug as a cream-filled cat. One thing she was certain of—she would not come to America.

Then, with exquisite slowness, their life had changed. Uncle Michael was fired from his hospital job. They were refused a passport to vacation in France. Their German maid was forced to leave them. They were restricted to buying food in certain shops. Margot could not stay at her school. They could not go into the parks or ride the trams. Their new passports were stamped with a large *J* for *Jude;* Margot and Aunt Anna were given the first name of Sarah, as were all Jewish women, and Uncle Michael, the name of Israel, as were all Jewish men. Finally, he was not allowed to treat any patients at all. For the past six months they had been living by selling all the beautiful things Aunt Anna had not wanted to leave and by the fees Uncle Michael was paid by drug addicts for getting them illegal drugs.

Elly had heard this through the years; she knew that Pop had been working and paying to get them out of Germany, but it had seemed remote at first and surely something that could be taken care of. She had been ten when it all started and young enough to believe that adults could make things better the next day. Not all the next days of five years had made this better. Still, what could *she* do? "Oh, to have to leave *everything* behind!" she exclaimed again. That bothered her even more than she understood. Thank goodness it could never happen here!

Mama passed the platter of venison in sour cream. Last week Henry Kocinski and his sons had brought some deer meat to Mama the way they did each autumn. Mama fattened two pigs for the Kocinskis every year and helped them slaughter the plump, squealing animals after the first hard frost; in return, they cleaned out the barn, spreading the manure on the fields, and shared their deer meat. They admired Mama.

"Sonya, my stomach is already touching the table," Pop said, "and my waist has vanished under a mountain of sour cream. Delicious! Mamushka, your pickled tomatoes are the best ever."

"Hold the potatoes," Elly said, and Mama frowned at her.

"Give it here, then," said Phil, digging down into the bowl. He never had enough food. He was not fat, though, but tall, past six feet and towering over the rest of them. "Eat, drink, and be merry, eh? So what are we going to do with this Anna, Pop? Bomb her out? Doesn't she see what's happening, now that Czechoslovakia's gone under? England! They won't do a damn thing to help!" Phil banged his fist on the table.

"Phil, such talking!" Mama said reproachfully. "Calling names does *nothing* to help, believe me."

Elly felt the familiar nausea sweep over her. Must they talk about the same things all the time? Oh, she wished that times were better! If it wasn't the depression, it was the situation in Europe, except in September, when everyone talked of the hurricane and the floods and the tidal wave in Rhode Island. They had been fortunate; only their bottomland by the creek had been flooded, the barn roof had held, and the electricity, run into the valley only last summer, had not gone out. In Providence, hundreds had been killed. Pop's grocery store had missed flooding by inches when the Ibanaki River crested above its high banks.

"God is angry," Baba had said, shaking her head as she read about the damage.

"But not with us," Elly said. "Or at least not *very* angry."

And Mama had told her not to joke about serious matters. Only everything was serious these days, too serious. Maybe in Hollywood things were different. How would she know? She would be stuck here forever in this old-fashioned farm kitchen, throwing mash to the chickens, slopping the pigs, galumphing around in mud to her knees, and arguing with her mother. Pretty soon she'd be too fat to get out of the kitchen door!

Then she drifted off into a daydream about her cousin Margot's arrival and the two of them becoming friends and sharing everything, and she imagined Margot's silky blond hair and gray eyes and heard her voice, with its fascinating accent, so unlike the foreign accents she heard around her all day. When Elly dreamed, she could shut the others out. Automatically, she asked for seconds on the meat and bit into the cake for dessert.

Even the radio was a background blur until she caught the tension in the room and the sharp edge of excitement in the voice of the announcer talking over static from Germany. "I'm looking down at an incredible scene here in Berlin, one being duplicated in cities and towns all over Germany, wherever Jews live and have their businesses. A few blocks away a synagogue is burning, and the columns of black smoke twisting over the roofs add to the eeriness of the scene. The street is covered with piles of broken glass from smashed shop fronts, and SS men with tommy guns are forcing Jews to sweep up the glass, using their hands as shovels. Just a few minutes ago one man protested and was kicked headfirst into a pile of glass."

As if in response, Elly let her milk glass slide, and it shattered on the floor. She jumped up for the dustpan, but Mama hushed her and motioned her to sit down again. A thin trickle of milk dripped from the edge of the table to the floor, and the glass crunched under her chair.

"The man is still lying on the street," the announcer said, sparing them nothing, "blood streaming from his face . . ."

Baba pushed her plate away. "Who would have imagined . . . ?"

"Plenty . . ." Phil began.

"Shut up!" Pop said, with such unusual force that Phil responded at once.

The voice on the radio was relentless. "Reports from Frankfurt, with its large Jewish community, speak of several deaths, and in Stuttgart men are being rounded up and taken to camps. Reporters have seen old men humiliated and beards pulled, but things are quieter in Berlin as many Germans remain indoors, possibly fearing for their own safety, possibly unwilling to join in this outburst of public fury triggered by last week's murder at the German Embassy in Paris of Third Secretary Ernest von Rath by the young Polish Jew, Herschel Grynszpan."

"Violence makes violence," Mama said, "as I am telling you . . ."

"Sonya!" Pop said. "Spare me, my dear! This is larger than any words we can make. Please be quiet!" he begged.

"All indications are," said the announcer, "that the government is behind these actions, which are too well coordinated to depend on popular indignation."

Phil snorted. Elly giggled nervously.

"What will happen next remains to be seen. It is possible that Hitler is waiting for protests from France, England, and America to determine future policy. As of this moment, no official protests have been received at the Chancellery, although it is reported that the American ambassador visited Foreign Minister von Ribbentrop . . ."

"That pig!" Phil said.

". . . to express, unofficially, his shock at behavior so much beneath what he had expected from so civilized a power as Germany."

"Civilized!" Baba cried out. "Our goats are more civilized!"

Then the announcer's voice became even more breathless and hurried. The tension grew in his listeners sitting in the silent kitchen while deep November night covered them. "Wait! Wait! New York, can you hear me? Listen! A troop of soldiers is marching down the street—that's the noise you hear in the background. Will they stop when they reach the man lying in the street? No! He's been kicked out of the way, back into the broken glass, he's rolling over and over in the glass; he looks dead, he must be dead! The other men are being rounded up; they are being marched at gun point down the street; women are leaning out of the empty window frames and screaming. The last line of soldiers has stopped, they are wheeling about, dropping down on one knee, and aiming at the windows across the street from me. These are second-floor and third-floor windows, lined with women and children, some crying, some shouting, some absolutely silent. And they are firing!"

There was a crackling sound, then silence. Booming, the New York announcer said, "Our transmission from Berlin has been interrupted. We will stand by for further news. Meanwhile, let's switch to our Washington correspondent, Bob Falkner. Come in, Bob, in the nation's capital."

"Thank you, Harry. Down here all the talk is about increasing bad feeling between President Roosevelt and one of the leading Southerners in the Senate, Walter George of Georgia. During committee hearings . . ."

Pop snapped the radio off. The silence was like the one that settled over the land in autumn after the great flocks of honking geese rose up and flew south, leaving behind them a stillness as sudden as a blow. They all sat around the table as before, and the world flooded in on them, getting at them through the closed windows, mocking the quiet fields and the moon in the sky, pushing aside the comfortable rustle of familiar sounds.

"So much for Tolstoy," Phil murmured, so quietly that no one was quite sure he had spoken. Elly knew what he meant. Mama had tried to protect them from worldly contamination by moving them to a farm far away from New York where she had met and married Pop. "Live by the soil and your hands," she said, and "Do not want and you will not be disappointed," and

"Follow Christ in all things and the kingdom will be yours." And what difference did it all make now?

Mama wiped her eyes; Baba let the tears trickle down her plump cheeks. Pop sighed. Then they began to talk about what to do, where to go, how to save three people from what was to come—if they still could be saved. Elly spoke, too, and listened, but she did not measure any of the words; she was caught up in her inner pictures of heel-clicking Nazi soldiers played by Robert Montgomery and Franchot Tone and pathetic refugees looking like Margaret Sullavan, and she imagined herself in the film, too, noble and suffering and rescued at the end. Because that's the way it always was in the movies, and she didn't know more than she had watched on the screen.

"Well, there it is," Pop said. "Oh, Sonya, if only we had some money . . . !"

"What would you do, Leo? Go and pull them out yourself? And how? No, no, my dear, it is beyond man's hands now, and there is only God that we must turn to. *Seek and ye shall find . . .*"

"I blame myself," Pop said, his face white.

"What has God done so far?" Elly cried out savagely, and Pop gripped her hands with his and motioned her to be still.

"You are ignorant, child," Baba said, standing up to clear the table. "And we are at fault."

"Imagine it," Phil said. "This could be us, do you understand, Mama?"

Mama nodded. "Persecution is always the lot of the just."

"Oh, Mom, you sound like a preacher!"

Mama laughed. "That I do not want, Phil, believe me. So tell me, my genius, what should we do?"

Pop's shoulders were shaking. "Don't you see, Sonya, we can't stand by and do nothing? For yourself, yes, absolutely, I agree with you, you have the right to die rather than fight evil. Yes! But for the others—no, no, no! Some day soon there will be—ach—such a reckoning! We will pay in blood for each day we did not bring Hitler down!"

Mama shook her head with the pliant stubbornness that would never yield. "Leo, does one wrong justify another? How do such things begin—war, hatred? From just such an excuse. Others, who can speak for others? This is difficult, I know. For myself, I would not be rescued through violence."

"What would you do then? Speak, my dear! What would you do?"

"Gently, Leo, you will blow up like a sail in a north wind! You mean if I could do anything? Oh, my dear, we have such money in this country, even now, this depression is from the rich, the money is being wasted, beautiful land is being wasted!" Mama got up to do the dishes and beckoned Elly to help her. The accustomed task counterpointed her words as she moved from table to sink, the new electric lights shining on her round face and neat hair. "I? I would rescue those people, every last one, take them into our house, give them life, not death. Only so shall people live. Watch those plates, Elly, they will fall!" She took the huge kettle of hot water off the stove and poured some into a dishpan. "The gun is death, it does not ask which hands use it, but life, life is from people, from Christ who wishes us to love each other." She washed the dishes quickly in a dishpan with soapy water, then dipped them into a pan of clear water, working fiercely, her shoulders shaking.

"And who was killed." Pop sighed. His mustache

drooped on either side of his mouth. "Sonya, you will never believe this, but not so many people are as good as you and your mamushka. Very few, my dear. Even where my poor sister is concerned, does she wish to come?" He brooded silently, staring into his cup, then filling it again with hot coffee.

Elly rushed to defend her father. "Mama, you are such a romantic!" She stacked the dishes in the cupboard any old way, and they began to fall over. Baba grabbed the plates just in time, and that gave Mama a fine chance to scold.

"*You* are the romantic," Mama began, not for the first time, "living in a dream world. Look at you! In town there is real hunger . . ."

"Oh, Mama, I know that!" Elly said, spreading the dish towel to dry on a rack near the wood stove. "And in China, too!"

"So you know! Still you spend a dime, *ten cents*, every time I turn around, and on what? Movie magazines!"

"It's my money," Elly said in a trembling voice. Pop paid her a nickel for every dozen eggs she gathered and candled for him and a quarter a week for sweeping out the grocery store each morning before school began. Phil earned five dollars each week for washing the big front window and floor of the store and delivering orders after school and on Saturdays. No one complained about what he did with his money. "It's not fair," Elly said. "You let Phil get away with murder because he's a boy."

Phil would have said something, only he had gone out to the barn to milk the two cows and water the animals for the night. Mama also kept two goats, Weber and Fields, and made a chalky and strong-smelling goat cheese, which Elly hated and which Baba and Pop and Mama ate with sliced onions on dark bread. And they had the Kocinskis' pigs and the two plough horses, Sasha and Masha, whom Elly almost never got to ride, but whom she had to curry and groom every week without fail. And she fed the chickens, of course, in the chicken house next to the barn, which was home to a noisy, filthy flock of Rhode Island Reds.

Mama dried her hands carefully. "You have a lot to learn, Eleanor. Fifteen and such a child! At fifteen I had full charge—full charge!—of the dairy at Green Branch Farm every Saturday and Sunday when the regular dairymaid was off. And during the week I went to school, not only American school but Russian, too—and oh, how I studied! And learned to sew and look after the chickens besides. And made bread each Monday in my turn." Mama was smiling the way she always did when she remembered life on the Tolstoyan farm in New Jersey where she had lived after she and Baba had fled from Russia in 1905. Her father had been killed by the police during the uprising of 1905, when Mama was only ten, "for no reason at all, only that he would teach the peasants," Baba said, wiping her eyes, "and we were afraid."

"Mama, I don't *want* to do those things!" Elly said. "Don't you see? What do I care about all of that? I have another destiny . . . oh, Mama, I wish you'd understand! If we could live in town . . ."

"You'd still have to do your homework, even there. Leo, let's hear again at ten o'clock the news. They have their passports, maybe they are on the way out, pray God."

"When Margot gets here," Elly said, opening her French book, "everything will be different." She had seen a photograph of Margot, taken last year on a Baltic beach, showing a beautiful, smiling girl with long, fair hair hanging loosely around a small face, and she had tacked the picture up in her room next to photographs of Luise Rainer and Garbo.

Phil stamped in. "Frost tonight. What a sky! I'm going out with my telescope. Coming, Elly?"

He had not asked her for a long time. The homework was easy, she had already finished her English essay, and Phil would help her later with the math assignment. History was a snap and the French not really work at all. She nodded.

"Get your gloves, then," Phil said.

Cold air hit them on the doorstep, streaming steadily down from the north and bringing winter with it. So much had happened since Elly had left her chilly room for dinner that she welcomed the peaceful dark and the chance to sort it all out. Phil worked quietly setting up the telescope and taking sightings while Elly wrapped herself in an old carriage blanket and leaned back against a crumpled maple tree.

She thought mostly of Margot, trying to feel what it was like to be her cousin, living first in a kind of luxury Elly had never known, then falling into such fear and despair that no one had words for it; even the newspaper articles and radio reports were banal and unfeeling.

"I'm certain they'll get here," she said into the darkness.

"What? Oh, yes. Come here and look at this, will you?" Elly saw a sprinkling of stars enlarge themselves in the telescope's mirror and stand out as if moving closer to her unwinking eye. "Do you see the Pleiades?" Phil asked. "That cluster close together? Got it? Now, look below it—here, here! The huge star, the twinkling one, Aldebaran. Now swing it over this way, to the left, along an arc—like this, follow my arm—no, let me. All set? Below Aldebaran and to the left, that's Bellatrix, then the big one to the left of that and slightly down in the sky . . . Orion. See the three stars of the belt at a slant there? My God, you don't even need a telescope for that! And Betelgeuse, over at the very edge of the sky, just before the pines block the horizon. Yes, that's it!" Phil sighed with happiness.

Elly looked and tried to feel the expected thrill. The star-spattered sky *was* glorious—as a background to her own dreams of glory, no more than that. It was too remote from the human world that she clung to. But she was pleased that Phil had invited her to share his pleasures. Once they had been this close all the time, depending on each other for support and friendship, sharing the chores, walking the fields and woods in every season to discover wildflowers and animal tracks. It had all changed in the past two years as Phil grew more silent and absorbed in his love of science and she put all her energy into her acting. They met and crossed and went apart again, unable to touch each other as they had so easily when they were younger.

"What will Margot be like?" Elly asked.

"Hmm? Look at those stars! They just shine up there, and by the time we even *see* their light, maybe millions of years have passed since they gave it off. Millions!"

Elly shivered. "That scares me. I like things to be . . . well, smaller—things I can touch."

"*That's* where you're wrong. It's safe up there in those big spaces and millions of years. Nothing counts for much. Especially not people. And you can be safe too if you get as close to the stars as you can—nobody can touch you there."

"Do you really think that?" Elly asked, horrified, getting up and letting the blanket slide to the ground. "Oh, Phil!" She was speechless, and that happened very seldom. To turn your back on all the confusing clutter of people—no, that was unthinkable! She let the night and silence flow around her, far from the chattering radio reports and multiple strands of family relationships; she liked the separation and the peace, but only as a change from the real business of life—people and understanding them. How could she ever give that up? Even when she was miserable, she would not wish it otherwise; she was gaining insights into herself that, dearly bought, were precious.

Mrs. Wilbur, the drama teacher at school, preached constant awareness. "Everything, you can use everything that happens to you, if only you take care to observe and to feel *honestly*. You can fool yourself, but if you want to be an actor—and a good one—you won't be able to fool anyone else." Remembering, Elly nodded agreement.

Phil had turned his back on her and was gazing at the stars once more. "Can you imagine," he asked, so softly that she had to strain to hear him, "the horrible things that are being done right now? Can you imagine living in Germany—I am being taken away by soldiers, Pop has died from a beating, you are all alone, can you imagine? Elly?"

"I'm here," she answered, too loud. "I imagine things like that all the time—that's when I think about movies, and you all laugh at me. In the movies, it's all right in the end. I like it that way."

Phil chuckled. "Let's go in."

How comforting it was—the homework, the crowded kitchen, the expected words, the hot cocoa before bedtime, the orderly pages of French verbs, the excitement of opening a book for the first time as Elly smoothed down the title page of *Death Comes for the Archbishop*, the rhythmic click of Baba's knitting needles, the hiss of the fire!

When Pop turned on the ten o'clock news, Elly went upstairs to run away from the voice, but not before she heard the staccato voice from Germany say, "It is estimated that 25,000 Jewish men were rounded up today and taken to detention camps. Border patrols report that they have turned back many thousands of Jews trying to flee, and in response to a formal request from the Jewish Agency, French government officials announced that they could not allow entry of any German citizens who did not have valid French entry permits and current visas."

Then the kitchen door closed, and the words faded. As quickly as possible she jumped into bed and huddled under the featherbed, rubbing the goose bumps on her arms. In bed, she heard nothing. When would Pop get a heater for this room? Never. She laughed, practicing that deep, throaty laugh that her favorite actresses had, and stretched and turned over, thinking *Margot, Margot,* then drifted off to sleep wondering what this cousin would be like when she came. For of course she would come. It was part of the happy ending.

2

"MEN, LIONS, EAGLES, and partridges, horned deer, geese, spiders, silent fish that dwell in the deep, starfish, and creatures invisible to the eye—these and all living things, all, all living things, having completed their sad cycle, are no more. . . . For thousands of years, the earth has borne no living creature. And now in vain this poor moon lights her lamp."

"All right, Elly!" Mrs. Wilbur called from the darkened auditorium. Laughter trembled at the very edge of her deep voice. "Cut! Enough!"

Elly stood hesitantly on the stage, peering down into the seats. "Should I come down now?"

"Yes, indeed. Come here, let me talk to you. Stand straight, don't slouch! Child, whatever made you choose something from Chekhov? I didn't know anyone in Franklin had even *heard* of him!"

"My mother and grandmother are Russian," Elly reminded the drama teacher.

"So they are. I forget you have parents sometimes; I think of all of you as my little students and nothing more."

Elly tossed her head. "Well? How did I do?"

"You certainly were clear enough, your breathing has improved enormously. Doing those exercises I gave you? Good! Why did you choose that speech?"

Elly shrugged. "I wasn't sure," she said slowly, "whether it was supposed to be romantic or just silly; it seemed so remote, and I wanted to find out by saying it."

"And?"

"Well, I couldn't do it any other way than all romantic and poetic, but just now, listening to it, I think it was supposed to be silly. Not funny."

Mrs. Wilbur tapped her pencil against her chin. "How to make it silly without being funny, that's the challenge. Who's left? Laura? Do your stuff!"

Elly slid down in the seat next to Mrs. Wilbur, relaxed after the long tension before her tryout, and gave herself over to deep happiness. She loved to look at and listen to Laura Fitzgerald. They were the last to audition for the big school play, planning it that way so they could walk home with Mrs. Wilbur. For the past hour they had done their homework backstage, listening to the other students and agreeing that they had no serious competition at all. Now Laura came forward on the stage and let out all her breath to say, "By my troth, Nerissa, my little body is aweary of this great world," then waited before launching into Portia's speech a bit later, skipping the dialogue since she had no Nerissa with her. "If to do were as easy as to know what were good to do, chapels had been churches and poor men's cottages princes' palaces. It is a good divine that follows his own instructions; I can easier teach twenty what were good to be done, than be one of the twenty to follow mine own teaching. . . ."

Again the laughter hid behind Mrs. Wilbur's voice as she stopped Laura. "You touch me to the quick," she said. "Here I sit, teaching drama, but acting not. Come along, girls, the janitor will sweep us out in a minute."

"Don't you just love that—*By my troth, Nerissa, my little body is aweary of this great world,*" Laura asked. "I think it's gorgeous!"

Elly caught her breath in delight as they walked out of the school into the dusk. New Franklin High School was built on a hill almost directly above the shops on Station and Lower Main Streets, and they could see the points of light from houses and street lamps shining through the chill fog that spoke of frost to come. The daily plainness of the town had vanished, only the outlines of some sparkling dream remained, and they were looking down on all of it.

"What play will you do?" Elly asked. "*Mary of Scotland?*"

"Don't know yet," Mrs. Wilbur replied. "Depends on what the fees are—budget's tighter than usual this year, and my husband'll kill me if I take any of my salary to pay for rights, my stupendous one hundred dollars a month! What would you think of *You Can't Take It With You*? Either of you girls up to comedy? You seem so solemn!"

"Are there a lot of parts?" Laura asked.

"Yes, my pretty, that's another consideration. We need something lighthearted this year, I do believe, and with plenty of parts so that the parents will come to see their darlings perform."

"But who will you get to play in it? Besides Laura and me, I mean."

Mrs. Wilbur laughed out loud. "Think you two are the only ones with talent? Stand up straight, Elly!"

"Yes," Laura said simply.

"Oh. Mrs. Wilbur," Elly said, "I keep trying, but I'm

so fat I hate the way I stick out all over. What will I do?"

"Eat less," Mrs. Wilbur said promptly. "And exercise more. Why, some of the greatest actresses in the world overcame all kinds of physical problems—Rachel wasn't even beautiful, not in the least—with willpower, hard work, and that mysterious something we call talent."

"Not glasses," Elly said miserably, pushing hers up on her nose.

"Even glasses. Most actors seem to be shortsighted. They manage. But stand up, for heaven's sake!"

They had a regular routine when they stayed late, walking down the long flight of stone steps to Lower Main Street, then going around the corner to Angelo's, where Mrs. Wilbur had a small pot of espresso coffee while Laura and Elly had cokes. Mrs. Wilbur liked the atmosphere of the small restaurant, the checked tablecloths, the candles stuck in empty Chianti bottles, the pervasive smell of tomatoes and parmesan cheese. "Takes me back to my days in the Village, children. The only civilized place in this whole town." And she waved to Angelo, who stood behind the bar. If Mama knew that Elly came in here, she would forbid it. But she didn't know.

Mrs. Wilbur never invited them to her big house in Yankeetown, the best part of Franklin, where her husband also had his dentist's office. "This is another me," she had said grandly, "a private, special me, and I want to keep it that way."

Both girls wondered why she had ever married Dr. Wilbur and left New York for Franklin, but she never told them. They wouldn't have asked her for the world.

Mrs. Wilbur appreciatively sniffed the smell of strong coffee that rose from her tiny cup. "Well, my dears, work begins in earnest quite soon. No more laryngitis, Laura; keep out of drafts. I'm counting on you. And Elly, no more coughs. We're going to do something great this year—mark my words. Put it on the bill, Angelo."

Mrs. Wilbur went one way toward Upper Main Street and the wide streets, neat lawns, and spacious houses of Yankeetown, built on the bluffs of the Ibanaki River just where it made a graceful loop and began to flow east instead of south. Laura and Elly went toward the railroad station and Pop's grocery store, darted in the back door that opened off the alley, and grabbed some stale doughnuts from the jar on the scarred table in the center of the back room.

"Helloooo!" Elly called. She picked up the filled paper sack on the table. An enormous eggplant stuck out of the top. "Is this stuff for me? Here's Laura."

"Hello, Laura," Pop said, "hello, Elly. Yes, take that food up with you, why don't you? No good to me any more."

"Busy? See you at six."

"A little busy. Take care!"

From the alley they turned onto a steep brick-paved street to the oldest part of Franklin, the Federal and Georgian houses grouped around the Green. Narrow twisted streets and alleys lay behind the open beauty of the Green, with its clipped hedges and ancient oak and maple trees. On one side of the square was the town library where they often stopped for books, and on the second side was Miss Wright's Female Seminary, the famous girls' finishing school where Laura's father taught art and her mother French. The other two sides were rimmed with houses, and in one of these Laura had lived ever since her family had moved to Franklin from France last spring.

Coming into school near the close of the year with her strange, dark coloring and foreign ways picked up from two years in France, Laura found herself shut out by most of the Franklin kids and even by some of the teachers. They felt that she was putting on airs when everyone knew that her father was a drunken artist who had been given the job at Miss Wright's only because his wife was a cousin of the present headmistress, Alma Fox. How did the news get around so quickly? Within a week of Laura's entry into high school, this information was common knowledge. She took refuge in the drama club where Elly welcomed her with obvious joy, finding in Laura the ideal friend she had been waiting for all her life. And that friendship had not yet wavered.

Laura's house was a narrow clapboard colonial. Her parents had painted it a gleaming barn red with white cornerboards, black shutters, and a bright blue door. They hadn't done much to the inside yet. The front parlor was painted ivory and filled with their delicate old French furniture, the kitchen was all torn up, and the dining room completely empty. Laura had a tiny downstairs bedroom off the kitchen, cozy with a faded oriental rug on the floor, a batik spread on her narrow brass bed, and an old pine dresser that she had refinished.

"Hello!" Laura sang out. "Brought Elly home. For a change." And she giggled nervously, unlike her usual calm self. Elly had been coming here every afternoon since school started in September and had seen Laura's transformation each time, wondering at it.

Elly gave Mrs. Fitzgerald the food she had picked up at Pop's store, some cracked eggs and bruised fruit, along with the eggplant. "My savior," Mrs. Fitzgerald said. "I was beginning to feel like old Mother Hubbard—now we'll have a feast! Too bad you can't stay for supper,

Elly; go on down later and see if your mean old daddy will let you stay the night. Look here, I've just got the bread out of this awful oven, and it's not too burnt, is it?" she asked, looking at the loaves. "No, it's not, and there's bean soup, and now I see before me eggs for an omelet and fruit for dessert. Guide Michelin, one star!"

"Where can I sleep if I stay?" Elly asked. Laura's room was too small for a chair, and her bookcase had to stand in the unheated back entry.

Mrs. Fitzgerald rushed in to answer before Laura could say anything. "We'll make you a little nest on the floor with that beautiful sheepskin rug up in the studio. Oh, do stay, Elly! How nice it would be if you lived in town all the time!"

"That's my wish, too," Elly said. "But Mama . . . she would *die* off the farm."

Mrs. Fitzgerald had long black hair and dark eyes, and she never seemed to get upset. Laura called her by her name, Glenna, and said that she often posed for Owen Fitzgerald's pictures. Elly thought that if she were a painter, she would paint Glenna Fitzgerald all the time, too.

"Glenna, you can't imagine, Elly's house," Laura said. "It's a regular European farm—like the place we stayed at near Loches, remember?"

"Oh, yes," Mrs. Fitzgerald said dreamily, "a real peasant life, so terribly Old World. Is your Mama *really* like that, Elly?"

Elly grew hot and would not answer. Mrs. Fitzgerald's tone of voice was clearly mocking; what was more, for a minute, Elly agreed with her. She was ashamed of Mama and wished with all her heart that her mother was like Glenna—slender and beautiful. She was disloyal and knew she was disloyal but kept right on wishing for

Mama's transformation, anyway. And she did not really like Glenna Fitzgerald at all.

Finally, Laura broke the silence. "Elly wants to be an actress, Glenna; remember when I told you that?"

"From my life with an artist," Mrs. Fitzgerald said, stirring the bean soup, "a peasant is the best kind of mother to have—you'll get food baskets wherever you are! And food's one thing that never goes out of style. There are days when I myself could write an ode to my granddaddy's pigs if only one would lie down in the oven and roast himself for dinner!"

She blew the girls a kiss. "Go on, my pets, you don't want to stay and talk to an old lady like me. I opened the register in Laura's room, and it's nice and warm." Sometimes she forgot, and they froze until the heat came through the open register from the stove pipe in the kitchen.

"She's squiffy again," Laura whispered as they left the kitchen, and now she was embarrassed and angry, too. "Glenna can't help it, she *hates* this place! But we've got to stay . . ."

Elly felt stupid trying to understand this so different way of living. Dreaming about an artist's life was one thing, it seemed, and seeing it, much less living it, quite something else. "Oh, I *wish* I could go to France!" she exclaimed, making too much of it. But she was grateful to her parents that they didn't drink. "What if you went away?"

Laura stretched out on her bed. "Oh, we shall, sooner or later," she laughed. "That's the way they are. Don't even think of it." She drifted off into her own world. Elly sat on the rug and looked at her. She did not look like anyone else in school. She had black hair and dark eyes like her mother, but her skin was dark, almost olive, and her features were enormous in her bony face, not set delicately in soft white skin. From the side she looked like an Egyptian painted head, remote and noble.

"Elly, she won't do *You Can't Take It With You,* will she?"

"Mrs. Wilbur? Why not? Lots of parts."

Laura groaned. "It's so . . . it's what you'd expect, such a typical play. She's so much more, don't you think?"

"Oh, I do!" Elly said fervently. "But what can she do? I mean, *we're* the only ones she can count on. I was hoping for *Mary of Scotland,* it's so *romantic!* You could be Mary and I, Elizabeth."

Laura lay back and gazed at the ceiling. "Ye-es, that's a possibility. You know what I wanted? *Romeo and Juliet.* Wait a minute, where's my book?"

Darkness settled into the room, and Elly turned on the lamp, sending pink light over the creamy walls and striped green and yellow curtains. The girls lounged side by side on the bed, reading out from a tattered copy of the play, enchanted by the words, which they repeated as Laura played Juliet first and Elly, Romeo; then they changed parts and dazzled themselves with the brilliance of the language and the intensity of their acting. When they finished, they sat silent and stunned.

"*Quelle* play!" Laura murmured.

"You're so beautiful," Elly said. "You don't belong in Franklin. You're going to have some great, romantic life." And she laughed shakily.

"Hah! You're the only one who thinks so then! I don't know . . . let me see, Elly, come into the light."

Laura looked closely at Elly's face, then touched her cheeks lightly, and stroked her hair. They stood in the light of the lamp like two people in a film, distant and romantic. Elly was warm with pleasure. "Wait," Laura said. "Someday men will find you interesting."

"Interesting? Thanks! I want to be desirable, not interesting! I'll never get rid of my glasses—and this fat."

"Ho, even Garbo was a plump teenager—Garbo! It doesn't mean a thing, wearing glasses. It's what you *are* that counts, the way your soul burns through your eyes. That's what Owen paints in his portraits—the person's soul; he says *that's* the true resemblance. It comes from suffering—you must suffer."

"The only question is: how?" They sat in silence. "It's so . . . so ordinary here, so dull. Nothing ever happens in Franklin, much less on the farm. Mama won't listen when I talk about moving to town, and I never get the chance to go anywhere—no money, no money, no money." Elly drummed on the wall behind her.

"Yes," Laura said placidly, brushing her hair, "we never have any money, either. Not for sensible things."

"You went to France," Elly pointed out, envying her.

"It was cheap, cheaper than New York. It was like here; we lived in a village in Normandy. We couldn't afford Paris. Only we had no plumbing, and Glenna had to cook on an awful woodstove—not that she cooked much—and applejack was cheap enough for her and Owen to drink it all the time. *He'd* go to Paris to deliver a picture, but we never had enough money for all of us to go—except once. The hotel room crawled with roaches. And bedbugs. And the toilet stank."

Elly squirmed. Thanks to Mama's and Baba's superlative housekeeping, she'd never get used to that. Even this household disturbed her; yet how could she be a great actress without being Bohemian? "Do you know I've never been away from this area in my entire life? I can't stand it—I won't be finished with high school until 1941. 1941!"

"Well, Owen got away from some awful town in Louisiana. He ran away from home. He says he was only sixteen."

"Then, let's ask him!"

Laura's face closed tight. "Let's not. He wouldn't tell, anyway; that's the way he is."

"Love," Elly said after a moment. "Love leads to suffering."

They laughed wildly. Love! What was the connection between the two of them and love? "That's just it," Elly said sadly, "all those fascinating things are happening, and we're too young. We'll miss the best part."

She was thinking of Margot, living out all that Elly herself wished for: first the rich life in Berlin with piano lessons and travel, now the loss and suffering that an artist had to know. All the books Elly read insisted on that. "My cousin from Germany will be here soon. Margot. Margot Blum. Isn't that lovely?" Without looking at Laura, Elly told her about Margot the beautiful, Margot the lost, Margot the smiling blonde posing on a Baltic beach for the camera. "Oh, don't like her," she cried out, saying words she didn't even know she was thinking. "Don't like her! There won't be any room for me, then, and I don't know what I'd do."

Embarrassed, she stopped. In the silence, Laura unbraided Elly's hair and combed it out into a fan rippling over her shoulders. "Here's a mirror. Now smile." Elly practiced getting a remote, mysterious smile on her lips, the smile of Garbo or Madeleine Carroll. With the pink light shining at her back and shadowing her cheekbones, she thought that she looked beautiful, at least for a moment, until she put the mirror down and the image vanished.

"It's a terrible world," she sighed.

Laura said nothing, only picked up the copy of *Romeo and Juliet*, and began to read. "O then I see Queen Mab hath been with you! She is the fairies' midwife, and she comes in shape no bigger than an agate stone on the forefinger of an alderman . . ."

"Come off it, Laura." Her father stood in the doorway, mocking. He was tall and red-faced with a busy mustache and beard streaked with gray. Elly drew back into a corner. Laura stopped at once, turned white, then pink, and kept her eyes down on the floor.

"Some actress! What do you think, Elly? I bet you agree with me—women are meant to be beautiful and quiet. The most beautiful thing in the world is a woman's body, all that naked flesh shining, begging to be touched, to be put on canvas, but are they content with that? No, they want more. Education! Books!"

The girls said nothing until, frustrated by their silence, he turned away. "I guess I'd better not stay here tonight," Elly said quietly, unable to look at her friend. Laura was afraid of her father, and he knew it and took advantage of it. And Elly was afraid of him, too. Pop would never do a thing like that. She had a sudden longing for Pop's comforting voice and touch. "What time is it?"

"Almost six," Laura said, dragging each word out. She looked miserable, blotchy and tired.

As the girls walked out into the hall, they could hear Owen racketing around the kitchen. "What slop are you putting together for supper today, Glenna? Got anything to drink? This place is dead, *dead,* and it's killing me, too!"

"You keep forgetting that we're not in France any more, with wine pouring down the streets."

"Gin'll do for me."

"Don't I know it!" Then Mrs. Fitzgerald laughed, and all the bitterness fell away from her voice. "Leave me be, Owen, you stink of turp! I'll hit you with this skillet if you make me break the eggs!"

"Come on," Laura said, "I'll walk you down to your father's store. I think it's time we went now."

Something was going on that Laura didn't want Elly to see; she blocked her view of the kitchen and hustled her toward the front door. But Elly still saw a little. Owen had Glenna pinned against a wall and was pressing hard against her, pushing her head back and kissing her mouth. Elly had never seen her parents like this; she could not imagine it. She looked at Laura's averted face and knew she could not ask her friend how she felt about it. There was so much silence in the world and so much to learn!

All around the Green, lights shone out of house windows. The bare branches of trees rose up high against the brick walls of the Female Seminary and tapped against the walls of the town library. Below them lay Upper Main Street and its intermittent flashes, then the train station with dim yellow lamps flaring in the center of darkness, and the river, a shining black pasted on a duller black, and the deep pine forests on the other bank. *That's what we are,* Elly thought, stepping carefully down the bumpy stone steps to Lower Main, *two specks of light in the darkness all around us.*

"See you tomorrow," Laura said, in a carefully neutral voice, and Elly shouted back, her eyes straining in the darkness for the lights that meant Pop's store. The damp fog slid down her nose and throat and made her eyes tear.

3

POP WAS ALONE in the room behind the store, dozing in his rocker with his feet propped on an old pickle barrel.

Elly let the door slam. "What's the matter, Pop? You don't look so good. Anything wrong?"

"What?" Pop asked groggily. "Oh, it's you. What time is it? Six. Phil'll be back soon, took the last orders out a little while ago. Then we can leave. Have a good afternoon? Hungry? Take an apple."

"A little," Elly admitted, biting into the apple. "I'm going to be in the play—Mrs. Wilbur doesn't know which one yet, but I'm sure to improve it. Right?"

Pop smiled. "You want to be in the play? Naturally! Then I'm pleased for you. How's your little friend?"

A customer came in at that moment, and Elly ran to serve her. Four rolls and two cans of soup. Pop marked the rolls to half-price just before closing, and a few people waited until the last minute to buy them.

"Not much business tonight," Elly said.

"Might as well lock up. Pull down the shade, too. You should be here from four to five, though, when Northeastern Mills gets out—maybe twenty people in at a time. Can't complain about business these days. Doubled my order for cases of tuna since the spring. Laura, how's she?"

Elly shrugged. "I don't like her father," she said rapidly. "He scares me."

"Drinks too much," Pop said. "Yes, word gets around. Pity. Bad for the child. But you like this Laura?"

"Pop, I've *never* had a friend like her! We read the same books, and she knows just how I feel and—it's wonderful!"

"Such friends are hard to find," Pop said gravely. "Stick to her. Come, let me clear the register and finish up; your Mama will worry if we are too late." He walked wearily into the store.

"Pop, what's the matter?" Elly asked again. He had deliberately not answered before. "Oh, I wish we lived in town! You wouldn't have to make such a long drive. We could live right upstairs—it would be so easy for you."

"Who knows? We might have to. Just today Harry Pelzer told me the Pelzers'll be leaving January first. A job he's got driving trucks from Allentown, Pennsylvania. Ever heard of it? His wife's father got it, they're from Allentown. So it's also on my mind getting the place fixed up and painted and rented. With so much extra expense, I can't afford to let that twenty-five dollars a month go by."

"Pop, why *couldn't* we live up there?"

He let his hand rest on her head. "No use asking, Elly, your Mama would not agree. Besides, it's not big enough. Not with Anna and Margot and Michael. The big front room, a nice kitchen—brand new linoleum on the floor—a bathroom, two small bedrooms in the back, and the one good-sized one. No, it's too small for us."

"But there's the third floor, the attic!"

Pop laughed. "Oh, such an expense to fix that up! Rich people we are not, my dear." He looked at her sharply. "You really want to live in Franklin?"

"I hate it in the country, Pop. There's nothing for me to do on weekends, my friends are here . . ."

"You used to love it. Remember?"

"Umm, when I was a kid. Not now."

"Phil, he's unhappy there, too?"

"Do I hear my name taken in vain?" Phil asked, banging the door. "Brr, it's cold, in case you don't know it. Pop, Mrs. LaBelle says put it on the bill, she'll pay you next Friday. What about me?"

"You don't even notice where you live," Elly said. "It's all the same to you." She was disappointed at the end of this conversation; she'd have to bring it up another time and push Pop harder.

Phil held his hands out over the kerosene stove. "Don't be too sure. I might notice it if I was in a refugee camp in England. Did you tell her about the letter, Pop?"

"Not yet."

"What letter?" Elly asked. "Did something . . . happen? Is it awful?"

"They got out," Phil said.

"You certainly don't look very happy," Elly told Pop.

"Anna and the child did," Pop said slowly. "They are in England. She writes from there."

"Then it's a miracle," Elly said happily.

Phil and Pop both laughed. "Not quite," Pop said. "It's only the beginning."

"What does it say? Can I read it, Pop?"

"In German? To tell the truth, it's even hard for me to read. She writes the Gothic script, and I've forgotten a lot. Strange, how that happens. Well . . . never mind. I'll read it to you. I'm not sure exactly what to do, it's on my mind." He read slowly, rustling the crinkly air mail paper.

Dear Brother Leo!

If only we had left earlier, Michael would be with us. They took him away 15th November, where we do not know, nor whether we are to wait here for him or sail to America. No one tells us anything, Margot and I have to share only a tiny cubicle in a big barracks, an old army camp, with washrooms and toilets at the end of the hall. There are no closets and our bedding is army blankets and rough sheets—they made me leave in Berlin all my lovely linen. Did you know we could take out nothing, only clothes and some small things. No one would even buy, what could we do with the marks?

Our apartment was taken by a doctor in Michael's clinic, he always seemed so nice to us, you never can tell, can you? But his wife was nothing more than a peasant from Swabia and she was burning with envy since the first time she saw all my lovely things. The finest Rosenthal porcelain, my trousseau linens—that this Swabian should have them, no! no! It should not be!

We are supposed to be learning English. It is not hard for Margot, of course, she knows it from school, she is like an assistant to work with the younger children. I too had a little in gymnasium, *but not the way they speak it here, these English who swallow their vowels and cluck like chickens! They raise their voices as if* then *they could be understood. I had always believed the English did everything so well—they praise themselves, they are so marvelous, but all here is the most awful mess, the Germans would* never do *things so! In our barracks are one or at the most two good families, one from Hanover, a newspaper owner (the man, too, was taken away, but the wife is educated), one from Breslau, the man owned a furniture factory that made only the best. The others are who knows what? Such manners! Such ways of living, you would never believe! I see it every day and still do not believe.*

I tried three times to explain to the English dame *. . . the woman in charge . . . that in England is classes; I have heard they would not, these people, sleep in the same room with their cooks and maids, with shopkeepers and peasants, and that is what these people were like, not our kind. The first time she listened coldly, as the English do, and did nothing. The second time, she said she would see what she could do. Also nothing. The third time she answered me first in Yiddish. Imagine! I told her I do not speak Yiddish, what does she take me for, I speak German, and she said she did not speak German, she was sorry, she heard the Nazis spoke very good German, maybe they would understand.*

I told her I did not know of what she was speaking and she grew angry, really, it was without conscience, the way she spoke. She said they were trying to save as many people as possible and send them to new homes, they had not much money (what a lie! when we all know how much the English and Americans have, how much they took from Germany after 1918!) and were doing the best they could. I said I see they are trying to bring us down low, to finish what Hitler started, that we are down now and all hate us

Jews. Then she said, as cold as ice, But I am Jewish myself. *Of course, it is not possible to believe her, except for the Yiddish.*

So we are still here in this same room, eating three times a day unbelievable food. At first they made for us coffee but with the grounds in it, weak and cold, now we drink tea, which is what they wished in the first place, with toast cold and dry and eggs and butter and marmalade for breakfast, never any meat, which they keep for themselves. There is a kosher table; naturally, I would not eat there, with the worst element in the camp. The other meals are stringy meat, watery vegetables, tinned desserts, everything boiled and cold. What I need most of all, Leo, is some money so I can send Margot to the town to buy some food, if they have anything fit to eat in this country. It rains all the time and, believe it or not, there is no heating in these barracks, the Englische dame *tries to tell me the English do not like central heating, it is this way everywhere, but it cannot be so in such a damp, cold climate. Why do they lie so much, these English?*

We look very much forward to come to you and wait with hope to hear news of Michael. If you get word, you will let us know, yes? I do not think they steal the mail.

Your loving sister,
Anna.

P.S. Margot asks to be remembered to her cousins and says soon she will see them and be happy again.

"Wow!" Elly said. "How awful!"

"What's awful?" Phil asked, amused.

"Everything! Don't you see? They had to leave all their stuff behind and now look where they are! No Uncle Michael. And . . . she sounds so . . . I don't know. The things she makes a fuss about! It's true, too, you know, at the end what the English lady said. Our English teacher, Miss Folger, goes there every summer, and she told us, they do use fireplaces and little heaters and that's all. I mean, she should know, shouldn't she?"

Pop wasn't listening. He folded the letter up and put it in his jacket pocket. "I'll see what Sonya thinks," he said softly. "Let's go."

In silence they turned out the lights, locked the door, and got into the car. The letter was a heaviness among them, hanging in the air like their frozen breaths.

"How much money?" Phil asked.

"Don't you worry about it," Pop said. "I'll manage. Some. Sooner or later she'll find out that we're not so rich ourselves."

"You know, Pop," Elly said, "it just occurred to me. You never talk about your family. Mama, she tells us plenty about *her* life, but you . . ."

"What's to say? Anna was a child when I left, a pretty, pretty child. Already my mother was talking about how she would marry well; it was all she cared about for the girls. It was natural, of course, that was the way they were. I was the outcast, with such different feelings and ideas from theirs. I did not regret leaving, if that is what you mean."

"Didn't you ever want to go back?"

Pop laughed. "Want? I would have to walk on the water, believe me! The other side of not wanting to be rich is to be—poor. Where would I find the money to go back? No, it's no loss. So here I am, as you find me."

"And there Aunt Anna is," Phil said. "In a refugee camp."

"Poor Anna! That's not fair," Pop answered. "Although they *could* have left earlier. Still, your Mama is right, you know. Things are like a chain to drag you down. I remember my mother and her diamond earrings . . . she loved them . . ."

Then Elly had a thought, which clarified something that had been puzzling her for a long time. "Is that why you married Mama?"

"I married her because I loved her, silly."

"Oh, I know that! But was that because of what you said . . . the way she was about things. And money. Not caring."

Pop was silent for a while. "You may be right. I never thought of it quite that way, but, yes . . . possibly it was so. She was so fresh, so open."

"I always wondered," Elly said. Her parents had seemed so oddly matched to her, with her father liking city living so much and her mother happy only in the country, that she wondered what had caused her father to settle on the farm and without complaint. Now she had a little insight, something to chew over and think about.

"My mother and her diamond earrings," Pop said into the darkness, "my father and his bales of wool, my aunt Trude and her big house in Hamburg, my cousin Karl and his photography shop, and little, pretty Anna. Yes, they all did well. My brother Walter was killed in 1916, of course. Otherwise . . ."

"What will it be like having Aunt Anna here after so many years?" Phil wondered.

Pop shrugged. "That I do not know. It troubles me. It is funny that now I am the only one left besides her. It is like smoke—poof! the wind blows, and it is gone—wool business, photography shop, house."

"And all those years," Elly wondered. "Won't it be strange having them come? I mean, they're almost strangers. Isn't there another place for them?"

Pop shook his head. "Strange? But they come, anyway—there is no other place. We'll fix up the storage room, make a nice bedroom, your mama is already full of ideas. All we need is a little money. Hah! All! And the car needs fixing—listen to that knock."

Obligingly, the car bucked at that moment, almost stalled, then leaped forward again. "Won't make the snow," Phil warned.

"Fifty dollars here, fifty dollars there, the Pelzers leaving . . ."

"I'll paint the place for you, Pop," Phil said. "A couple of weekends, and it'll be done."

"No, thanks. Such a smart boy I have doesn't paint. You do enough with the store. We'll manage." The car skidded on the mud and gravel around the sharp turn to their driveway. "Thank God we're home again! May Anna say the same when she sees this place!"

"It doesn't sound promising, does it, Pop?" Elly asked. The house looked tiny and poor to her also, with its unpainted boards silvering in the weather. At least when it was dark, you couldn't see the messy front yard and the crumbling walls of the old barn and chicken houses, replaced ten years ago but left to rot or be used for firewood. There was nothing picturesque or charming about the place, Elly had to admit that. Even in her most romantic mood, she could make little out of it except what it was: her home and certainly loved. Nevertheless, she wondered if that would be enough for Margot and her mother.

"We'll see," Pop said shortly. "Get out, moony, if you please, so we can go in and eat. Soon will be Fibber McGee and Molly, which I don't want we should miss." He opened the door to the kitchen. "Sonya! Where are you? A letter came to the store today from Anna. . . ."

Elly lingered outside the door, surrounded by the night. Bits of gravel crunched beneath her feet, and her nose began to run. Her stomach rumbled. Her imagination was working at full steam, however, and she did not want to be interrupted by reminders to take off her coat, wash her hands, or eat her potatoes. She forced her mind into the refugee camp she had quickly assembled—unpainted wooden houses knocked together, drafty and smelly, yes, but she hurried past that to focus on the people milling about aimlessly, talking, complaining, bolting down food, sitting dully on their camp beds. But how did they feel? There she drew a blank. How humiliating! She did not have the experience and could not make the leap. She kicked at a stone.

A beam of light shone from the open kitchen door. "Elly—we're sitting down! Hurry!"

How did Margot feel? Oh, she couldn't wait to find out! They'd have long, lovely secret talks in the dark, she was sure of that. Couldn't Margot speak English? Aunt Anna . . . well, that would be interesting, too, but it wouldn't matter so much. Margot would teach her so many things!

She pushed away her doubts. What good would they do? Already she was forgetting the letter with its indications of difficulties ahead, for she could not bear to think about it. Who outlawed imagination, anyway? Mama called it daydreaming, but then, Mama wasn't always right, either.

"I'm coming, I'm coming," Elly called, pausing on the threshold to listen to the far-off noises of the evening train rushing through the valley on its way from New York.

"Soon they'll be on that train," she said happily. "Oh, Mama, what will we do?"

Mama looked up soberly from the big soup tureen. "Put this on the table and wash your hands. My dear, I do not know. But we will manage somehow. Why not? With God, all things are possible. I was reading only today that beautiful story of Ivan Ilyich by Count Tolstoy . . . do you know it yet?"

Elly shook her head. "Mm, this is good!"

"So please wait a minute! Then you should look for a copy in English in the library and tell me what you think."

"Mama, you know what I mean! What did you think of Aunt Anna's letter? She doesn't sound so nice, does she?"

"No," Mama said slowly, "she is frightened out of her wits, poor thing. And what makes you think you wouldn't be, young lady? It is not for *you* to judge older ones—wait until *you* must face such a . . . I don't know what to call it . . . there is nothing in my mind to make comparisons."

"Well, it doesn't make any difference what I think, anyway," Elly said grumpily.

"No," Mama said, "nor what any of us think, Anna included. That is what is so hard to accept."

4

❦❦ "AT THIS TIME of the year, what kind of crossing would we have?" Aunt Anna asked, weeping. "I was sick the entire time." Pop translated for her. "I am still sick. My stomach . . ." And she collapsed, groaning, on the parlor sofa, closing her eyes and leaning back against an old pillow. She and Margot had finally arrived in the midst of a January storm on the train from New York to Franklin, where Pop had picked them up for a harrowing drive through thickly falling flakes that leaped upon the windshield to block the road. "Margot, where are my pills?"

Margot stood surrounded by the piles of luggage Phil had lugged in from the car, snow melting on the fur collar of her dark coat and beading her damp blond hair. "I do not know, Mutti. Please! You did not, after all, wish to spend in the barracks all winter."

At that, Aunt Anna groaned again. "The worst of it is the thought of crossing once more that ocean. You would not believe . . ."

Suddenly Mama came to life. "My dear Anna, I would believe. I still remember when I came with my mother for even more days. Three weeks we were crossing—remember, Mamushka?—in the steerage, with no cabins and people sick all over the floor and babies crying and people dying in the very sight of America!" Mama shuddered. "No, one does not forget."

Aunt Anna sat bolt upright. "Well, I am sorry we did not have so hard a time as you did . . ."

Pop interrupted. "Anna, Sonya is only trying to say that she is understanding. We are all most sympathetic."

Elly turned away to giggle. She had this irresistible desire to laugh and was ashamed of it; what, after all, was funny? Only her own sense of anticlimax and of confusion, for nothing was as she had imagined. Margot had not even noticed her!

"Maybe I am not so used to the English language, so I make mistakes," Aunt Anna said with dignity.

Margot found the pill box. She had paid attention only to her mother, not even looking directly at the rest of them. "I took from the kitchen this water, I hope it is all right," she said stiffly. "Here, Mutti."

"All right? But this is your home now," Baba said quietly.

"You should have come last year," Elly chimed in, "when we had only the pump in the kitchen, before they ran the water lines through and we could put in the plumbing."

Margot lifted her eyebrows. "How quaint," she said. "But no, thank you. Of course, we cannot be any more choosers, eh?"

"Oh, my God!" Phil said under his breath.

Despite the exhaustion and unhappiness marked on her face, signs of Aunt Anna's old beauty could still be seen. Her lipstick had worn off, and her powder was caked with tears and mixed with grime; but her eyebrows were carefully plucked to pencil thinness, and she had managed, despite all the inconveniences of the refugee camp and overcrowded ocean liner, to have her faded blond hair cut short and waved close to her head. Even rows of small waves framed her round face with its trim little nose and snapping blue eyes. She was tiny, no more than five feet tall, and slightly plump, and she moved, even in her present state, with the air of a woman who expected admiration for her beauty and charm. The fact that she was not at all charming now made her pathetic, but it was clear that in other circumstances she could be formidable. It was also clear that she would not be an easy person to live with.

"Let me show you your room," Mama said nervously, "then you will have some coffee, yes? Leo loves his coffee, and we keep the best for him—and now for you."

"We grind our own . . ." Elly cut in hastily and was left in the silence with the rest of her sentence hanging. She blushed.

"This is a tiny house," Aunt Anna said accusingly to Pop.

Pop spoke gently. "You know we are not rich." Elly was astounded. Why wasn't he angry?

"You should have seen our apartment in Berlin . . . so beautiful it was . . ." Aunt Anna said.

Why was she talking this way? Elly looked at Mama; whenever Mama grew angry, her cheeks glowed red. She was the same Mama as always, looking at and listening to Aunt Anna with her usual calm expression. But Aunt Anna was wrong! Elly clenched her fists and started to say something, then stopped when her arm jostled Margot's. She wanted this cousin to like her; how could she manage that?

"This is the room we have fixed for you, Anna," Pop said. "We have done what we could and hope it will do well." Was Pop being apologetic? That was wrong, too!

Elly had admired the way Mama and Baba had fixed up the old storage room, painting the walls a pinky-white, laying soft, weathered boards from the barn for the floor, then covering them with rag rugs. They had made flowered curtains for the two windows and a matching spread for the bed, then upholstered two easy chairs and refinished the odd tables and dressers and chairs that filled the large room and shone in the light from the Franklin stove and the bridge lamp.

Elly had gone in each day while they worked, liking the sunny, pleasant room more and more. How could anyone not like its freshness and warmth?

Now she saw it through Aunt Anna's eyes, with everything second-hand and homemade, and she was ashamed of liking it before. How could it possibly compare with the bedrooms in that lost Berlin apartment? No wonder Aunt Anna looked so miserable as she stood in the doorway staring. She made all they had taken for granted look shabby.

Phil dumped the luggage on the floor with a series of thuds and pulled Elly's hair in passing. Their eyes met, and they grinned at each other.

"This is like the peasant house we stayed in at Hachterfelde—remember, Mutti?" Margot said. The faintest of smiles flickered on Margot's face and was gone. Elly stared in fascination at her cousin's changing expressions.

Mama laughed. "Well, that is what we are, peasants!" Little spots of red shone on her cheeks. "Perhaps you will be disappointed in us."

"Certainly not my brother!" Aunt Anna said. "Always we were town people. Leave everything here so, please." She looked around. "But where is for Margot? Not surely on this couch? *Mein Gott*, I am tired!"

Pop spoke rapidly, too rapidly. "Elly has a large room

upstairs, which she is most eager to share, so we have fixed up very nicely a place for both the girls. That is all right?" he asked, turning to Margot.

Margot shrugged. "Why not? What shall it matter?"

"Well, gee," Elly said, "it'll matter a lot if you don't like it, right? You're liable to be here years and years!"

Margot focused on Elly for the first time. "And if *you* do not like it?"

"Oh, no, I'm really looking forward to our sharing the room! Come on up and see it, why don't you?" How false her heartiness sounded in her ears! The truth was, she had absolutely no idea what to say and felt like a fool.

"Yes, and I go into the kitchen to make some coffee," Baba said. "Sit, Sonya, sit!"

Phil carried Margot's suitcases up the stairs and threw them, "Ooof!" onto the floor of the big bedroom. The girls followed. "I'm right next door," he said, smiling. "If you need anything, knock." He looked at Margot, then quickly turned away. "Your mother's a real lulu!"

"What does this mean—lulu?" Margot asked. "In here? But how cold it is!"

"Pop's going to get a heater next week—he promised. In honor of you. *I've* done without one for years." Elly knew she was gabbling on and on, yet she couldn't stop. "Oh, yes, the bathroom's right at the foot of the stairs—one for the seven of us. There's a wash basin in the corner here, for all the good it'll do you." She watched Margot for some reaction; all she could see was the same carefully composed pale face and the cool eyes that stared slightly above her head. With no clue, what could she say? "And here's room for your clothes." She continued with an apologetic little laugh, "Funny closet, I know but you'll get used to it." The deep closet had been cut into the wall under the slope of the roof. "Kind of dark. Can I help with your clothes?"

"Oh, I think I manage myself, after I wash a little and brush my hair, hmm? There is not, I think, such a hurry." Margot plumped down on her bed and lifted a small case to her lap.

"Well, no," Elly said, feeling more and more uncomfortable at this cousin's ungivingness. Yes, that was it, she was ungiving. How had she imagined Margot to be? Surely not like this. "Listen," she began desperately, "I'd like to . . ." then stopped. Margot had unpacked nothing but a photograph in a small frame.

"This is my dresser? There are not things on it, so I assume . . ."

It was the golden maple highboy from the auction that Elly had coveted; why couldn't Margot take over her scratched pine dresser and not be the wiser? Mama had insisted, though, and the piece was saved for Margot. Much good it did, Elly thought. She was unhappy with the highboy, too; she might as well have had the pine.

"Yes, we bought it all for *you*," she couldn't resist saying, and more sharply than she had imagined she could, "the highboy, the bed, and the chair. We can share the desk and bookcase, is that all right?"

Margot nodded. She set the photograph carefully on top of the highboy and stood looking at it. How vulnerable her back was! Elly walked over and stood beside her. The picture was of a severe-looking man who stared stiffly out at her behind a pair of rimless glasses. The head was fine-boned and narrow, the hair was clipped short and graying, and the jaw was firm.

"This is my vatti," Margot said softly.

"I see," Elly said, just as softly. Then she burst out,

"Oh, Margot, I hope you will be happy here! I wanted you so much to come!" She paused and turned away to speak in a whisper to the wall. "You didn't want to come, I know. Still, I wish . . ." She couldn't bear to look at her cousin for the confusion she herself felt as she tried to understand how her dream of Margot had shattered against her cousin's simple presence in this room.

Margot shrugged and continued unpacking her clothes, laying them out with meticulous care on her bed, stroking and caressing them, refusing to look up at Elly, who was standing over her and staring at the growing pile of clothes.

"I'll help you put them away," she said, grabbing some hangers and ignoring Margot's "No, no" for the sheer pleasure of feeling the wools and silks as she put the clothes away with more care than she had ever shown for her own things. But these were so beautiful!

"There will be no room to wear these here, I think, hmm?" Margot asked. "Pity."

"No room?" Elly was bewildered. "I think you mean place—no place."

Margot shrugged again. "Yes, possibly. My English is not yet so good. Well, this was the dress my vatti liked best; naturally I take it." It was a flowered blue with a long pleated skirt. "For the theatre in Berlin. Which you do not have here."

At once Elly forgot her clumsiness. "Theatre? Did you go a lot?" She forgot about the clothes, too, and almost sat on them. Margot gathered them up, and Elly moved farther away on the bed. "Sorry. What did you see? That's what I'm most interested in, the theatre . . ."

Margot stared at her until she flushed. "I am not so interested in the theatre at all. My vatti would take me, and I would not wish even to speak of it when he is . . ." and she dropped her eyes to look at her hands twisting in her lap. "I do not think I shall see my vatti again. I do not say so to my mutti, you understand, but I shall be surprised if he appears once more. There is no way you could know."

No, of course not, there *was* no way she could know. Elly tried her best to imagine Uncle Michael being tortured in a prison camp, but she could not. All she could feel was her own misery. How had Margot managed to make her feel so small and unfeeling? Oh, she had never imagined anything like this!

She was close to tears, putting away the clothes in silence, when Mama called upstairs that a little supper was ready, and they went down. Baba held Elly back at the kitchen door and whispered in her ear. "Do not listen to *what* they say but to their fright, so you will not answer them. It is terrible, we cannot know how terrible! Who would do better?"

"You!" Elly exclaimed, hugging her grandmother.

"No," Baba said, "not one of us without the grace of our dear Lord. Not you, dear child, not you at all."

Aunt Anna was hunched up over the table, her hands clasped around a mug of coffee. She spoke excitedly in German, her voice shrill, sweat breaking out on her powdered face. "Mutti, you must be learning English," Margot reminded her, but she could not stop, she had to speak, and now and in German. Pop translated, more and more upset, until his hands began to shake, and Mama clasped his hands in hers.

"She says at the end they had almost no food. They had to beg almost for the simplest things. There was no school for Margot of course . . . earlier in school the children would not speak with the Jewish children. Margot's best friend from infancy almost would no longer notice her . . ."

Margot shuddered. "The worst was when they came for Vatti." She shivered again. "We knew. Who did not know? In the building downstairs they waited; they looked at us with piggy little eyes and waited, adding up the sofa and the beds and the linens and the china, no longer remembering when Vatti would visit their sick children and send no bill, for they were neighbors, *nicht wahr?* And then, after the *Kristallnacht* . . ."

"We heard about it on the radio," Phil said.

"Ach, but *we* were there. To go down the next day and see smashed up the shops, the houses—everything! And painted signs all over the streets . . . where could Vatti hide?"

Mama spoke slowly. "Wouldn't anyone take him in even for a little time?"

"What is she saying?" Aunt Anna asked. "But there were so many to be hidden! And so few who would try!"

Margot slid her fingers through her hair. Absent-mindedly she put hot milk in her coffee and drank it quickly, greedily. "It was not so easy. No one who lived in an apartment building could hide a person, for the janitor would somehow know, and they were all Nazis, those little men from the cellars. At the country would be best, but in November? The Gestapo was already that morning at Vatti's clinic to check that the Jewish doctors would not go there. Police were at the train stations . . . ach, police were even on the ends of our streets, it was known that many Jews in the apartment buildings lived . . ."

"And it happened so fast," Aunt Anna said, twisting her hands nervously. She stared down at them. "At the border they took from me even my wedding ring," she said dully. "Even that."

"We could not call people by the telephone," Margot continued. "There was too many dangers, you see."

"Then they came. That same night." Aunt Anna closed her eyes and leaned back in her chair. The light shone eerily on her exhausted face. "We heard them. That was the worst. From downstairs. Bam! Bam! on the doors." She banged so hard on the table that the cups and saucers leaped into the air. Elly's heart beat fast. "All the way up to our floor. Behind the other doors, our dear neighbors waited."

"Afraid, too," Margot said. Her voice cracked. "Some men jumped from their windows, and even their families with them. We could not move. We sat like mice under a cat's paw, Vatti with his little case of clothing. . . ."

"We do not know where he is," Aunt Anna finished. "But we were able to go away in a week if we had a visa. All that was needed was to leave all behind—the money, the furniture, the jewels, the table silver, the pictures. All told to us how lucky we are that we are having this chance to go, maybe it is never again, and we are here with the new year."

"Let us hope it will be a good year, dear Anna," Pop said. Mama moved to bring plates of bread, cheese, and meat to the table, and the noise of these ordinary actions broke the spell.

"I do not think so," Margot said. "Nineteen thirty-nine. I am one week late, but I wish you a happy new year, anyway."

"I shall pray," Mama said quietly, "for his release. We can do that much. And you will be tired now. I hope with all my heart you will think this is your home."

Aunt Anna started to say something, then stopped. Mama went on, "I *know* you do not think you can. I say that I *hope* and I pray so."

However, Mama's prayers led to the next indication that life together would be far from simple. Aunt Anna held herself rigidly away from the table when Mama said grace and turned from the sign of the cross. She said nothing at the time but after dinner drew Pop into the parlor and spoke volubly, shrilly, emotionally. "Every night? No! Impossible! Leo, how could you? Our parents would never have . . ."

"Anna, be quiet!" Pop said. "You are so foolish I cannot believe it—what kind of a Jew are you? And what were our parents, may they rest in peace?"

"That is what is so funny," Aunt Anna said. "We were such good Germans. But now I see that it is not funny at all. . . . Still, I tell you, Leo, I do not like the prayers, I do not like this Jesus business. Never!"

"Then you must endure what you do not like. Even when you were a small child, you found this hard." For the first time Pop's voice was sharp.

Aunt Anna exclaimed in astonishment, "You are jealous, even after so many years! I would not have believed this."

"You think jealousy sent me away from home? No doubt our mother said that. Never could she accept that I did not wish to live her way—so closed up. It was like being in a coffin while you are alive."

"And this is better?" Aunt Anna asked. "I see how poor this is, and now I believe that one can be American and poor. I did not believe so. The little town, your store, this house in the middle of nowhere—this is better?"

"Much better," Pop said. "There is no comparison."

In the kitchen Mama smiled. "I think Margot wishes to help with the dishes also," she said. "Elly, wipe the table, please, sweep the floor, then take water to the chickens."

"Want to see the chickens?" Elly asked Margot.

Margot shook her head, her face closed tight, her long silky hair swinging from side to side as she bent and stretched to put the dishes away in the places Mama pointed out.

Baba was finishing a sweater. "There is no end to knitting for Christmas, even in January," she sighed. "Ah me, my back aches! Maybe I'll send a package for Easter down to Green Branch—oof, such a pain!"

Elly went to rub her grandmother's back. "Oh, I love you, Baba!" she said, feeling miserable. She could tell from the sound of the voices in the parlor that Pop was unhappy, and what little she understood of the conversation was enough to let her know that Aunt Anna was calling them *poor* in a way meant to hurt. And it did. That was the worst of it. She felt that Aunt Anna was right; they *were* poor, and it *was* awful.

"Margot, shall I make a sweater for you?" Baba asked. "If you had come for Christmas, you should have had one, with scarf and mittens and hat besides. Each year I make for Elly one and then for Phil, it is a family joke, eh, Elly?"

"But nice sweaters," Elly said, now sweeping the dust from one part of the kitchen to the other. How dreary it was doing the same chores, even with Margot here! How could she have imagined that Margot would make everything change? She was angry at her own folly, her own dreams, and angry with Margot for not living up to them.

"Thank you, I have still many clothes," Margot said,

without turning around.

Baba drew in her breath sharply. Her needles clicked faster.

There it was, Elly thought, in a nutshell. How little Margot gave! Could give, would give? Oh, what difference did it make in the end? Well, she would try again. "I've *never* seen nicer clothes," she said.

"Yes," said Margot, "that may well be so."

Mama poured the dirty dish water down the sink with a great *woosh*.

5

THE AWKWARD SILENCE that followed was the first of many. There was no escape in the tiny house, no chance to say what was on your mind and be done with it, for you could never go away and leave your words behind. When Elly awoke in the morning, Margot's head was on the pillow in the bed across the room. How beautiful and calm she looked before she opened her eyes and rearranged her features into the expression of cold reserve she tried to maintain all the time. All right, she had had a terrible experience. But why wouldn't she yield at least a little now?

Each morning Elly found it harder to ask. She grabbed her clothes and ran downstairs to the bathroom before the next person needed it, then dressed in Baba's room where the small stove sent out waves of toasty heat. Margot would not go to school until the new term began in February, and she had had a chance to grow accustomed to this new way of life.

While Elly was doing her morning chores in the barn, there was a chance to talk to Phil, both of them freezing in the bitter January cold but working slowly for the pleasure of the quiet time together.

"Well?" Elly asked, stamping her feet and cleaning her fingers of chicken mash with wisps of hay.

"Well, what?" Phil answered. "Hey, don't knock into that milk! It's going to be a long winter. Listen, it's not their fault. They're stuck out here, too—it's like the end of the world for them."

"I know but . . . why can't Aunt Anna be different at least? Then Margot would be, too."

"Maybe," Phil said. "Maybe." He forked a last load of hay into the cow's stall. "People are what they are, not what you'd like them to be."

"You sound like Pop," she said in disgust. "He said the same thing the other night to Aunt Anna. And I can't stand it to be like that!" she cried out, and the horses nickered and whinnied at the noise. She went to rub Sasha's coat while she talked, her loud voice half-muffled as she pressed her mouth to the horse's warm side. "I can't stand it here another day! Everything's changed . . ."

"Let's go in," Phil said. "Nothing's changed. You were the one who had all those great dreams, and now you're awake. That's all that's happened. You can't blame them for it, you know."

"Who can I blame? I've got to blame somebody!"

Phil laughed and laughed. The barn echoed to the sound. In the chicken house next door, the chickens squawked and flapped their wings. "Dumb birds," Elly said in despair. "Dumb, stupid birds. Don't you just hate them?"

"Well, I'm not crazy about living on this farm myself, you know. If you ask me, I think *that's* a romantic idea. Mama wouldn't admit it, and you'd bite my head off, wouldn't you," he asked, teasing Elly, "if I said that you and Mama are the same, both of you, wild romantics?"

Elly hooted. "Mama? I think you're balmy. Must be all the studying you do."

"Here, take the bucket in, O.K.? Don't just leave it for Baba to get. You know what I'm doing? I'm entering two exhibits in the Connecticut State Science Fair . . ."

"Yes, you've always got your work," Elly said, swinging the empty feed bucket fiercely back and forth. "Oh, it's so cold!"

"I'd like to win," Phil said. "There's the sun at last. Thought he might forget us today."

"You don't like it here any more than I do," Elly said.

"But don't blame Margot, it's not her fault, poor kid. She's scared stiff about school, you know."

"I didn't know."

"Then why don't you plain talk to her sometime without getting your ideas in the way?" Phil asked.

"Did you? When? I didn't know," Elly said accusingly.

"Hey! You're not my boss, remember that? I need help with my German for college, and we agreed I'd help her with her English—it's pretty good, though, don't you think?—and she'd work with me in German."

"You like Margot, don't you?" Elly said passionately. "She's beautiful, isn't she? Really beautiful."

"She's all right," Phil said. "Why shouldn't I like her?"

And they went in to eat, spooning down the hot oatmeal to warm themselves, thinking about the school day ahead.

"There is no end to this cold," Margot complained one evening. "I would not have believed it."

Pop looked up from the newspaper. "Poor Czechoslovakia. Finished. *Kaput.* I saw Prague on my way to America. . . ."

Aunt Anna was embroidering a tablecloth. "That is a most beautiful city. We are going there many times. How do you find my English?"

"Quaint, very quaint," Elly said, grinning. "Pop, when can we have a stove for our room?"

"Soon, soon. On Wednesday I'm picking up a big order of canned goods in Newchester, and I'll talk to Johannes at the junkyard and see what he's got. I don't want to get any old kerosene *firemacher,*" Pop said. "Not for you."

"Junkyard?" Margot asked, raising her eyebrows.

"Yes," Pop said. "Just that. What should I do? Buy a new one? Impossible. Do without? But you are both complaining about the cold." His voice was sharp again.

"It is difficult for us," Aunt Anna said, "to know such changed ways. That is all." She smiled sweetly at them. "It is all right if I heat now the stove in my room? Possibly you would wish to come in there with me," and she rose, gathering the long tail of tablecloth in one hand and the hoops in the other. "I am not in the kitchen easy."

"We could light the fire in the parlor," Pop said hesitantly.

"No!" Mama said. "There is not enough wood, Leo, it would mean that Phil would have to cut more, and when would he find the time? Leave it as it is, and call Johnny DiLeo for more coal tomorrow for Anna's stove and the kitchen. We'll manage his bill as we do everything—somehow."

Phil followed Margot into her mother's room. Elly sat in the kitchen studying and listened to Mama and Pop talking softly yet fiercely about money. When she tried to interrupt, they told her to concentrate on her school work, she could certainly do better in some subjects, and went on with their discussion, which wasn't about money at all but about what to do with Aunt Anna after Margot started school the next day.

"There is nothing for her to do here, poor woman. She cannot cook, she does not understand the English on the radio or in our books, she will not go out in the cold," Mama said. "Really, Leo, she will go crazy—and take me with her. You do not know what it is like around here!"

"Then let's move to town," Elly popped in, and went back to her books.

Pop thought. "I have friends in New York still. I'll write and ask one of them to look for some German books. Second-hand. And send them to me." He began to cut his thick, square nails with a paring knife. "Alma Fox sent me her meat order for February."

"Instead of going to the A&P in Newchester?" Mama exclaimed. "But you will have to give her their prices!"

"There is no profit in it, that's so, but enough maybe to pay for some German books for Anna."

"Always money!" Mama said, and they were off again. "Leo, you know I have *never* minded working as I do, it is my life, to make our clothes and grow our vegetables and live by ourselves. But once Anna and Margot come, then little by little it costs money, always money, that is all they know, how to spend money, not how to do for themselves . . ."

"Oh, I am so miserable," Elly exclaimed. "I don't want to hear about money any more! You know what, Mama? I'd like to *buy* my Easter clothes this year, just for once. Walk into Blessington's in Newchester and buy everything I want—a navy blue suit and a white piqué blouse and white gloves and navy blue patent leather shoes and a white straw hat with a red band and red flowers. . . ."

"What nonsense!" Mama said sharply. "What utter nonsense! Have you finished your homework?"

"Well," Elly said, hurt, "I need all the help I can get. Compared to Margot . . ."

"I begin to think you are a jewel!" Mama said, laughing.

Elly felt no better. In bed that night, she began to talk to Margot about clothes, about the Easter clothes she wanted, and suddenly her cousin's voice changed and grew warm as she told Elly in detail about the clothes she'd left behind.

"But you brought so many with you!" Elly said, astonished. Was this what her cousin came to life for? Clothes!

"The best was of camel hair, a skirt and a vest and cape with shoes and gloves and beret to match," Margot finished. "Fine wool. Too heavy for packing and for wearing too costly, it would call attention." Excitement sparked her voice as it caressed in words all those vanished beauties.

"Do you *really* like clothes that much?" Elly asked. "I mean . . . well, clothes . . . I hardly notice mine at all!"

"That," said Margot, "is obvious."

Elly didn't even care. "There are so many more important things than clothes—my God—it's such a waste of good time, I think . . . clothes."

"*Ach*, no, you are wrong," Margot said. "It is to me an endless fascination. Do you have here fashion journals? From where do you pick your clothes and buy?"

"Mama makes all of mine—I *hate* to sew!" Elly remembered seeing copies of *Vogue* strewn around the kitchen at Laura's house and began to tell Margot about them, then checked herself. She didn't want to talk about Laura. Or about *Vogue* magazine.

"Sew?" Margot asked, sitting up. "Brr, it is cold here." Elly could see her face in the light of the moon through the window, and it was open now, sparkling and almost friendly. How awful that it was *clothes* that made the difference! She felt the last of her wishes about her cousin steal away and regretted their going. How much nicer that Margot was who smiled eternally into the distance on a sunny Baltic beach! She had put that photograph safely away in her drawer; occasionally, she took it out and peered at it, trying to bridge the gap between that Margot and this one. In truth, she preferred the girl in the picture.

Margot was talking freely now. "I do not know how to sew, it is something I am sorry for, my mutti does not let me learn. She thinks it is for shopgirls. Your mother, would she teach me? I must learn, I wish to learn, I think it is necessary if one wishes to become *couturière*. What do you call it in English? A designer of clothing?"

"I haven't the foggiest notion," Elly said thoughtfully. "Is *that* what you want to be? I couldn't imagine!—well, good luck!" How could anyone want to spend a lifetime making clothes? "Mama show you how to sew? You bet—she'll eat you up alive. She's been dying to show me for years, and I wouldn't learn, so she'll absolutely adore you!" All right, there it was, Margot would never be what the girl in the picture promised, and Elly would have to learn to live with that. She snuggled down into the cold sheets and thumped her feet to warm up the bed a little.

Margot spoke quietly into the darkness. "I think then

I feel a little better. Only . . . only . . . I would wish two things. One, that my vatti should be here. And the other is that I did not need to enter into school tomorrow. This frightens me, and that I do not like."

"Well, gosh, no, who does? Listen, don't worry about it, though, you'll do fine. Better than I do, probably."

"You are having trouble?"

"The kids think I'm a nut," Elly admitted.

"I do not understand," Margot said, puzzled. "I fear I shall have not such a good time." She was silent for such a long while that Elly thought she had gone to sleep. When she spoke again, her voice was remote and tinny. "I would like, please, if you could say only that I am German. You understand? Not that I am Jewish."

Elly let this sink in. "Sure," she said easily. "But it doesn't make any difference here. Of course, everyone knows that Pop's Jewish, but he's not, if you know what I mean, not really. And you aren't either, not like the kids that go to the synagogue and everything. So it doesn't count."

"You think not?" Margot said. "It is what we thought in Germany, too. I asked the same question—how is it that I am Jewish when I know nothing of it? There was no answer, but here we are, anyway!"

"Oh, you don't have to worry about it. Honest! It's just not the same in America. Phil says he won't get into Yale because they've got a quota, but . . ."

"Ah, so it begins!" Margot said, sounding utterly miserable. "I did not think things here would be like this after all!"

Elly decided there was no point in continuing this conversation. "To tell the truth," she said frankly, "I did not think you and your mother would be like you are, either. Especially your mother!"

"My mother? But why do you speak of my mother? I shall tell you this. In Berlin she is a silly, spoiled woman. My . . . my vatti is adoring her. And so with other men who are coming to our house. She is going to theatres and operas and does not wish to think this is all coming to an end." Her voice grew husky. "You do not understand, you can never understand, what we are going through, and so you will not be understanding my mother, I think."

Elly thought that her family had lived through hard times, too, and what did Margot know about those? She sounded as if she alone had suffered, and Elly couldn't stand that! "If she is silly and spoiled, why do you defend her and go to her all the time?"

"You are mistaken," Margot said simply. "Several times at the table I am hearing you say that you wish to be an actress and are observing people for this. But you do not observe us so carefully, eh? I do not like so much my mother. Then what should I do? Shout at her the way you are doing to your mother? This we do not have in Germany."

"I don't shout," Elly said, stung. "It's just the way we are here." Imagine! She had no idea that Margot might have been as disappointed in her as she had been in her cousin; in her self-absorption she had never given a thought to the impression *she* might have been making. "Oh, Margot, I'll help you out in school if you need it, just wait and see. Everything will be all right."

"I like it that *you* are thinking so," Margot said bleakly. "Only I do not think you are right. Your brother is telling me other things."

"*He* is? It's true," Elly admitted, "that some of the teachers don't like anyone who's different in the least way. And foreigners . . . ! Not all of them, though.

And the kids are O.K. Well, most of them. Dull. They made life hard for Laura because of her folks and . . . you're different, anyway. There's a whole group of girls who live in Yankeetown—that's the fancy part of town —and you'll see, they will be simply crazy about you! They don't like me. But you're so . . . elegant!"

"Only we are here so far away from town. That is a problem, I think. *Mein Gott,* we are far away!"

At that, Elly jumped out of bed wrapped in her thick quilt and went to sit on her cousin's bed and pour out the story of her own unhappiness on the farm and desire to move to town. "It would be so much better for both of us . . . maybe we could convince Mama together . . . now that you're here."

"You have much faith," Margot said, "that you will do what you wish to do. This is charming. And very American, not so? I do not believe this any longer. So you must believe for the both of us. And so you will, it seems to me!"

She laughed, and Elly joined her. They sat close together in the dark, cold house, muffling their laughter in the quiet. It was the first time in the three weeks that Margot had been with them that she had laughed, and Elly was enormously pleased.

6

THE WIDE CORRIDOR leading to the auditorium wing stretched silent and empty ahead of them as Elly and Laura hurried to Mrs. Wilbur's office behind the auditorium to hear what play had been chosen and what their parts would be. The regular school day had fallen away from them along with the jostling crowds and the noise that had stopped at three o'clock as suddenly as if a magic cloak had fallen upon the building.

"All I hope is that there are good parts for *us!*" Elly said.

"Oh, I don't know," Laura objected, "I'd like it to be a play we could be proud of, too."

"Yes, but . . ." Elly began, and then saw Margot. Her cousin was leaning against the heavy doors to the auditorium, hugging a pile of books to her body. Elly knew that something was wrong when she saw Margot's coat buttoned wrong, hanging down on one side and scrunched up on the other. "My cousin," she said flatly, hating this moment when Laura and Margot would meet.

Before she had a chance to introduce them, Margot rushed up, pushing her hair back from her angry face and speaking so quickly and breathlessly that Elly could barely understand her. "What am I to do? They are putting me into such strange classes that I do not understand anything. This is my program—here!" And she thrust a crumpled card in front of Elly's eyes.

"Wait a minute," Elly said, annoyed. "I can't read it like this!" She yearned to open the doors and walk down the sloping aisle to the stage.

Margot seemed to notice nothing. "In English they are putting me with all those big boys who do not know how to read, and when I speak to the teacher of this class, he does not even look at me! Can I move to your sports class, is this possible? I think in my class are the girls you said I should like; but no, I do not like them at all, they are not cultured. They look at my underthings because such stitching and lace is strange to them, and they laugh in a most stupid way. This I do not like." She breathed several times sharply and shallowly, then plunged ahead. "The French class shall be simple. Boring but simple. But it is the mathematics, which makes no sense, and this I do not understand. I am already studying this entirely in *gymnasium*, and now what is happening?"

"Oh, Phil can help you . . ." Elly said, relieved.

"But it is sitting in the class so desperate," Margot went on, "I am thinking I cannot do this. For science I must go to the general science, and there are again these same boys who know nothing, and then I see they are putting me with the dunces when I am going to the best school for girls in Berlin! I go to the office and ask for a test, and again they do not even *see* me! I am missing my lunch for doing this. At the end is American history class, and the teacher is talking all the time of the badness of Europe and the goodness of America and is making little remarks to me." She said with bleak dignity, "I am not, after all, Europe."

"You've got Mr. Mather, don't you?" Laura asked, amused. "I have him, too, first period. He really gave it to me when I said I'd just come back from France. It's bad enough being a European, but you can't help that. To be an American and actually *go* there—he gave me a D first marking period just for *that!*"

"But this is terrible!" Margot wailed. "What is to be done?"

"Nothing," Elly said. "That's the way it is here. I'm used to it, and you will be. Some of the teachers really care, but not all that many. Listen, Margot, why don't you go down to Pop's store and wait there for me? I've got this meeting now, and Phil should be there soon. Look over your books, and then we can talk about it tonight. Phil will know what to do."

Margot took in Elly's impatience for the first time. "I am sorry," she said coldly. "You said that you would help."

"And so I shall," Elly assured her. "But, look, Margot what can I do now? Everyone's gone home except the drama people. Tomorrow I'll go to the office with you, I promise. Tomorrow." She practically shoved her cousin out of the door, pointing down the steep flight of steps to Station Street and Lower Main. "That way. Pop's expecting you. Have fun!" She let the door slam. "Honestly! You'd think I was her mother or something!"

"Well," Laura said mildly, "she does have problems—and she seems very nice."

"Thinking only of herself," Elly grumbled. "Let's go in. Mrs. Wilbur won't wait forever, you know how *she* is."

Elly put Laura's sharp look out of her mind in the excitement of finding out about the play.

"At last!" Mrs. Wilbur said. "I thought you girls didn't care. Well, it's to be *You Can't Take It With You*—I was able to get a good price thanks to my contacts in New York. Have you read it? Then here are copies to take home with you. See what you think. And whatever you do, don't lose these books! Penny is for you, Elly, and Alice for Laura. I don't usually give such big parts to sophomores, you understand, so you'd better make sure you can do them. Agreed? I've Rob McGuire down for Tony, and he's a senior. That's the usual way. I'm willing to try though . . . and we shall see, won't we girls? We'll have ourselves some work—and some fun!"

That was it. Mrs. Wilbur dismissed them. They were used to her moods. What bothered Elly was that Margot could have stayed with them, and they could have gone to Laura's house together and—but no! She felt thoroughly bad, as if she were a small child again, being scolded by her mother, and she hated her cousin for making her feel that way. It would be just the two of them, Elly and Laura, the way it had been.

"Well?" Laura asked when they finished the scripts. It was freezing in Laura's tiny room. "Have some of the blanket, kiddo—if only Glenna would remember to open the register!" She wrapped herself up and leaned against the pillow. "How humiliating!" she went on. "The ingenue lead. Really! Do I look like that simpering Alice to you?"

"Just think, though," Elly pointed out, "you've got Rob McGuire playing Tony with you. What more could you want?"

"Well, yes, he's the Clark Gable of Franklin High. Still . . ." Laura drank some hot chocolate. "I know what I'll do! I'll play against my natural personality, I'll really *create* this part."

"Shape it!" Elly said.

"Mold it!" Laura said.

"Carve it!" Elly said. "And now, tell me, how do I play Penny Sycamore? Do I look plump, middle-aged, and loony?"

"Why, yes, as a matter of fact you do!"

And they collapsed in laughter on Laura's bed. Elly thought that everything was all right again.

Only it wasn't. In the back of the store there was an unhappy Margot and a disapproving Pop, and at home there were all of them jammed together with winter blowing outside and tempers short inside. Phil went to the office with Margot the next morning and arranged a better class schedule for her, but still she was unhappy and complained that the girls did not talk to her and the boys laughed at her accent and the teachers did not like Jews, especially smart Jews.

Elly couldn't understand why Phil took Margot so seriously. "Got the same troubles myself," he said. "Yale won't take me, you know. I don't let myself get angry, though."

"Ah, but maybe you should!" Margot said warmly. "It is important, to get rightly angry. If only in Germany we had earlier!"

"Hey, you could be right . . ." Phil said, and Elly didn't hear any more; he and Margot went into the parlor to study together, Phil learning German and teaching trigonometry and American history. Aunt Anna went with them to embroider, explain grammar, and read Goethe's *Conversations with Eckermann*, which had come in a large parcel of German books from New York.

"You light the fire for *them!*" Elly mumbled, hunched over the kitchen table and her school books.

"Yes," Mama said tranquilly, "for they are our guests."

What made it worse was that Elly knew Mama was as unhappy as she was but would not talk about it, would offer no comfort. "You need time to study, not to talk," she said evening after evening. "With all the time you spend on your play, not even to stay with Margot one day after school, it is clear to me these hours must be for school work, not for talk."

Elly could say nothing, for her marks were indeed falling. She did not know why she had given up, maybe it was the relentless winter beating around her ears, or Baba's continual coughing from bronchitis, or the desire to lose herself completely in the routine of rehearsals without falling back into the world of marks and bells and classes. What she did well—English, French, history—was not any trouble, even if she no longer sparkled. But her science and math marks were moving steadily downward, and she responded to each test by refusing to study and turning away from the help her teachers offered. What difference did any of it make? She would show all of them by her brilliant performance, and the rest hardly counted. Why should she be a drudge like Margot and Phil?

One especially bitter morning Pop asked her to come out with him while he warmed up the car, and she would have gone at once except that she heard Margot and Phil laughing in the parlor as they wrapped themselves up in sweaters, scarves, mittens, coats, and boots, and she simply had to go in with them. "Can't," she told Pop and turned her back.

"Well, another time we will talk, eh?" was all he said, as he went slowly outside.

"Elly, Elly!" Margot cried out, "am I still alive or am I a mummy in these things? Never do I know such a cold time! My mutti does not come out of her room for a week until noontime, she is so cold!"

"You sound happy enough," Elly said sourly, and the laughing stopped. No one said anything, only Pop looked straight at her as the quiet trio slipped into the car.

The three weeks that passed this way seemed endless. Elly awakened each morning to a frozen room, arms and legs as heavy as lead, eyes stuffed with cotton. Dressed under the tent of featherbed smelling her own body's night sourness. Waited for the bathroom. Lunged through the bitter cold to the chicken house and the fug that greeted her as she felt around in the dirty straw for the eggs and fed the chittering birds with steamy mash and warm water. Mama and her farm! After the hurried breakfast, came the bucking ride to town in the first light. The days unrolled like a faded blanket, too thin to give warmth.

There were not even rehearsals to look forward to each day, for Mrs. Wilbur was dissatisfied with the cast and reopened auditions. Elly didn't mind spending the afternoons at Laura's house, but at those times she could not escape her guilt. Margot should have been with them. And she knew it. But she was afraid that Margot and Laura would like each other so much that there would be no room for her. Once she had said that to Laura, and it was true. She was wrong to feel this way; she did not need Mama to tell her that. O.K., she was wrong. But she didn't, wouldn't, couldn't, change. Was it her fault? She had been here first, this was *her* home, and Margot would be leaving as soon as she could, anyway, as soon as her father was released.

One drizzly morning Margot overslept. "You've got to get up!" Elly called.

"Too cold, too cold," Margot said, digging her head further into the pillow.

"Let her be," Phil said. "I'll wait and go on the bus

with her, and you can help Pop open the store. You haven't done much around here these days, anyway, Baby Snooks."

"So come, my moony daughter, stop looking at your feet, and keep me company," Pop teased, hurrying Elly out of the house. Her skin shrank against the damp cold of the car seats. "Sorry about the heater," he apologized. "Only the battery won't take it any more, and . . ." Pop shrugged.

All her dissatisfaction and unhappiness, which went back before Margot came, clumped together like a boil—and burst. "Oh, Pop, I hate this! Why can't we live in town? We wouldn't *need* a car then!" And she wouldn't have to keep Margot company in the back of the store or feel absolutely rotten. She didn't say that, though.

For a long time Pop said nothing. Elly wondered if he had heard her. Then he said, "Still on that? Yes, well . . . all right, I'll tell you something. It's not for children, but maybe you will understand more, be nicer to your Mama at home, if you see . . . Maybe we were wrong not to tell you. Since ten years I put aside one dollar a week for college for Phil. One dollar. We were crazy, Sonya and I. Oh, yes, to think of college, people like us. But he was such a brilliant boy, even then! So we put. Five hundred dollars it was, enough for his first year, and then, well, we would see. Never have I borrowed from a bank, never—did you know that? That's how we have managed this whole time, this depression. Owing no one. From the flat over the store I put into the savings for Phil. So! One hundred dollars from this money I had to give to the refugee agency against passage money for Anna and Margot. More I could not. They understood."

Elly nodded. The dun landscape slid past the window,

frozen, still, dead. Had they put aside any money for her?

"Then one hundred dollars Sonya needed for the room—the furniture, the stove, so on—and I had to take some of that for the car repair. Now we must give one hundred dollars more for Michael. . . ."

"Will he come then? Is he safe?"

"Well, they ask for the money—what am I to think? I pray it is so. Then there is the flat to be vacant while we repaint and the cost of that . . . and your heater. Yes, that was necessary. What is left then? A little more than one hundred dollars. Ten years! How is my Phil to go to college on that?" The question was torn from him with a sound very much like a sob.

"I didn't know," Elly said, feeling worse than ever.

"How would you know? That is why I tell you. Now, you tell me, smart girl, what shall I do? You know your brother begins next month a job in the library afternoons and gives up his chemistry class? From 12 to 6 he works four days a week, for nine dollars."

"I didn't know," Elly said again. "But Phil did. Why did you tell him and not me?"

"Because you are such a child, my dear. The way you act at home these days, to make everyone unhappy, I see this."

Elly ignored his gentle reproof. Normally, the slightest sign of disapproval from her father upset her, and she fiercely defended herself. Now, however, she was filled with the idea that had come to her as her father talked, and the words tumbled out one after the other as she stammered in her eagerness. "Listen, Pop, why don't you sell the farm? Just think—all the money you'd—we'd—get . . ." She went off into a delicious dream. "Money for college, oh, pots of money . . . we'd travel, I could even go to New York to see some plays, couldn't I? And we'd have heaps and heaps to give to Uncle Michael and Aunt Anna and Margot, right? Oh, Pop . . ."

"Seems to me," he said, "like you didn't wake up this morning. Still dreaming!"

"No, no! I'm serious. We'd buy a gorgeous house with a real refrigerator and a gas stove, maybe—it would be so easy for Mama! Don't you think so? And the rest of the money we could save, you wouldn't have to worry so much. Why, we'd be rich!" She was totally absorbed in her vision. How cozy it was to be in the car with Pop! Never mind the rain slashing down against the windows. Never mind the dampness and the chill. She could talk to Pop and he understood; he didn't like the farm any more than she did.

Pop could not answer right away. They had arrived at the store. This meant a few minutes of concentrated work—turning the heat up, unlocking the door and bringing in the fresh rolls and bread from the bakery, the milk in wooden boxes from the creamery, rolling up the green shade on the window, sweeping the floor, and waiting on the first customers who came in through the pelting rain for bread and rolls, fresh milk, sandwiches and doughnuts. The factory whistle blew. There was no time for talk until after eight, and Elly had to leave for school by 8:30 if she wanted to call for Laura on the way, and she did.

By the time Pop finally turned to her, she had lost her vision of the riches that would flow from selling the farm, and the damp realities of the day had chilled her hands. More than anything, she wanted him to understand what she was thinking and to see how much she cared for him—and how her plans were really intended to make things easier for him.

"You wouldn't have to worry," she repeated tentatively, trying to read in his expression what he thought of her idea and imagining that he could see how much she wanted the move for herself and would condemn her for her selfishness as he had done in the past with a single sharp glance that she could not meet.

However, his words were gentle. "You want this so much? I did not know that—and your Mama does not, either. No. She wishes for you only the best of everything. This is so important to you?"

Shamed, Elly nodded. "And I try to tell you," she said in a low voice, "and Mama doesn't listen, and you don't either, and I have no place to be alone . . ." Try as she might, she could not keep the note of trembling self-pity out of her voice; she stopped, furious at the betrayal.

Pop listened. "Yes, I see. We have been wrong, perhaps, in thinking so much of Margot and Anna, to save them. Your Mama . . ."

"Not wrong, Pop!" Elly said. "Not wrong! Mama loves everyone, I know that. Only . . ." Once again, she could not finish. It was too much for her to say, *Mama doesn't love me enough*. "Oh, Pop, why did you marry Mama and leave New York? Imagine if we lived there!"

Pop laughed. "Idiot! If I hadn't married your mother, where would you be? Not in New York certainly! Now go, so you won't be late. Go! And give my love to your crazy friend, Laura. I will talk to your Mama."

7

MRS. WILBUR'S VOICE boomed out at them from the dark auditorium. "Stop! Stop! I know this isn't exactly an immortal play, but it's a darn good one! No play should have to put up with this butchery! For one month—one month, let me remind you!—we have been working on the first act. At this rate the entire play won't be ready until 1940. Begin again!"

Frank Galliano, who played Mr. DePinna, shouted out, "From where?"

"Straight through from the opening! We've got to get the flow of the act before we worry about the details!"

"Oh, Christmas," he grumbled, and the others tittered behind him. Mrs. Wilbur came down front and stood by the stage, tapping her foot.

Reluctantly, they began. Elly moved out onto the bare stage to sit hunched over an imaginary typewriter. The trouble was with her; she could feel it. She had no rhythm at all, no lightness. She had lost control of the character. Her personal misery had slopped over into her performance, and that was unforgivable. It was only a matter of time before Mrs. Wilbur would attack her, and she braced herself for it. But the teacher let them stumble through to the end of the act before sighing dramatically and suggesting with irony that they cancel the entire play and do something simpler, like *Peter Rabbit*. "I suppose we can't *always* be at the top of our form," she said acidly, "but we needn't be so much on the bottom, eh?"

"It's five o'clock," someone on the stage mumbled.

"Glad to know you can tell time, at least," Mrs. Wilbur said. "Enough for today then. Oh, one more thing." They groaned. "Children, we have a problem. The Grand Duchess. True, she doesn't appear until Act III, and we may never get there. Lily Musgrove is out, though. She's failing math and biology, which means no extra activities this semester. So put on your thinking caps and find me a new Grand Duchess, a brilliant Grand Duchess—in other words, someone who can learn the lines and stand up on the stage. Dismissed! Oh, Elly, will you see me in my office for a minute?"

Now it would come! She had been awful, no doubt of it. "Go ahead," she said, "lay into me. I fell apart and I know it."

"What? Oh, that. Yes, we all have those days, don't we? I'm glad you could see it and not let it throw you. Just loosen up for tomorrow." Then her manner changed. "What I *would* like to know, though, is what *this* means?"

Elly looked at the yellow sheet of paper. There it was in black typing: a warning notice. As of February 10, 1939, she was failing in math and had a D average in chemistry; she knew that in the intervening three weeks, she had done no better. It was just as if she were like that dopey Lily Musgrove! She needed a C in her final chemistry exam and a C+ in math to earn a passing grade for the marking period and remain in the drama club. And if she did not do even better, she would jeopardize her advanced standing, her position on the honor roll, and her chance to graduate a semester early.

"Well?" Mrs. Wilbur prodded her. "What happened?"

"Nothing," Elly said in a low voice. She was ashamed to put on an act with her teacher.

"Any problems at home? Don't you have relatives staying with you? Get on well with them?"

"No, not really," Elly said reluctantly, forcing the words out, acting a part again. "And I don't even have my own room any longer." Her voice quavered out of control.

"You're no worse off than many another," Mrs. Wilbur said. "Quintus Fry, for example, or Rose LaBelle. Can't you work in school? Your brother will help you, won't he?"

"He's busy helping my cousin!" Elly said hotly.

"I see." She paused. "You know, my child, I don't care about your math or chemistry. But to lose you for the play . . . ! And it would be entirely out of my hands. Let me tell you, I've been thinking quite seriously about having you and Laura play a scene from *Mary of Scotland* for the June Show if you like it so much. But this! You can do better . . . all over a bit of feeling here or there."

Then Elly burst out, "It's more than that! I'm so unhappy at home, they don't understand me . . ."

Mrs. Wilbur cut her off. "No one understands anybody else. You know why I bother with you? Because I think you really might be an actress someday. Maybe. Not if you wallow in all this flummery, though. Discipline! Work! That's my motto. And while you're at it, child, pass your subjects, please. For my sake, at least."

Elly kept her eyes down. "Yes, ma'am," was all she could say without crying. She would simply have to pass. There was no pretending any longer. This meant an end to her delicious evening reading of Colette's books in French, which Mme. Graves, the French teacher, had slipped to her privately. There would be time only for work, work, and more work. Scuffing along and noticing how worn her shoes were, she went to gather up her books, muttering, "The last straw, the absolute last straw." There was no money for new shoes.

But that wasn't the last straw. Laura was waiting for her, sure enough, but so was Margot!

"What did *she* want?" Laura asked.

"I have decided to watch a rehearsal," Margot said, smiling. "It is not forbidden, no?"

"You saw *that!*" Elly exclaimed. "Oh no!" Why, of all possible days to watch, did Margot have to choose today? "It's not exactly forbidden but . . . well, it's . . . private . . ."

"Why don't we *all* go to my house?" Laura suggested quickly.

"Oh, sure," Elly grumbled. "Why don't we all go to my grave?"

"What happened?" Laura repeated.

Elly shrugged. "Oh, nothing at all. Would you like to cut off my head while you're at it?"

"I shall not come," Margot said. "I shall visit the library, I think."

"Won't hear of it," Laura said. In the long silence she made bright conversation. "Ever been to Paris, Margot? Isn't it romantic?"

"Yes, I have been," Margot said softly, "but I do not think it is romantic. My vatti—my father—is saying there is appallingly much tuberculosis rate with the poor, higher even than in Berlin, which has many poor."

"You don't say?" Laura exclaimed. "My God, I didn't know that!"

Elly giggled. At that moment Laura sounded exactly like Glenna in one of her more sarcastic moods. Elly squeezed her friend's arm, but Laura shook her off and talked to Margot about the play. "It stank today," she said frankly, "but we're not always that bad."

"This is supposed to be a funny play?" Margot asked. "I think maybe I do not understand American humor."

She and Laura talked all the way to Laura's house. Neither of them kept Elly out of the conversation, she had to admit that. But she was so shaken by her marks and by the knowledge of the warning slip coming to her parents in the mail that she could think of nothing else —and she resented the talk going on without her.

Glenna called out to them the minute they walked in the door. "I'm making my original, good old-fashioned hot chocolate; come and have some. Who knows? Maybe I'll open a restaurant, eh? Or would you rather try the egg nog with real rum?" She talked to them quite a long time, speaking faster and faster, not letting them go until Laura said, "We've got only a few minutes, Glenna," and walked out of the room.

In her bedroom she murmured, "Glenna *is* a pain sometimes. Rum!" She twisted her bedspread.

"Oh, she is delightful, your mother. Someday you shall meet *mine*," Margot said. "Right, Elly? Have you a cigarette, Laura? And I tell you about my mother."

Laura opened a desk drawer. "Here they are. Old Gold all right? Glenna doesn't like me to smoke, actually, but Owen says it's O.K. He's for all the vices."

Elly pressed her head against the cold wall. Laura did not think to offer her a cigarette. Naturally. They thought of her as such a pure baby; it was the way Mama had brought her up. She would never break free.

How easily they lit their cigarettes and puffed them, crinkling their eyes up at the corners and blowing smoke into the room! She would not ask. All that she was afraid of in herself was focused on that single point of a glowing cigarette tip. Her head ached. She had been sitting in the same position for so long that she had lost touch with her arms and legs. There it was! She would be on the outside forever, it was her fate, while all around her others went off to their destinies, not even looking behind at her retreating figure. Saliva rose into her mouth. "It's almost time to go," she said loudly.

Laura nodded. "Wait a minute. Margot, let me ask you a question. Did you ever act in plays?"

"Never! In my school we did not do such things."

Laura jumped up. "Elly, *listen* to her! Don't you hear it?"

"Hear what? Smoking gone to your brain?" Elly asked sullenly. She concentrated fiercely on a spot on her skirt. Hardened egg, probably. Mama was right, she could be neater. For what? To marry a farmer, someone like Stan Kocinski, and slop hogs all her life? She might as well fail, too, and abondon *all* of her hopes.

"Margot, you loon!" Laura said. "She could be the Grand Duchess. Why, you'd be splendid!"

"A Russian accent is not quite the same thing as a German accent," Elly pointed out.

"Oh, who'd notice? Besides, Margot could learn—couldn't you? Then you could stay for rehearsals every day and not go off to the library by yourself."

"No, I do not think so. It is nice of you to ask. But, no. What do you think, Elly, eh?" Margot squatted down on the floor next to where Elly sprawled on the bed and smiled up into her cousin's face. "You think I have this talent?"

"How do I know?" Elly cried out. "What difference

does it make? Don't you need all your time to study?"

"Study? Ha! Not at all," Margot assured her merrily. "It is not so hard as I thought. We have had much harder at *gymnasium*. I think I shall do well enough."

That was the last straw! Now it had come—for Margot to do better in school than she did! "If it was so much better in Berlin, why did you leave?" Elly asked, as she swallowed tears that stung her throat. There! Now it had been said!

"Elly!" Laura exclaimed, "what's the matter with you?"

"Nothing," Elly said, moving to the door, half-blinded by her tears. "Margot would be good, oh; very good. She is an experienced actress, and I am so wrong!"

"I told you," Margot said quietly, "you would be not so happy I am here after a while. It is all right, I will not be in this play."

Elly believed that her legs would give way under her and she would drop to the floor. To be forgiven, and in such even tones! It was too much. She had no resources left. "I feel sick," she whispered. "I think I'm getting the curse." She sank down again on Laura's bed. "Excuse me," she said to the opposite wall.

Laura was ominously quiet. "I don't want to talk about it," she said into the cold silence.

"Did I tell you about my mutti after all?" Margot asked. "It is quite funny, Laura, *you* would understand."

"Ah, you think I don't understand anything," Elly said.

Margot shook her head. "Your parents are so happy together, I have not seen this before. I enjoy to watch. Maybe I do not say so. My vatti . . . I have told you this . . . is adoring my mutti, she is very beautiful. Do you not think so? But I do not think she cares so much for him." Margot twisted a strand of hair around and around her finger. "He is too serious for her, he is working too hard, and what she is loving is the theatre and parties—which *he* does not like. *Ach*, they had many fights!"

Laura was idly playing with some brown wooden beads. "Fights? Ho! Glenna took a lover once. He brought me boxes of French chocolates." She spoke flatly, as if reciting a speech.

Margot's thoughts retreated behind the shield of her blank eyes. "My mutti has liked the younger men but for theatre only, for parties. I think it is that my vatti would kill her—yes," she insisted. "Such terrible things happen."

"But not here!" Laura said, snapping out of her mood. "You tell her, Elly! Franklin is a safe place, isn't it?"

Elly nodded and gulped. She couldn't talk. Without warning she began to cry, not the false surface tears so easily summoned, but slow, deep tears of despair as genuine as any she had ever felt. She began by crying for herself, for her poor grades, for her exclusion from all that had happened between Margot and Laura. She cried for her meanness and her fat middle, her freezing bedroom and the stinking chicken house. She sat and let the ugly tears run down her face while she hiccuped and sniffed. Then she was crying for more—for poor Aunt Anna and Uncle Michael, and for Glenna Fitzgerald and the man with the box of French chocolates, until it seemed that she was crying for everyone in this sad world; for all the men out of work, for the tramps who hopped off freight trains and came into the grocery for sandwiches and warmth; for Phil who had to work in the library and for Pop worried about money. It was all jumbled up and pressed on her like a pain, and through it all she felt the hard exultation of certainty that someday she would be an actress and would play it out, this sadness and joy, for thousands of people to see.

"Well, golly," Laura said, embarrassed, "nothing's that tragic. Here, have a hanky. Better now?"

Elly nodded and sniffed. "Oh, Laura, remember when we talked about suffering? Remember? It's awful!" she wailed, staring at the wall without blinking until it wavered behind her tears. "I'm sorry, Margot," she whispered. "I'm really sorry. I wish you would try out for the play."

Margot hesitated. "I will think about it," she said, "but I shall not say yes." She paused again. "It is lonely waiting in the store." She made no other reproach.

She didn't have to, both Elly and Laura knew what she meant. They could no longer remain two, no matter how much Elly wanted them to.

8

“THEN IT’S ALL settled,” Baba said, coughing. “I’m taking your meld, Leo. I think I’ve won.”

“Nothing is settled, Mamushka,” Mama said.

“Elly, hear your Baba?” Pop said. “If she goes, I’ll lose my pinochle partner, and you’ll have to learn to play with me, eh?” He held out his cup. “Some more coffee, if you please. What’s on the radio for tonight?”

Elly sniffled. “Darn cold! Pop, you drink too much coffee. *One Man’s Family* is next, how’s that?”

“No, thank you, I’m one man with my own family, it’s enough. Without coffee I could not live—do you think maybe Maxwell House will sponsor *me* a program? Your play, Freda,” he said to Baba.

“Are you really going away, Baba?” Elly asked.

“No, she’s not. I never heard anything so foolish,” Mama said.

“Yes, I am, until spring. Listen to me, Sonya! For a long time you do not listen to me.” She coughed again. “At Green Branch Farm is first of all a doctor. Second of all is they need me with so many refugees coming in, and here you do not need me . . .”

Mama broke in. “Mamushka, such a thing to say!”

Baba laid out a fan of cards. "Look to your hand, Leo. But true, Sonya. What do I do until spring but sit and eat? And cough. Already the cellar is filled with so many hundreds of jars we canned. What more do you need now? Anna is here and Margot and soon Michael, I am certain."

Aunt Anna burst out in German. "*Ach*, if only this comes to be! How much I worry . . . where do I turn, I ask myself over and again, and there is nothing out there . . . nothing!" she pointed to the night and the slowly falling snow. "More and more I think this—I shall end here. Alone."

Baba sat tranquilly, sipping her tea. "I tell you otherwise, Anna," she said, putting her sturdy, wrinkled hand over the other woman's thin one. "These are bad times, and maybe they will get worse. But they will not go on. Well! Add up the score, Leo. I knew it! Won a game from you at last. Another?"

"Not tonight, Freda. A little heartburn, the food didn't set so right in my stomach. I think I'll just read the paper, sit a while. Here, Anna," and he handed a section to his sister. "To keep improving your English. You do so well now."

Baba scooped up the cards. "Come with me a minute, Elly, to my room. I put these away."

Baba's snug room smelled faintly of flowery toilet water and tart apples. She coughed and panted, patting her chest. "This is a bad one, eh?"

"Oh, Baba, I wish you weren't sick and would stay," Elly said, clasping her knees as she leaned forward on the stuffed hassock. For the past three days, while Elly had been home from school with a cold, her grandmother had been listening to her lines and cuing her in, even though she had no idea of the play at all, as she admitted.

"A little cold? Nothing. Much worse have I had than such a little cold! No, I wish to go for other reasons. I'll tell you. At Green Branch there is a great need for help . . ."

"But Mama doesn't want you to work so hard in their kitchen!"

"Your Mama doesn't want? I know. But *I* want. You understand? And there are too many people in this small house, your Mama will be better with me away for a short time. And me, too. I am not often away, think of that."

"I am thinking," Elly said. "You're right, I guess, only I wish . . ." She straightened herself up. "Baba, is Uncle Michael really coming? You sounded so sure! Was that for Aunt Anna?"

Baba stopped rocking. "It is not for children to worry themselves over."

"I'm not a child," Elly pointed out.

"Only sometimes you act like one," her grandmother teased. "Your father hears that in May will be released many of the men—if they are still alive—to leave Germany at once. We think it is that war will start, and Hitler does not want so many in prisons, for he will need the guards."

"May? You'll be back by then, won't you? And see my play?"

"Maybe you will be so glad without me you will wish me to stay away," Baba said, smiling. "One thing I do not tell you: I want to give you my room for a little privacy when you need it. Here, take the key. Sonya says you cannot sleep in here, it would be an insult to Margot, and she is right. But have your friend Laura stay if you wish. Only be careful—I am leaving all my things here."

Elly jumped up. "Oh, Baba, thank you, thank you!"

she cried, kissing and hugging her grandmother. "I can . . . oh, thank you!"

"One more thing. I keep forgetting. Getting old. Here is five dollars for you. I want you should buy that nice Shakespeare book you are talking about, all the plays. You can buy this in Franklin?"

"It's about the only book you *can* buy—Shakespeare and the Bible and Webster's Dictionary. Yes, Mr. Plotkin at the drugstore ordered some for Christmas, and he's got a few copies left over."

"Then buy. From me."

Elly squeezed her grandmother again. "You're simply wonderful!"

"You will not be failing in school then?" Baba asked.

Elly whirled around. "How did you know?"

"Your Mama had a letter from school—not that we were surprised. But two subjects in danger!"

"Why didn't she say anything? Oh, she's so *sneaky!*" Now that the big scene of anger and reproach hadn't taken place, Elly felt cheated.

"Eleanor! Your Mama does not wish to make you more unhappy. She said to me herself she understands very well—it is because of all the upset in the house. Which is not to say she is happy. Or your dear father. From you we expect more." She took Elly by the shoulders and turned her around. "I'm tired now. I rest, I pack, I go. Two more days. But do not for your mother make difficulties. Poor Sonya! Her life does not go as she wishes, and she wishes so well."

Elly clutched Baba's key as a talisman. Tomorrow the big black volume of Shakespeare's plays would be on her desk. Suddenly from the kitchen came an hysterical wail. Aunt Anna! Elly didn't want to face her now and started down the hall toward the stairs. But Mama saw her through the kitchen doorway and beckoned her to help with the dishes.

Mama's face was red and wisps of hair escaped from the neat coil at her neck. "Anna, you make much nonsense," she said in her quiet way. "For Margot it is not good such a burden."

"And what about me?" Aunt Anna asked. "To sit alone all day in that room waiting. For what? And never to have a kind word from you because I do not read the Bible or make crosses? What difference from this to jail?"

Her lovely face twisted with anger as she ran out of the kitchen back into her room, calling Margot to follow her.

Margot remained, staring fixedly at the fire in the stove. "Uncle Leo," she said, "my mother is a sick woman. It is too bad no one understands that."

Pop was dazed with tiredness and brought himself back to the waking world only slowly. "Understand? We understand. Only we do not know what to do, we are not such complicated people here. Let me tell you a story. Once was a rabbi, famous all over for his judgment. One day two men fighting for a long time came to him to settle this fight. The rabbi listens to one man's story and at the end says to him, 'You know, you're right.' The other man says, 'Wait a minute, *my* story you haven't heard,' and tells *his* side to the rabbi. And at the end the rabbi says, 'You know, you're right.' A man standing by hears this and asks the rabbi, 'So, how can both be right?' And the rabbi turns to the third man and says, 'You know something? You're right, too.' Do I make myself clear? What is to be done?"

"The chores, for one thing," Phil said, pushing himself back from the table and fleeing the room.

"This is a small house," Mama said, appealing to Margot. "Each one must crunch into himself a little and so . . ."

"Oh, it is easy for you to say," Margot said in a despairing voice. "And you think it should be easy for us, too. But it is not. That is the simple truth. And so we rub against each other until we strike a spark."

Elly kept wiping the dishes and putting them away. Yes, all that had happened was as interesting as she had imagined it would be, almost like a movie, really, one of those dark, brooding dramas with Ida Lupino or Bette Davis. Except there was something else she hadn't counted on, and that was the nerve-jangling unpleasantness of the relations among them. All the edges were rough and grating, apparently beyond smoothing by any of them. The most trivial conversation would end by upsetting somebody; even Mama and Baba, usually so even-tempered, had ended up shouting, not only at Aunt Anna, but also at each other. And now Baba was going away. Elly stacked the glasses on the top shelf. Could there be such a thing as too much intensity? And look how it was affecting Pop! He was always tired these days, spoke apologetically when he spoke at all, and could not even be rallied by Mama's quiet talk and the cups of coffee he usually enjoyed so much.

Without Mama telling her, she wiped the counter clean, folded up the cloth, and put it on the drying rack. Of course, she had noticed all the tension because she had been home from school all day, stuck in the house, and too miserable to lose herself in her books. Now she *had* to notice it, could not stop seeing and hearing and feeling, for it was as if a drum throbbed constantly in the house, beating out its intense and chilling message through the rooms in which they lived.

"I think this war comes soon," Pop said into the silence. "If only Michael will get out in time." He lifted his hands and let them fall into his lap. "I'm going to bed, Sonya. Maybe I am getting this famous cold."

Mama was concerned at once. "Leo, let me give you something . . ." and she followed him out of the kitchen and down the hall to their room.

Saying no more, Margot went upstairs, walking slowly and painfully, as if her bones were hurting. Elly was alone in the kitchen. She turned out the light and sat in darkness broken only by the glow coming from the wood stove and the white streak made by the moon shining through the kitchen window. How still it was at last! She sat at the cleared table, breathing in and out for a long time, not moving, not thinking.

Her feet made no sound when she finally mounted the stairs. "Margot?" she whispered into the dark bedroom. "Are you asleep?"

Margot sat up in bed, the quilt pulled to her chin, and stared at Elly. "No, I am simply enjoying being unhappy. That is what you think, no?"

"No." Her voice was too loud in the room. "For a long time I wished you would come," she said shyly, and stopped. She had wanted to tell Margot her dreams, but where was that Margot she had imagined talking to? This Margot, huddled in a cold bed in a cold room, was a different person entirely, and what had Elly to say to her? In the darkness she blushed for her discarded dreams. She never looked at the old photograph of Margot any longer; it was no more real than the face of Garbo on the screen pretending to be Anna Karenina. "I thought . . ." she said with a nervous laugh, and stopped again.

"Well, here we are," Margot said.

There was a long silence. Elly shivered. How hard to say what she wanted to say! "What can I do about your mother?"

"Do?" Margot asked scornfully. "Nothing. Let her be unhappy. She has good reason. Why must you always *do?* To be unhappy sometimes is good, I think."

"Oh, I couldn't bear to think that . . ." Elly began, moving to the window and looking out at the cold moon.

"*You* couldn't bear? But what has it to do with *you?* How like your mother you are! You wish to do always, and this is fine, only for one thing—there is no room for other people to do as they wish in this so good world you make. You have wished me to come, but in what way are you thinking of *me?*" she asked quietly.

Elly was stung. She remembered with terrible clarity the afternoon at Laura's house; after all, she knew more about her mixed motives than Margot did! "You!" she said hotly. "You don't think of anyone else! And *your* mother is the worst of all."

"So she is," Margot said indifferently. Then her voice quickened. "Only—I do not go around as holy as you."

"I do not!" Once more Elly remembered that afternoon at Laura's where she had sat on the bed, forgotten, while the other two smoked cigarettes and talked around her.

Margot laughed. "Ha! You should see yourself. How graciously you allow me time with your precious brother—*his* time you have given me, and I am to be grateful!"

Only the most desperate shame prevented Elly from bursting out into the tears of childhood. "It's not that way at all, it can't be!" Her last image of Margot—the cousin who would like her and enter into her dreams—was crumbling, and there was nothing she could do about it.

Margot's voice dropped. "As you wish. You cannot help this. I did not know what it is to really suffer, either. . . . But, oh, I love my vatti, and he is maybe dying, you understand? And freezing cold and having no food. And no one else is caring for me like he is . . ." Now she spoke almost in a whisper. "I promised I would not do this—complain over small things, for in truth, I am grateful to be out of that . . . horror . . ." and she visibly shuddered. "It happens yet that such small things bother me, no matter what I think, and so . . ." She dropped quietly back on her bed.

"Well, yes," Elly said uncomfortably. She hated to feel so awkward and at sea. What could she say? "Oh, damn!" she exclaimed and hoped that Mama did not hear. The electric heater glowed faintly against the far wall, fighting a losing battle against the wind and snow. Why couldn't Margot be easier? Why couldn't everything be easier? She took a deep breath. "I think you could play the Grand Duchess very well," she said jerkily. "We c-could help if you needed it. Then your father c-could see you act."

Margot did not answer. The clock ticked. Elly blushed in the dark for her foolishness in leaving herself so open to rebuff.

Mama entered, stepping softly as she always did, but Elly jumped at the sound. "I have brought extra blankets, I think you'll need them tonight." After she unfolded them on the beds, she stood in the middle of the room, looking awkward with her idle hands hanging down by her sides. Elly's mind made a sudden leap toward her mother's, and she knew that Mama would like to stay with them and become part of their conversation, but what could she say to them?

Mama pulled at her apron. "Homework all done? Shall I make cocoa?" Margot faced the wall. Elly stared out at the starry sky. Mama murmured, "Leo is not feeling so good. I don't know what to do for tomorrow."

"I am sorry we are so much trouble, Aunt Sonya," Margot said in a voice that seemed to come from far away.

Mama opened her hands, palms out. "No trouble," she said. "Not like you think. There is so much on my mind . . . and Leo not well. I speak to God," she added with simplicity, then said, as shy as a young girl, "but I know you do not like this." She started to say something else, then abruptly stopped. "I am *so* tired."

"Then you must go to sleep," Margot said. "As I myself am doing. Thank you for the blankets."

"I'll have cocoa," Elly said, walking downstairs with Mama. She squeezed her mother's hand, and Mama managed a smile in return.

"Shall Phil drive me in tomorrow to the store, and we let Leo sleep?" Mama asked. "Yes, I think so. I manage by myself, or I ask Krystyna Kocinski to help a little. If only *Anna* could do something . . . she is not so helpless, I am sure of that!" She poked the kitchen fire down and raked ashes over the smoldering wood. "I shall go in, yes, I shall. If Leo were to be sick . . ." She sighed. "I have managed before." She pulled a chair over to the window and sat heavily on it to read her worn Gospel book by the moonlight.

"I'll help, Mama," Elly said. "I promise."

"If I need, I will ask," Mama said. "What I most want is you to be happy."

What had Margot said about being unhappy at times? Why should Elly always be happy? But that was Mama! How had Margot seen Elly like her mother? Impossible! She finished her cocoa and grabbed a bunch of carrots, buttoned her coat and stepped out into the freezing night. Several inches of snow lay lightly on the ground. More would fall tomorrow; already the air was still and moist. The sky glittered with frosty stars. Far off across the valley came the whistle of a freight train.

"Oh, you smelly barn," Elly said into the gloomy interior.

"Warm, though. And quiet."

"Phil, what are you doing here? Gosh, you scared me!"

"Hey, don't get all worked up—my lord, you do jump!"

She fed the carrots to the horses, rubbing their familiar flanks with her cold hands until the heat of the animals' bodies warmed her. "I guess I am," she admitted. "But, gosh, it's been an *awful* time, simply awful."

"Nonsense," he said lazily. "The trouble with you is you've got to have a big scene once a week or so to set you up. And you get mad if the rest of us don't play along."

"This is different," she said, not bothering to argue with him. They sat side by side on the hay, looking out the barn door into the still, breathless night and the white stars. "What are we going to do, Phil? I mean, that's a real problem, right? Like Aunt Anna—she's impossible, don't you think so? Margot, too. And how long will we all be together jammed up like this?"

"Aunt Anna's not the greatest person I've ever met," he admitted. "But what's wrong with Margot? Oh, I know—you imagined some fantastic person . . ."

"Stop it!" She pummeled the heavy mackinaw he wore.

"Well, you did," he said imperturbably. "Don't blame her if she's different. I like her myself. She's tough. After all they've been through! And stuck way out here!"

"We're stuck out here, too!" she pointed out passionately. "I asked Pop, seriously, you know, if we could move to town. Even you'd approve of how calm I was! He said he'd talk to Mama, but of course, he never did!"

Phil was serious. "Elly, Pop's not feeling well. Damn it, *you* know that! Don't push him, eh? Why should he go against Mama for you? It just makes things hard for him."

"But still," she spluttered in her eagerness to defend herself, "he doesn't like living on the farm either. Maybe if he knew how we felt, he'd . . ."

"He'd do what Mama wants. Meanwhile, you push at him, and he gets dizzy from all the talking. *That's* the main problem I see in that house—too much talking! Listen to the night. Isn't it nicer here than in the house?"

They listened to the animal sounds from the dark barn, the thump of a hoof, the breathing, the snorting. No talk, no need to talk, yet life was all around them. They sat quietly for a long time, thinking together without words, before they went out of the barn. They could almost touch the silence in the crystal night outside. The cold, clear air opened Elly's nose so that she breathed in its sharp clarity in big gulps. "Someday when I'm in Hollywood, I'll think of this. When I'm swimming in my pool—oh!"

"Meanwhile, watch your step. Ice here."

"And snow! Glorious snow!" She stood on a little hillock to one side of the path, spread her arms, and jumped into the virgin snow, gasping as the cold struck her face and dampness slithered down her neck. "Snow angels," she cried, sputtering and shaking her head. "Be-yoo-ti-ful snow angels!"

"Hey, you really *are* living in the past," Phil called,

and jumped then to make one, too, on the other side of the hillock. "It's been years," he shouted, laughing, and hit Elly in the back with a soft snowball.

She ducked and ran and fell into the snow again. "Full moon!" she shouted. "Crazy!" Phil ran after her, both of them floundering in the soft snow that covered the humpy meadow, and they jumped again and again, laughing and hooting, until their coats were soaked through and the snow was patterned all over with their angel shapes.

9

❦❦ "ALL FOR TODAY, children," Mrs. Wilbur called up to the stage. "Would you believe that it's snowing outside? And April upon us—beautiful! Hurry on home." Her voice dropped. "Listen, Margot, could you stay for a few minutes, and I'll work on the Grand Duchess with you? You'll do fine, once you get a little confidence, hmm?"

Margot turned pink with pleasure. "I do not think I can act very well. This is something I discover from now. All I am doing before this is singing and playing the piano."

"Ah, yes, Germans and music . . ." Mrs. Wilbur murmured, without paying much attention. "Elly can work with you. Look at this . . ."

Elly walked slowly to the dressing room. There had been a full rehearsal of the first act, and she had used make-up and costume to make her *feel* nutty Penny Sycamore. And she *had*. She could tell. So could the others. Quintus Fry, who played her husband Paul, was at her elbow, waving his long arms and talking.

"You were really good, you know, Elly. How do you do it? I think acting's kinda fun, but I'm not much good at it."

"Oh, Quinny, you'll do fine," Elly said, brushing her hair vigorously. "Let me take off my dress." She pushed him out and closed the door. When she was finished, he was still standing in the hall. Laura, however, wasn't anywhere in sight. "Seen Laura?"

"I told her not to bother waiting today." He paused, staring at the peeling paint of the green corridor. "Elly, how'd you like to have a soda or something at the drugstore? I'd of asked you before, but you know how it is, no dough."

"How's your dad doing?" Elly asked, remembering the work Mr. Fry had done in fixing up their storage room. Mama liked Mrs. Fry and sorrowed when times got bad for them with five children and Mr. Fry, who was a carpenter, out of work for two years.

Quinny shrugged. "Some better. Repair work. Furniture—just chairs and tables and stuff. Ain't no one can afford what he really does best—cabinetmaking. Kitchen dresser your Ma bought couple of years back was the last one he sold."

"Did your dad make that? Why, I never knew! Wait a minute, there's Laura going back to the auditorium. Wait up—Laura!" she called after the disappearing figure of her friend.

"Hi, Elly!" Laura turned to call back, "I'm going to wait for Margot, then we'll go on up to my house, right? See you!"

Elly looked back with a pang, but already Quintus was grabbing her arm and opening the door for her. "Mrs. Wilbur certainly was right," he said, caught in the whirling downpour of thick flakes. "Ain't it the damndest!"

"It's beautiful, though," Elly said, tasting the snow on her tongue.

They didn't talk much as they ran through the snow to the drugstore. Elly was astonished that Quinny liked her. Imagine! And she had never given him a thought! When she wiped the steam off her glasses in one of the booths at the end of the soda fountain, she casually left them on the table.

"Ain't you forgetting something?" Quintus asked, grinning and handing her the glasses. "Never could figure out this thing about glasses, anyway. My Ma always wears 'em, and my Pa thinks the world of her."

"Wasn't she a Latin teacher?" Elly asked.

"Sure was. In the old county high school before they built this new one. How'd you think I got my name? I was the fifth kid—Virgil, Lavinia, Horace, Paula, and me. Ma always liked things a little fancy. So I kinda favor girls with a good head on their shoulders. Your Ma's like that, too—she'd come and talk to mine about books. They had a right old time."

"Mama never said a word to us, not about the dresser being from your dad or anything else."

"You like chocolate? O.K., two chocolate ice cream sodas," Quinny ordered, then blushed. Elly noticed that his ears turned very red. "Not likely she would, your Ma. She was helping us, you know, and she liked to keep it quiet."

He looked straight at Elly, and she thought his eyes were bright and kind. "She had Pa make her the dresser and paid him in food. She was always bringing food—chickens, vegetables, potatoes, bread, soup—you know. It's O.K. now, my Pa's working some, and Virgil's got a good job pumping gas over in Newchester, and Vinny's living with Ma's sister in Boston and working at the phone company."

He laughed. "Now all we do is get credit from your

Pa, so I guess we're still tangled up with your folks. Besides, I kinda had my eye on you for a long time. Only you know how it is." He shrugged and smiled.

Elly sipped her soda. "I didn't know," she said, feeling very strange. "I've been so busy, and then, not living in town, you miss out on things." She was almost dropping into Quinny's drawling speech; it was easy for her to mimic any kind of accent, she heard so many of them at home. Suppose he thought she was teasing him? "Of course, I don't have much in common with my parents," she said primly, smiling a little. What were Margot and Laura talking about, she wondered. Yet, she would not have been there with them to find out. Far better to be sipping an ice cream soda with this boy, someone she hardly knew and wasn't even sure that she liked. But he liked her! "I'm glad you're in the play, though."

"Oh, that! I'm not much of an actor, am I? Not like you, that's for sure. You're a regular little actress, anyone could tell that."

Elly puckered up her face and made Penny Sycamore's vague little voice come out of her mouth. "Why, Paul, Grandpa himself said that talent runs in our family like some Gowanus Canal."

"Oh, you're making that up, I swear," he said admiringly, and laughed again. Elly thought his laugh was too loud, then she squelched the disloyal thought. After all, no one else in the drug store seemed to notice.

After a pause, she asked, "What do you want to be when you graduate, Quinny? You've only got another year, right?"

He nodded. "Glad for it, too. You really interested?"

Elly wasn't, but she said, "Why not? I mean I'm getting to know you, right, and that's important, what you're going to do."

"You betcha. First off, I ain't leaving Franklin. I like it here—hunting in the fall, fishing in the summer—nothing like it. Then, I sorta know everyone in town, a bunch of fellas I've been going around with since I've been born practically, so you might say I've got ready-made friends. I like to work with my hands like my Pa, but I don't think I'll stick to carpenter work. Too unsteady. I aim to fix myself up good, and any family I get the same. I got my eye on a coupla things. One's auto mechanic, if I can get a spot down at Hardy's Garage. Might. Fix farm machines. Then when times get better, I'm going to try for an auto dealership. Don't you laugh at me now," he said, brushing her hand with his.

She left her hand on the table for him to touch again; that first grazing had made the hairs on her arm rise slightly, and she liked the new sensation.

"I'm not laughing, Quinny." All the while he was talking she had been thinking, *Oh no, this can't be me listening to him;* however, she gave him a big, sincere smile that led to an answering smile on his face.

"I got big plans, you see. This town's going places, the factories opening up again, and that's what I'm going to do, get a piece of it right here where I want to be."

Elly hardly recognized the breathy voice that came out of her. "Not me! I'm leaving for New York just as fast as I can."

Quinny shook his head. "Nice girl like you don't belong in New York. What you want to go there for?"

"Study acting. You said yourself I was good. I know it. I *am* good. Not good enough, though. Not by half. What Mrs. Wilbur did—studying in New York, then marrying back here—you won't catch me doing that for anything."

"Make a bet with you, O.K.? You should stop seeing

that Laura Fitzgerald, get away from her crazy ideas."

"Why, she's my best friend!" Elly said, angry.

"Sure she is," he said soothingly. "Nice enough girl, too, for all I know. But her folks—hah! Just plain phonies, if you ask me. She can't help but pick up some of their phony ideas. Know what I mean?"

"I know what you mean very well, Quintus Fry!" Elly said, standing up to leave. "And I don't agree with you at all!"

"Hey, does you good to get mad—you're not so prissy then. Think I'm going to make you mad a lot." He reached out to help her with her coat, and his hands lingered on her shoulders. She was in no hurry to move; the touch was solid this time—a man's hands touching her, and she knew that she liked it.

"Ladies *should* be interested in things like acting," Quinny said. "Why, you could get a drama society going right in this town. I'd help out in it myself. All I'm saying is, don't listen to Laura and go rushing off to New York. New York!" He finished with deep scorn.

Elly couldn't answer because the wind blew snow thickly into her face and took her breath from her. They struggled down Main Street to the station, slipping and sliding on the first layer of packed snow. "I guess I'll go to the store," she panted. "We'll have to stay in town tonight." It was a regular arrangement. Whenever the weather was really bad, Phil, Pop, and Elly camped out behind the grocery store. Where would they put Margot? Maybe she'd stay with Laura! Elly agonized over that thought.

"Won't your Ma worry?"

Elly turned from the wind and pulled her wet scarf up over her mouth. "She knows. We don't have a phone, but she's got the radio. And she can *see*." Elly was irritated with him now, with herself, with the insistent cold that poured down her neck and slipped up her skirt and gripped her wrists between glove and coat. "Thanks Quinny. I enjoyed it," she said at the door. She had to get away from him and call Laura from the phone in the store; they could talk about Quinny and laugh together.

"Next time maybe I'll be able to raise fifty cents, and we can go to the movies. *Dodge City* is coming up. Sound good?"

"Love to!"

While they talked, Quinny pushed open the door and followed her into the store. How could she shove him out into the bitter wind and snow? "Come on in and get warm. Pop's always got coffee on the stove." She shook the wet out of her hair and wiped her glasses before she realized that something was odd. The silence. Her heart leaped. With the wind shut out, silence thickened in the store. "Pop?" she called. "Pop? Where are you?"

"Maybe your Pa's out delivering," Quinny suggested. "Awful time for that, though."

"Not and leave the store alone! Hang your coat up here," she said, pointing to a board wall with hooks in it that separated the front of the store from the back room. Pop had only been back in the store for two days; Mama had gone in all last week to make sure he recovered fully from his cold and upset stomach, and some of Mama's concern had entered into Elly, making her extra jumpy. "There! That's better, nice and dry now." She shivered. Had Pop let the fire go down, too? "Pop?" she called. No answer.

"Here's a light," Quinny said, standing at the top of the cellar stairs. "And a light to upstairs, too."

"Oh, good, he's probably checking out the work on

the flat upstairs. Painters were supposed to finish up today. They took enough time as it is, and we've got tenants moving in on the 15th. For a minute I was . . . worried. Pop!" she called up into the stairwell.

And then she did hear something. Breathing. Down in the cellar. Rough, harsh breathing. The way Baba breathed when she had bronchitis. Stertorous. That was the word. Her mind clicked it off on one level. On another, her heart beat rapidly and her palms were clammy.

Quinny was already pushing past her and running down the steps to the cellar.

A burglary! she thought wildly. And Pop had been hurt! But who would want to steal anything from him? "Oh, Pop!" she cried and clattered downstairs.

"Best hurry," Quinny called, crouched on the floor and doing something to the still figure lying there. "Where's your brother? Don't he help out here?"

Elly shook her head. She couldn't form any words. "Oh, Pop! He's breathing, isn't he? What happened?" But his lips were blue.

"He's awful cold, Elly." Quinny was rubbing the back of his neck. "Some kinda attack . . ."

"I'll get a blanket," and before he could stop her, she had raced up the stairs again to bring back the old afghan flung over the back of Pop's chair. "Here."

"Give a hand, will you?" Quinny asked. "I'll lift him up, and you wrap the blanket around him. There!"

Through all of this the harsh, labored breathing continued.

"Don't rightly remember what else I should be doing," Quinny said.

"Is it bad? Is he shot? What happened?"

"Shot? Lord, no! Sick, more likely. I'm not a doctor, you know. Best get one. And my Ma. She'll know what to do."

Then Elly remembered. "Phil works at the library until six."

"Best get him then, too. I'll have to leave you alone down here while I call. O.K.? Just keep holding his head up like this. Looks to me he breathes somewhat better this way."

"Oh, I can't. Dear God, I can't," Elly mumbled. "Pop? Can you hear me?" His chest rose and fell in a shuddering, irregular rhythm. Each breath could be his last. Elly felt the struggle through her hand at the base of his neck. How cold the cellar was and how damp! Some cans lay on the floor next to Pop; he must have dropped them when he fell. Beans and chicken soup. Beans and chicken soup. Where was Quinny? What had happened to the snowstorm? The coal fire in the furnace crackled, the lumps shifted, ashes dropped into the grate. Elly massaged the back of Pop's neck with one hand and held his head up with the other. Her legs were cramped, and she shifted slightly but could not move much. Prickling pains stung her feet.

Another slow and painful breath. Pop opened his lips and panted. His fingernails were blue. How soft the sounds upstairs were through the wood floor! Where was everyone? "Quinny!" she called. "Oh, Phil!"

"Soon an ambulance comes."

Who was that? For a minute Elly was confused. She could not turn around to see. "Margot!" She had completely forgotten her cousin.

"Quinny said to come down. He goes for his mother, the snow is very bad." Margot knelt down beside Elly and began rubbing Pop's hands vigorously. "Maybe this is a heart attack. Yes . . ." and she stared blankly at the wall, remembering. "The stomach pains . . . I'm not surprised. Lucky you found him."

Elly groaned with the aches in her feet and legs.

"Here, I'll take him," Margot offered.

"No!"

Margot didn't argue. "Only let me hold his head while you move a little. Better? I try rubbing his chest, hmm?"

"You'll hurt him!" Elly cried. She thought, *you'll kill him,* but there was no way she could force those words through the locked doors of her mind.

"Nonsense. Sometimes I watch my vatti when he has clinic. There is no good pulse, but it is steady. Well, we see."

Margot said no more but moved rapidly and expertly to wrap him in the afghan Elly had taken off the rocker upstairs, shifting him only a little at a time, humming abstractedly to herself. "There! I think this is somewhat better, how much I do not know." She dimpled. "I am not a nurse—too bad, eh?"

Elly's own heart and pulse beat had slowed down a little; her hands were numb, and she was shaking all over. "Oh, Margot, we knew he was sick—I didn't do anything about it!" She had promised to help Mama and what had she actually done all of last week? No more than she usually did: help open the store and sweep up at the end of the day. Oh, she had let Pop teach her how to play pinochle one night, when all she wanted to do was read her book, but then she had offset that by shouting at Mama only a few minutes later, when Mama asked her to take the school bus home the next day and prepare dinner. Miss a rehearsal? Impossible! Her hands grew clammy. She heard the door open and close upstairs, open and close. Footsteps. "Customers! Oh, God, I'll have to go up."

"Quinny's there. Or Phil. Watch out!"

Then Elly remembered it was Pop's head she was holding. "Oh, yes!" Margot was still rhythmically massaging his chest, then his hands, then his feet. Elly was swept by a sense of warmth and release as she watched her cousin's strong, competent actions, and she was able to reach across all the barriers she had built up, unconcerned at this time with what impression she would make, unable to focus her mind on anything but the minutes grating by on the sounds of Pop's breathing. "You'd make a good doctor, Margot. I wish I didn't get flustered—you're so calm. Even the first day you came, after that long trip and the time in England—I remember it so well! How calm you were! In control."

Margot laughed, and the sound made the cellar seem warmer. "Only I was not, believe me. Look, I am shaking now! We are different, that is all. Since I am a child I think to be a doctor to make my father love me, so I watch him and learn a little. I learn I do not wish to be a doctor—and still I am afraid to tell him. You are not, I think, afraid of your father?"

Elly shook her head vigorously. "Oh, Margot, I'm scared! I can't bear to think . . ."

Margot reached over to grasp her hand. "Then don't," she whispered. "I don't think, either, of such things. I have little games I play—later I tell you about them . . ."

"I'm so *glad* you're here!" Elly burst out.

"Thank you," Margot said with great dignity. "I am glad to hear you say it."

Was she imagining it, or did Pop's breath come more slowly, more painfully? His mouth puckered and opened like a fish's, searching for air. Elly held his head higher. Why hadn't she kept her unhappiness to herself? Phil was right; what could Pop do about it on top of all his other worries? "Where are they? What's taking them so long? What time is it?"

"Ten past five."

Then it had been only ten minutes! "Oh, dear God, please make Pop well again," she prayed, just as she had as a child, wanting impossibilities. What would they do without Pop? Why hadn't she been more thoughtful last week or last month? Her head drooped.

"The snow is very bad. That is what is taking time," Margot said, yawning. "Beans and chicken soup." She put the cans back on the shelf.

This time, when she offered, Elly let her hold Pop's head up while she herself straightened her cramped muscles.

"Yoo-hoo, Elly, you down there? Mathilda Fry up here. Hello! I'll put on some tea for all of us. Wait a minute. Poor child, what a shock! Such a good man . . ." and her voice dropped as she talked to someone upstairs. "Go on down, Phil. Quinny'll keep store for you."

Elly painfully shifted her cramped position. "Phil, thank God you're here!" How white *he* looked. "You're not sick, too?"

"No," he said with great effort. "Worst snowstorm all year out there. What happened?"

"I don't know. Pop was lying like this when Quinny and I got here," Elly said.

"Heart attack," Margot said.

Phil hit his closed fist against his head. "I never should have taken that stupid job and left him here alone. Never! Too much work for one man. And he wouldn't admit it. All he talked about was me, sending me to college. And I let him."

Nobody said anything. What could they say? It wasn't true, not the way he put it, but there was no arguing with his grief.

Elly reached over to touch him. After a time she spoke softly. "What's the use of all that? Pop thinks you're great, he wants to do something for you." She carefully avoided using the past tense. "He told me once about the money he saved . . ." and she trailed off, remembering what had happened to that money.

"It is a terrible thing to love someone," Margot said quietly. "I am thinking about my vatti."

Elly told herself *I will not cry.* Pop's lips and nails were still blue. For a moment he almost opened his eyes, then the lids sagged again. Phil crouched where she had been, and she walked around the cellar, stamping her feet, feeling as if they were all buried in an enormous grave.

The muted noises continued upstairs, then were replaced by louder noises, shouts and clumping feet, and doors slamming, then, suddenly, two men dressed in white loomed on the narrow staircase holding the furled stretcher between them.

Elly pointed, unable to talk; moving with practiced speed, the men unfurled the stretcher and in one smooth movement eased Pop onto it. "Problem here," one of them said, pointing to the narrow stairs and odd-angled space at the top.

"Do it this way," the other said, backing up. "Seen worse."

"Right. Have to take him out the front, snow's blocked the alley. Got it, Charlie? All right, here we go! Alley—oop!"

"Clear the way, up there, clear the way!"

Elly and Phil dashed up behind them, rushing out into the snow. "Let me go with you," Phil said, shivering. "He's all alone."

"Please," Elly said. "Please."

The men were in a hurry to get away. "Every minute counts," one of them said, shuffling his feet. "Gotta give him oxygen, need the space."

"He'll be waiting when you get there, don't worry about that!" the other one said, chortling a little. "See ya!"

And in a minute the ambulance doors were slammed shut, and they were on their way, sirens screaming and lights blinking. And the street was dark and empty again, muffled by the steadily falling snow.

"Children, come in, you'll freeze out there with no coats on," called Mrs. Fry. "Here's sandwiches and tea. After you eat, you go on down to the hospital, all three of you. I'll lock up here." While she talked, Mrs. Fry bustled about setting the food out. "Don't know if you should walk or drive. What do you think, Lucas?" she asked her husband, who was sitting silently in the shadows. "Quinny went on home to tell Horace and Paula what happened. How will you let your mother know? Pity she's got no phone."

"I'll drive out there in the morning with the pickup truck," Mr. Fry said from his corner. "Why don't we talk about that later, Tilly?"

"Yes, yes," Mrs. Fry said quickly. She was a tall, thin woman with frizzy brown hair and alert dark eyes behind her thick glasses, and she moved in a series of quick jerks, never sitting down. "Now look, don't you worry about anything, do you understand? You all come home with us tonight once you leave the hospital, hear? I'll fix beds for the three of you and breakfast tomorrow, and you go right on back to the hospital, and I'll call the school, and Luke here will open the store, and everything will work out just fine. It's a pleasure to help out Leo and Sonya for a change when they've done—oh, my! so much—for us. Eat up!"

Phil ate slowly but steadily. He was always hungry. Margot ate sparingly as she always did, her eyes fixed on a point somewhere outside the room. To Elly the food tasted of sawdust. She chewed but couldn't swallow. The hot tea was good; it reminded her of Mama and Baba and the kitchen at home. She could drink that.

"Ready? Let's go." Lucas Fry rose from his corner. "Take you in the truck. Can't get your car out nohow, and driving's even worse."

No one said a word on the way to the hospital. The old truck groaned and sweated up the snowy hills and screeched as it slithered on the down sides. The streets were swept clean of people. A few cars crawled along, their headlights peering into the flying mass of snow like blind eyes into the darkness. The truck cab was freezing cold. They huddled together in the narrow space, glad of the close comfort. The spire of St. Joseph's Church loomed out of the snow as they turned, skidding, and went up Cannon Hill behind the church, past the parochial school and the Italian Social Hall, past Wickerham Park and the medical building to the hospital. At last. Elly was stunned at how big the town had become.

"Last stop here, kids," Mr. Fry said. "When you leave the hospital, whatever time it is, all you got to do is bear right down the hill one long block. Got that? Then skirt past the Eye-talian place and cross the street. King Street it is. We're right there, house next the corner, upstairs. Can't miss us. Got my sign in the window downstairs.

Lucas Fry. Cabinetmaking, Carpentry. Want me to come in with you?"

"No, thank you," Elly said politely. "If we need you, we'll call."

Straining and protesting, the truck lumbered off into the storm.

"Now what do we do?" Elly asked, turning to the others. "We should get out of the snow, don't you think?"

The hospital smelled of hospital, of all the sicknesses they had ever had or heard of, of alcohol rubs and high fevers, of chicken soup, and of something unknown and sickly sweet. Because Margot's father was a doctor, they deferred to her.

The black-and-white tiled lobby was cold and cheerless. Muddy water pooled on the floor. The nurse on duty looked at them sharply as they hesitantly told their business. *As if she didn't trust us,* Elly thought. Already Pop seemed far away, in another world. Was this what death was like? She shivered. How sick Phil looked! He leaned on the nurse's desk, dazed. Margot was calm in her wool beret, brushing wet hair out of her face. They went where they were told to go—a small waiting room on the second floor—and sat like wet lumps on three slippery leather chairs, listening to doors bang and carts rattle down the halls. The voice of the paging operator sounded regularly, and they heard beeps and telephone rings and whispered conversations. Nurses passed them briskly and doctors loped by, but no one came in to see them.

"Oh, we've been forgotten, we'll sit here all night," Elly moaned. She yawned and her eyes closed. "No one wants to tell us anything." She refused to believe that Pop was dead; all this time meant they were taking care of him.

"Shall I find out what's going on?" Phil went out of the room and up and down the halls, returning baffled. "Nothing. Let's wait a while longer. It's only seven o'clock, it just seems later."

Margot touched Elly lightly. "This waiting is the worst. I know *that*—there is no worse."

Elly allowed herself to relax against the back of the chair. She tried desperately to remember everything she had done today, each class and teacher, the rehearsal, her time with Quinny, as if, by pinning it all down, she could use it as some warmth against the cold displacement of this evening in a room cut off from everything she had ever known. No use. What swarmed into her mind were other scenes—Pop listening to her complaints; Pop arguing with Aunt Anna; Pop lugging home the heater for their bedroom; Pop and Mama adding up expenses every week; Pop falling asleep over his evening cup of coffee. Everything was speeded up as if in a nightmare, but all of it was true. She shivered with grief and exhaustion. Her own chest hurt. They had all done it to him, and now what would they do without him? It didn't bear thinking about.

The clock hands slowly turned around to mark the minutes and then the hour. Eight o'clock. "If he was . . . dead, they'd tell us right away, wouldn't they?" Phil asked no one in particular.

"Oh, yes," Margot said, too loudly. "Of course," she added in a lower voice.

When the doctor finally came in to them, he wasn't anyone they knew. He stood in the doorway, hands thrust into the pockets of his coat, young, pale, and weary, and kept looking around the room even after he had seen them. He consulted a slip of paper in his hand. "Joseph?" he asked.

"Josephs," Phil said. "Leo Josephs. How is he?"

The doctor was startled. "Is there a wife?"

"My mother," Elly said, explaining. "We live in the country, and the storm . . ."

"Of course. So you are the family?"

They nodded. "Can we see him?" Phil asked.

"All in good time," the doctor said. "I'm Dr. Berger. He's resting quietly now. Would you tell me exactly what happened?"

Since Elly had gotten to Pop first, she told all she knew from the first minute she heard that terrible breathing. When she finished, Dr. Berger nodded. "Very good. You did the right things—and none too soon. Wish some of the older people we get here could do as well." He led them down the hall and whispered something to the nurse who stood at the door of the room. Room 218. "Just for a minute," he said. "Then you'd better go home and get some sleep. He's not out of the woods yet. When can your mother get to town? Tomorrow? That might be a good idea."

They tiptoed into the tiny dim room. Elly didn't want to look, but when she did, it was all right. That still figure on the bed couldn't be Pop; it was all some sort of joke. It lay, white as the sheet, with tubes in its nose and taped to its arms and an oxygen tent enveloping its face like a great balloon. Pop would never allow himself to get into a situation like that! Elly almost laughed, then smothered it behind her hand. Everything in the room discouraged laughter.

But he was breathing. The nurse assured them that they would be reached if they were needed during the night, then hurried them downstairs and out the door into the freezing night. Only a few big flakes still drifted lazily down. The northern sky was clear and bright.

Margot began to sing a melancholy song in German. "*Am Brunnen vor dem Tore, da steht ein Lindenbaum/ Ich traumt' in seinem Schatten, so manchen sussen Traum.*" When Phil asked her what the words meant, she did not answer, only continued to sing, hunched forward, hands in her pockets, striding ahead of them down the hill to the Frys' house. The mood of the song possessed them, the strong minor key sadness. Margot broke off. "Sorry. I love our German songs. This is not right, to sing at such a time?"

"No!" Phil said, "I liked it—it seemed just right. Do you know any others?"

"Hundreds!" Margot assured him. "Happy ones, too. But I do not think for now, eh?"

Elly wanted to stay burrowed deep into her sadness; hadn't Margot once said that being unhappy was right at times? "Sing that one again," she ordered, and Margot did, carrying them along with her as they climbed the steps to the Frys' flat, feeling with each step their extreme exhaustion.

"Well, young folks, what happened?" Mrs. Fry asked, buttering bread, slicing apples, and pouring cocoa for them. She seemed to be content only when she was feeding people. "Well, that's not such bad news, is it?" she commented, when she heard. "Quinny, the beds made up? Good! Phil, you'll sleep in with Quinny and Horace; we've made up Virgil's old cot for you. Whyn't you boys clear out of the bathroom first and leave it for the girls? Paula's got her cot and I'm spending the night on Vinny's old bed in with her. You two chicks get to sleep in the double bed right here."

"Where's Mr. Fry?" Phil asked.

Mrs. Fry looked uncomfortable. "Why, honey, he went on down to your store to spend the night. That way he can open up bright and early. Hope you don't mind?"

"But that's not a very comfortable couch," Phil protested.

"No matter. Lucas has slept plenty of places and managed to get him a good night's sleep. Now, scoot!"

Mrs. Fry's bustle and competence, her air of believing that every disorder and tragedy would yield to clean sheets and food, reminded Elly unbearably of Mama. She clung to Phil. "If only Mama were here!" she cried out. "What are we going to do?"

PART TWO

A Changeable Spring

10

“NO,” MAMA SAID, and it was difficult to tell whether she was saying *no* to God or to their questions. “My mother is still not well; she is not to come here. So she is not to know.”

Mama sat on an upturned milk crate in the back of the store. After four days Pop was no better, no worse; Mama had just come from the hospital and was rubbing her forehead with her palms.

“But, yes,” Aunt Anna said firmly. “Things must be done.”

Mama closed her eyes. Elly handed her a cup of hot tea. “Thank you,” Mama whispered. She did not seem to be in the same room with them. Then she went to the phone, dialed, waited for the answer, and spoke in Russian to someone at the other end. The soft and then harsh sounds rolled from her throat. “Da, Yermolay,” she said, “. . . nah n'yeh-d'yeh-l'yoo.” She listened for a long time before she hung up.

“God be praised,” she said smiling. “It is clearer in my mind now, after talking to Yermolay. Anna, you were saying . . . ?”

“Listen to me, Sonya. To tend store I will not do. I

am sorry, but I will not. Since I was a child in my father's store, I am knowing this. And I am not able to go to the animals, I am absolutely frightened."

Aunt Anna's face dimpled as she smiled at her own fears. Her hair was longer, and she wore it smoothed back from her pale face, pulled into a French twist at her neck. She was thinner and wore almost no makeup. She looked older, yes, but also, Elly thought, really beautiful, without the slightly brassy look given by too much makeup and the waved blond hair. She spoke more forcefully now and without the whining tone in her voice, making an effort to speak in English.

"But, of course, I shall take over the house, and you must all eat as I cook. At which I am very good." Her humor was as heavy as ever; Phil winced and winked at Elly. "Also the cleaning," Aunt Anna went on, pursing her lips. "It is no disrespect, Sonya, to say this, but what is for a Russian clean is for a German still dirty."

Elly groaned. At such a time to go on like that!

"Why did you not say this before?" Mama asked simply, too tired to protest, although red spots glowed on her cheeks.

"I did not think you would like it," Aunt Anna said, with equal frankness. "Now there is no room for liking or caring, there is only Leo to think of, so I go ahead and speak." She shrugged. "Not even one person like you can do everything."

Elly was astonished again at her own anger—that Aunt Anna should be judging *them!*—just as she had been when she realized that Margot had found *her* wanting. How dare they? And she blushed, hoping the others would not notice. For she was wrong to be angry, and she knew she was wrong. "Why don't we move upstairs? We could find another place for the Cummings family, couldn't we?" They had moved in two days ago during all the concern over Pop, Elly hadn't met them, and they had no reality for her. "They're not even unpacked yet."

"Absolutely not."

Mama kept saying no to all their suggestions. They would make no changes for a week at least. "Until we see if Leo shall live," she said openly, not hiding behind the euphemisms used at the hospital. "Next week is the Easter vacation." Phil would help her in the store. "Yermolay will come after Easter from the Tolstoy farm at Newchester to help." She smiled again. "He is their storekeeper, he knows about groceries." Meanwhile, Elly would do the farm chores and make the Easter paskha and kolachi. Mama did not ask any questions or wait for any responses. Anna could indeed do the cooking and cleaning if she wished, the house certainly could use a good spring turnout. As for Margot, lucky that Mama had taught her a little about sewing, for she could use that week to make Easter outfits for herself and Elly. "And then we shall see what to do."

"You're waiting for God to tell you," Phil teased.

Mama opened her eyes wide and stared at him. "Well, *you* certainly are not going to!" she exclaimed.

And, despite their exhaustion, they all laughed.

They pushed through that first week following Mama's plans, and the steady rhythms of work were comforting. In the midst of scrubbing the living room walls, Aunt Anna turned around, a scarf tied crookedly over her hair, and said, "You know it is astonishing. I remember my mother saying to me one day that no matter what the rabbis say and the laws say, to be a woman is best, for countries fall, battles are lost, kings die, but through all this, women go on dusting and cooking, and that is the very root of life. Of course, I did not believe her, just as you do not believe me, but here I am as if such cleaning would make a difference—and for a minute I even forget about Michael . . ." her voice trailed off, "about Leo . . ." and she went back to scrubbing.

In the kitchen Elly smiled. She kneaded the dough for the Easter bread, the kolachi; the house smelled of yeast and strong cleanser. Propped up on the counter in front of her was a copy of Maxwell Anderson's play, *Mary of Scotland*. Glenn Miller's music was on the radio. Margot worked the treadle of the sewing machine in Baba's empty room, and the house hummed with activity. Aunt Anna had climbed the ladder to clean the outside windows, and the countryside, barely touched with the first faint green of spring, shone into the room between freshly ironed white curtains.

It was a miracle, what Aunt Anna had done in five days to the house and, even more, to herself. The floors had been scrubbed, waxed, and polished; the windows cleaned, the curtains washed, starched crisp, and ironed, and Aunt Anna was working on the walls. Tomorrow she would whitewash the kitchen and cellar. "You think I cannot do this? Oho! I have done in my childhood. I do not *like* to do but . . ." and she shrugged again in her funny way. "Then we take the furniture outside, air it all, beat the rugs and bedding, and all will be fresh and sweet again."

Mama had given it into her hands. There was the store, and there was Pop, and nothing else mattered. "It is good to open the hands and give it all away," Mama said, as she and Elly walked through the muddy fields one evening. "Freely. I was wrong not to do this before. Shall we have time to plant this spring?" she murmured. "Yes, no matter what, we put in the vegetables."

They walked through the fields and back past the barn and were at peace, as night came down on them with its sharp chill and, underneath, the hints of spring growing stronger. Mama seemed content to rest for a time from the burden of work and worry and hospital visits, but Elly still pushed on, talking about the future, about next week, and next month, and finally, about not planting vegetables but moving to town, where it would be easier. She saw Mama frown and grow silent, and still she could not stop.

"No, no, no!" Mama said, shaking her head. "What we have to do, we will do for the best of all of us, but until it is necessary, we shall stay here." Mama looked out over the fields and the rim of woods behind them. "Stan Kocinski will help me plant. I am thinking I will give him the cows, anyway. The milking *is* hard." She was talking to herself, not waiting for Elly to answer. "Yes, he will help. Not for the cows . . . let him have them for a start. How much milk do we need? There's no telling about Michael, of course . . . to feed him up . . ."

"When is he coming?" Elly asked, kicking at the mud on her shoes. "You know I forgot . . . isn't it awful . . . you don't *say* anything to me . . . I think about Pop all the time, but I can't imagine Uncle Michael."

"Much use telling you!" Mama said sharply. "What has come over you, anyway? All right, you had a great shock with Leo, I understand. But my father was *shot* when I was ten, and we had to come, my Mamushka and I, to a strange land . . . do you see? You were not always so . . . so thinking of yourself all the time—even at such a time like this. Is it Laura who makes you so? I do not like her parents at all, but I say nothing."

"Oh, Mama, I don't know what you mean! I'm just different from you, don't you see? When you blame it on

Laura, you make it sound as if I'm nothing, just a follower . . ."

Mama interrupted. "Don't shout so! Please. I would like us to be friends. Will you come with me to Newchester for Easter? I need to visit the Tolstoy farm."

Elly kicked at a rock in the path. "Yes," she said finally. "It'll be someplace to go."

For with Mama, Phil, and the car gone all day, the other three were confined to the farm for the entire ten-day Easter vacation that began with Good Friday, went on past Easter Sunday, and ended with the Russian Orthodox Easter celebration a week later, the day before they went back to school. "Not even a phone," Elly grumbled. "And no one to call, besides." Laura and Glenna were going to New York for the week.

They talked only in spurts around the work, for talking would mean thinking, and there was no use in thinking, not as long as Pop remained the same. "No better, no worse," the doctors said, pointing out that actually it meant he *was* better as he was still fighting.

"No," Mama said, "we will still not write to Mamushka, there is no point in it. I shall send her an Easter letter, that is all."

Phil argued with her. "We could use the help." He said almost nothing these days, more silent and drawn into himself than ever, desperate to find the time for his studies and to keep a part of himself separate from the voracious demands of the family.

"Absolutely not." Mama walked into the parlor. "Anna, you agree?" She paused and breathed deeply. "You have made a miracle here."

Aunt Anna put down her book. "Your mother would be in the way," she said. "It is better so." She sighed and leaned back in her chair, looking at the sparkling windows and white walls and polished floor. "I think maybe I become a chambermaid, hmm? When Michael comes, how he will laugh! I do not think it can be much longer now, am I right, Sonya?"

Margot turned away. "Mutti, do not count on it."

"Ha!" her mother said. "Since this with Leo, I do not count on anything. But when I read Goethe, how reasonable the world seems! And then I hope a little."

Phil would drive them to Newchester after supper on Saturday. He asked Margot to come with them, but she would not leave her mother alone. Aunt Anna listened to Mama's shy explanations of the Easter service and nodded her head. "This is not in a church?"

"In the community hall. We decorate it, of course. And with candles and singing. After is a great feast—Elly, you made the kolachi very good. And the eggs? Bring extra."

"We all come," Aunt Anna said decisively. "Yes, I too wish to go out. Soon I will be afraid of streets and people. God knows . . ." and she shuddered.

Aunt Anna had made soup with dumplings for supper. Mama did not eat but came home from the store and went to shower and wash her hair. She came into the kitchen beaming, her embroidered Russian blouse shining white and crisp, and her graying hair plaited into two thick braids crossed over the top of her head. How foreign she looked! Elly thought. How terribly foreign—and how old.

Margot had made clothes for herself and Elly from the same pattern, varying the colors and details; the skirts and blouses looked stylish, even though they did not begin to compare, in Elly's mind, with the clothes in the stores.

"It is not perfect," Margot admitted ruefully, showing

Mama where the seams were not flat. "There is so much to learn! But for setting in the sleeves I follow my own way—see, here—it it easier than the pattern, and the shoulder does not bunch up, so!" She crumpled the material in her fingers. "But it lies smooth."

Elly's skirt was camel color and her blouse a light fawn. She did not care for the colors, but Margot had insisted. "These subtle colors are the best for you with your dark hair; you shall learn to like them. And very simple. That is most elegant. Not like the puffed sleeves in fashion. Plain, like the line on these sleeves, close to the wrist."

"You are losing weight," Mama said, admiring her.

Margot's skirt was in a dusty blue wool and her blouse was pink cotton, bringing out the color of her fair skin. They were a complete contrast, and when they stood together, Aunt Anna called them flowers of spring. She wore her navy blue Schiaparelli suit, still beautiful, though very old.

"And Phil wore his old jacket and slacks," Phil said. "Hurry up, if you don't want to be late. Got all the food? Off we go!"

It was funny, Elly thought, how quickly Pop's open space had closed up. Where was there room for him? They filled the entire car. "A family," she said quietly, "and to think, four months ago, we did not know each other at all."

They stopped at the hospital, and Mama dashed in with an armful of damp lilacs. They waited for a long time. "Something is wrong, I know it," Elly said through clenched teeth. *Please,* she prayed silently, *please, make Pop be all right.*

Mama hurried back, apologizing. "The nurse said he was awake a little today, so I waited to see if I could talk to him, but not quite yet. Tomorrow. This is true Easter news!"

They drove the thirty miles to Newchester through farmland and stands of maple trees putting out their leaves. Aunt Anna exclaimed at the beauty of the land, saying how different it was from the awful wintertime of their arrival. Elly thought that she was wrong—it was nothing in the land that had changed, but Aunt Anna herself; *she* was the difference. A depressing thought, really, considering how much she herself had changed, and surely for the worse; the spring countryside was remote from her, as if she were looking at it through panes of glass, and nothing was real but the beat of her own desires.

All the way to Newchester, all through the lengthy preparations for the feast and the incomprehensible talk in Russian around her, the standing from one foot to another, the staring and the smiling, she brooded about her weaknesses and wondered whether her preoccupation with herself was indeed a failure or a necessity if she were to be an actress. She saw all the activity through a haze, saw Phil and Margot walk down a path among the pine trees, saw Aunt Anna's eyes glaze over as she sat at a rustic wooden table, chin resting on her hand, lost in memories, and she felt the gradual quickening of emotion as the members of the community slowly gathered together, bringing bread and eggs to be blessed, but everything took place behind the screen of self-absorption.

Turn and twist as she might, she could not shake the suspicion that Mama was right, she was increasingly selfish and now was the time to stop. Why did Mama always make her feel so . . . so wrong? She had no answer except that maybe she *was* wrong. But to give up her acting? Impossible! That was what, in the end, Mama wanted. Never! But . . . there she was, judging Margot and look what her cousin had given up! Had she any right to criticize, even to herself? Suppose she had to leave Franklin, leave her language—just like that? Oh, it didn't bear thinking about! Leave Pop—but then, dear Pop . . . she walked quickly to the edge of the clearing and blinked away her tears, unable to forget his breathing and blue lips on that awful day.

Suppose she gave up her acting in return for Pop's health . . . ? A bargain with God. The worst possible thought. Besides, how much was her acting worth to anyone but herself? Except for Laura, who else took her seriously? She had seen the skepticism in Margot's face, the laughter brimming in her eyes. But what was Margot's opinion, that it should matter so much? Still, her face burned as she remembered some of the foolish things she had done. And said. Showing off her French when Margot's was infinitely better; when Margot and Laura talked to each other in French, she understood almost nothing. Coming upon Margot and Phil laughing together, their faces close, and seeing Phil's face open up the way it never did with her. Walking through the auditorium doors and leaving her cousin outside on that first day of the spring term. What was the use of going on? It all only confirmed her misery.

The candles flickered around her, wavering and growing in the pull of the wind that came through the pine trees. About one hundred people were moving toward the plain frame community center that stood in the clearing; thirty or forty were members of the Tolstoy farm, and the others were followers, like Mama, or guests, who came for the Easter celebration. Elly had known many of the residents since she was a child and had loved visiting with Mama and receiving pennies, kisses, food, and admiration, but when she grew older and it became clear to her and to the Tolstoyans that she was not interested in their beliefs, a distance spread between her and the community. The members, feeling sorry for Mama, did not hide their sense that Elly and Phil, too, were unworthy children. Nothing was said, everything was intimated, but the meaning was clear. For the past two years Mama and Baba had gone to Newchester on the bus alone, staying the entire weekend. Remembering that, Elly was sad. She could have come; these were good people. But she had not. Well, she would do her best now.

Her feet moved with the others. Slowly, then more quickly, the clusters of people joined together into one mass flowing through the open doors of the community center, each one holding a candle. Where were Margot and Phil? Elly could not see them, so she took Aunt Anna's dry hand and whispered that she would explain the service. Mama was far away, in front with the other believers.

Without warning the singing began, barely above the threshold of silence, then growing inexorably in volume, with the deep bass voices reverberating throughout the small room, echoing from the corners and sounding again, coming out with infinite slowness and comfort, calling on God over and over to have mercy, to bless, to receive this worship. Elly heard nothing but the singing. Then the incense filled up the cracks in the air and drifted in clouds over her head. Singing and incense. The swell of the congregation responding, the priest's thin voice chanting, then the bass voices once more making the candles dip and sway. The silence between the sounds grew thicker, not only in the room but also inside her head. She was no longer thinking of anything. *Gospodi, poilehmu,* begged the singers, and like waves of the ocean, the people knelt, bowing and crossing themselves. Aunt Anna stood, confused, then she knelt, but she did not cross herself. She stared, lips closed tightly, at the iconostasis behind which the priest moved.

Elly was swept up in the intense emotion that filled the room. She looked around at the faces, some of them known to her for all her life. Old, many of them, or looking older than they would have if life had been easier. Bearded men. Women without make-up. Kerchiefs and gray hair. Sun- and wind-burned faces and twisted hands. Heavy bodies. Not one of these people had an easy life.

Yet, in the light of the candles, their faces shone. By standing on tiptoes and craning her neck, she could see Mama, guarding her candle flame with a cupped hand, and on Mama's face was a look of utter peace and contentment. It was a strong face, withdrawn behind the barrier of its hooded eyes, a face that lived an independent existence, a face that had its deepest relations privately, inside its bones and skin. Its inaccessibility to Elly and her needs at this moment was total, and Elly gasped slightly, as if cold water had been thrown in her face. She wanted to cry out, to do something to attract Mama's attention—hadn't she done just that when she was two or three and frightened by the shapes the candles made on the walls?—but she did not. The time for it was finally past.

She steadied herself and looked at other faces, shining, rapt, refreshed. Mama had never forced her beliefs on Elly and Phil, and they had been grateful; had they missed something extraordinary in not knowing with all their hearts the power that could so transform hardworking, quite ordinary people into such radiant figures? She squeezed her aunt's hand and nodded at the answering squeeze. Phil and Margot were at the very back of the room near the door, whispering to each other, holding hands, smiling. She felt remote from them, she felt remote from her own self.

Had Christ really risen? She had never thought that the familiar story could be literally true; it had been merely a story that made Mama and Baba happy. But what about tomorrow, when the lighted faces would go out? Mama said that people on earth had to continue Christ's work, but tomorrow many of these people would be the same quarrelsome or lazy people they had been yesterday. Then what difference did it all make?

She brushed her forehead with the back of her hand, wiping off the sweat that dripped from her hair. No, what she was seeing here was real, and tomorrow wouldn't change it. There were people—all the adults she knew in Franklin—who believed that art wasn't real, that acting was foolishness and worse, that reality was only the ordinary business of life, the eating and sleeping and washing and talking that you did day after day until the end. If that were all, why bother? She knew there was more, she had felt it herself, not only when she was on stage, but also when she was listening to the Metropolitan Opera broadcasts on Saturday, and suddenly a phrase of music would linger beyond the touch of time, or when she opened a book and felt her skin prickle with the fire burning inside her. Could she ever forget the first time she had seen the words, "Out of the cradle endlessly rocking," and had gone on to read the rest of the Whitman poem, hardly breathing until she finished? Her skin prickled at the memory.

There *was* something more, then, and whatever it was, it was even more real than what passed for life; she would stake her own life on that. *All right, you are being dramatic, maybe melodramatic; why not?* This was the perfect place for it, in the midst of a great swell of feeling; would she ever be able to remember it?

Bells tinkled, incense blew over them, and a great sigh swept through the people, as voiceless as the sigh of wind through fields of corn in August. After the deep silence, the bass voices boomed out again, the bells rang, the people rose, again in waves, and the happy cry was taken up and spread from one to the other, "*Christos voskres,*" with the response, "*Voistinu voskres!*"

She sighed and blinked. The greeting and response went around and around, hands were clasped, people were kissing and being kissed, embracing and being embraced, their candles tipping dangerously. Some were crying, and Elly discovered, to her astonishment, that she was one of them. She sniffed and wiped her eyes with her hand, standing in the center of the jostling crowd, her candle high, wax dripping on her wrist. She would try to get over to Mama.

Aunt Anna tugged at her. She looked peevish and tired. "This was for me a mistake. I try, yes, you must admit that. But I cannot. I am so hungry for people that I think this must be a way." She bit her lips. "To bow down to this Christ . . . ! I do not wish to spoil your mother's time, but is there a place I may go to rest?"

For a split second, Elly winced at the old whining note in her aunt's voice, then she pulled herself up, and with Aunt Anna trailing after her, worked her way outside into the clear, chilly night. "There's a meal next, you know, in the dining hall; don't you want to eat?"

"*Mein Gott,* no! At this time of night? These Russians are truly crazy!"

Elly laughed heartily. Aunt Anna had not changed

completely; the old querulousness was still there. "This is the best time—we won't go home before dawn."

"With so much work to do—and Leo so sick! Well, who am I to say?" Aunt Anna hunched into her jacket, cold.

Phil and Margot came up, beaming.

"Where were you?" Aunt Anna asked sharply. "Back in the woods? Alone?"

"I showed Margot the greenhouses," Phil said. "Remember how we loved them, Elly? Especially in winter—we couldn't believe it, the way flowers grew with snow on the ground."

Elly remembered that. But Phil hadn't taken her this time. "Aunt Anna wants to lie down," she said quietly, trying to keep the reproach out of her voice and not entirely succeeding, for Phil stared at her, then blushed.

"I'll take her to the infirmary," he said. "Why don't you look for Mama . . . it's right this way; there's always an extra bed made up in the guest room," and he walked off into the night with his aunt, explaining that they would indeed come and wake her when they left.

"Did you like it?" Elly asked, feeling the exaltation come over her again.

"Very interesting," Margot said. "There were in Berlin many Russians, almost certainly they are all dead now, and they would have such celebrations, and always I wanted to know what it would be like. Now I know."

"Don't you *feel* anything?" Elly asked, amazed.

"Should I? I am tired, very hungry, a little bored. That is not what you mean, eh? Listen, Elly, I am sorry to disappoint you. It was good. Can't that be enough?"

"Not for me." And then Mama came out, and Elly was able to kiss and hug her without rancor for the first time in many months. When Phil came back, they went to eat and snooze and watch the Russian dancing; and then to eat some more, until every muscle was tired, and their faces hung slack, mouths half-open, too exhausted to talk.

The spell was broken, but Elly did not lose the feelings she had been gathering into herself during the service. She did not entirely understand them. She did not analyze them. She simply let them grow into her. Driving back in the early Sunday dawn, she saw the countryside freshly, looking closely at the flowers beginning to emerge from their long winter. They were not thinking, either. They were just growing.

Seeing them, she knew what she had to do to set the seal on this day. But she could not tell the others—not yet.

11

❦❦ "I'M TOO OLD to cry," Mrs. Wilbur said through gritted teeth, "but . . . I have a headache. And I know *why* it aches!" She gave them a frosty smile. "A week's vacation and—this! Am I to be grateful that some of you —*some* of you—still remember your lines?"

"Gee, I thought we were pretty good," Rob McGuire said, and the others laughed nervously. He didn't care and didn't mind who knew it; what difference did it make to him? He was handsome and easy-going, his father was the leading realtor in Franklin, and he let Rob drive his new Chrysler. On top of it all, Rob did well in the classroom and at football, and now here he was in the play, where he was one of those who did remember the lines. But he wanted it understood that none of it mattered very much to him.

Even Mrs. Wilbur was amenable to his charm. Her anger cracked ever so slightly, and she slumped back in her seat. "You have the makings of a drama critic, young man," she said, her mouth twitching, "but not of a director—or an actor. Come on, all of you, don't you have any pride?"

They agreed to do better tomorrow and began to move

off-stage, eager to be outside in the spring day. Elly lingered behind, putting Quinny off with a promise to see him before school tomorrow. "Not enough time," she murmured, making exaggerated gestures to let him know how sorry she was. She turned her back on Laura and Margot and moved toward the drama teacher on shaky legs, licking her dry lips.

"You, at least, know the lines," Mrs. Wilbur greeted her. "Let's go to Angelo's," she said abruptly. Catching sight of the other girls at the back of the stage, she called to them. "Time to bring back the old days—come along!"

"I wanted to talk to you alone—just for a minute," Elly pleaded. "I've got a problem."

Mrs. Wilbur strode ahead of them down the hill, sniffing at the air. "About time. Buds on my lilacs. Who hasn't got problems? Not your grades, I hope—not at this stage. Middle of April's too late to do anything about them."

Elly attempted a laugh. "I'm passing!"

"Oh, you are doing better than that," Margot said. Laura was silent.

From the clear sunlight they entered the dark room that was Angelo's, leaving behind spring for the seasonless time of the restaurant and the fervent greetings of the waiter, who had not seen them for a long time.

"The usual," Mrs. Wilbur said. She turned to Margot. "You like cokes?"

"I have never had one," Margot confessed. "Since three months in America! So I am glad to try."

Mrs. Wilbur moved briskly. "Problem from Elly. Oops, wait a minute! Laura, do you mind giving me the slightest hint as to what happened? You were the worst today—if you don't mind my bluntness."

Laura kept her eyes on the red-checked tablecloth.

"What if I do mind? What do you know of it?"

No one had answered when Elly had rapped at the door of Laura's house that morning, and Laura had not come to school until she slipped into the French class at the end of the day, looking paler than usual and with the hem of her skirt hanging down. She had avoided Elly and was doing so now, stubbornly keeping silent and marking the tablecloth with the tines of a fork.

"We're leaving here," she said. "On May 31st. That's the day classes end at Glenna's school. So the scene is out."

"The Mary and Elizabeth?" Elly asked. "But why?"

"I told you," Laura said, "we're leaving. That's the way Glenna and Owen are—you know that. Or should. I've warned you often enough, Elly. We've already rented the house for the summer—a friend of Owen's, a weaver, Lia Temorio. Then—who knows? Maybe Miss Fox can rent it to a teacher or sell it or something," she finished indifferently.

Elly was stunned. "You won't be back in the fall." She wiped her wet palms on a napkin.

"Don't be such a slow learner." A flush spread slowly over Laura's olive cheeks. "My God, how do *I* know *where* we'll be in the fall?"

"I heard something," Mrs. Wilbur said, then stopped.

"Probably true," Laura said, and shivered. "I'll do Alice as well as I can, Mrs. Wilbur," she added formally, and was silent again. She seemed to be dragging the words out one by one, with great difficulty. "I'm sorry about the scene—maybe you can find something for Elly to do by herself."

"You sound as if you've gone away already," Elly said sadly. "What happened? Your mother wanted to stay . . ."

"*Glenna* did—but Owen didn't." Laura shrugged.

"Whenever he doesn't want to stay in a place, Owen gets his way. Oh, he's a horrible man!"

The cokes and silver pot of espresso arrived, accompanied by a plate of pale round cookies.

"To say this about your father!" Margot exclaimed, shocked despite herself and what she knew of the Fitzgeralds. It was an instinctive reaction.

"Eat, eat," Mrs. Wilbur urged. The crisp cookies tasted of lemon and were delicious.

"I suppose you've got an angel father," Laura said in despair, her eyes opening wide. "Lucky you." Her bitterness softened. "And lucky Elly, who doesn't appreciate her luck. *My* father's not sick, and he's not in a prison camp—but I wish he were both. Go ahead, kill me for it, why don't you? He's here and he's awful. What more can I say? I'm stuck with him—three years to go before I'm eighteen—and we're stone broke."

Delicious as they were, the cookies brought no comfort.

Mrs. Wilbur spoke dryly into the awkward silence. "Can't fault your analysis. They were true, then, the stories? No. Forget that. None of my business. Do your best in the play, that's all, really. Yes, that's the best. Elly, watch what you say, or I'll cancel the entire show."

"I wanted to talk to you alone, I don't know how I can say it, especially now . . . Laura . . . oh, Mrs. Wilbur, maybe you *should* cancel the play, it might be a good idea. I want to withdraw. Or let Annette Soames do it, she'd be great—and she knows all the lines."

"Great, eh?" Mrs. Wilbur laughed. "You may not be an actress yet—or ever—but you're certainly learning the show business habit of exaggeration. Annette Soames! No, without you, we'd have to cancel. But you're not going to withdraw, of course; there's no point in even talking about it. Check, please, Claudio."

Nothing was as she had planned, but Elly plunged in, anyway, trying to ignore Margot and Laura. She would not see them; like Laura, she kept her eyes down and fiddled with the fork. And as she spoke, the past weeks kept intruding in her mind until she forgot what she was saying and stopped, to begin again with an absent-minded clumsiness. She had no choice, she said, there was simply too much to do—and she saw her father still and white in the hospital bed—housework, schoolwork, helping in the store, going to the hospital—and she was in the spotlessly clean house yesterday, with the sun shining in from each window, and all of them a family in the moment after Mama said that Pop was much better.

"Don't you see how it is?" Elly said, caught up in that memory. "I didn't do enough for him, and now I've got to try!" And the Easter service flooded in all at once, the sounds and scents almost overwhelming her. "I *have* to do it—to give up what I want . . ." She came out of her dream and looked around. Impossible to explain. She had recaptured something, only for a minute, and like a soap bubble, it slipped from her hands as she touched it and popped. "I feel . . ." No use telling about the bargain she had made when she prayed that Pop would live; even she was ashamed of it now. "I'm sorry, I don't know what to say. But it's real what I feel, giving this up, helping my mother more. Can't you see that?" But of course not. The sunny house, the Easter service, had meaning only for her in the way she saw them. She had not been able to make the others see. "I know I wasn't very good today," she told Mrs. Wilbur directly. "I've got too many things on my mind. It's true. I might as well quit. I guess you'll say I'm giving up—but I don't know *what* I can do." She finished lamely and kept her eyes down.

Mrs. Wilbur drew back in distaste. "I've made a mistake with you, that much is clear," she said coldly. "All of your talk about a career was just that—talk. Too bad. I'm sorry, but you can't pull out of the play. There's no question of that."

"Your big scene ruined," Laura murmured.

"Ah, no!" Margot put her hand on Elly's arm.

Elly's face seemed to fall apart. "I didn't deserve that," she said, struggling to keep control. "I don't know what happened to *you*, but . . ." She began again, "Oh, Laura, come back. Please."

"I do not like scenes—except on the stage," Mrs. Wilbur said. "And I must get along home. The Elizabeth and Mary scene is definitely out, am I right? Pity. But I expect excellent performances in the play from *all* of you. I hear that you have troubles," she said bitterly. "Who hasn't? That's all I hear! What kind of life would we have if we turned tail and ran at the sign of a little trouble? I'll tell you, Elly, *you* would have a life like mine, and you would hate yourself. Please believe me."

Elly was bewildered. "My goodness. I didn't know . . ."

Mrs. Wilbur reached across the table to tap her wrist. "There's nothing *to* know—no big romantic secret. What did you think? Oh, I know. I used to think the same way when I was young. But it's never romantic . . ."

"Elly won't believe that," Laura said, smiling crookedly.

Mrs. Wilbur shrugged. "My mother needed me; she was afraid to stay in the house by herself after my father died. I came home. Temporarily." Mrs. Wilbur spoke with difficulty. "Do you know where our house was?" she asked, laughing, looking like a young girl again.

"Where the library is now! The day after Mama died, I sold it to Lou McGuire, and he turned around and sold it to the town for the library! Made a mint on it, I wouldn't doubt. That's Lou's way. So. The house is gone, and I'm still here."

"Why didn't you leave then?" Elly asked, fascinated. Margot kicked her under the table, but she paid no attention.

Mrs. Wilbur's face closed like a shutter over a window. "I had . . . other obligations by then. That's what I mean. Giving up is the easiest thing of all. Let me tell you something, all of you girls. When you're fifteen or sixteen, talent is common. You'd be surprised how many people have it." She reached into her purse for the money, laid a tip on the bill, and closed her eyes wearily. "I had it. No, what makes the difference is something else."

"My father talks always of persistence," Margot said, sipping the last of her coke.

"And more," Mrs. Wilbur said. She rubbed her fingertips together. "A quality . . . I don't know. The great ones create themselves all over again out of what they know about themselves. They don't give up. Does that make any sense? I'm afraid not. Look, I'm tired. But *you* don't have to go. See you tomorrow."

She paused before she went. "Elly, I'm angry with you, don't think I'm not. I don't intend to let you get away with anything." Her hand lingered lightly on Laura's black hair. She looked as if she wanted to say something more, but she did not and left in silence.

"What did you mean?" Elly asked, turning to Laura. "I *had* to do it—I made a promise at Easter. It was *so* beautiful! I don't know . . . I wanted to give up something important. And you—you made it so shabby!"

Blinking in the bright sunlight, the three girls walked out into the street and the softness of an early spring day. Tiny furled buds dotted the trees along Main Street, and spears of fresh green grass poked their way up among last year's brown stumps. A languid breeze floated in from the river to lift their hair lightly off their necks as they went up the long cobbled hill street toward the Green.

Laura's back was stiff. "I'm so sick and tired of your playing games. That's all. My God, when will you grow up? Jeanette MacDonald and Nelson Eddy at the movies this weekend—what a town! I'm glad to be leaving, if you want to know. Owen's right. There's nothing here. *You Can't Take It With You*! Probably we'll be living in New York, and I'll take classes at the American Academy. Why not?"

Margot strode along, her hands stuck jauntily into the large pockets of her spring jacket. She was humming a gay tune. "The first American spring," she remarked to the air. "Is it true what I am being told—no matter how bad the winter, the spring comes? Yes," she answered herself, "it is true. Remarkable." She rolled her R's and laughed.

"What did your father do that was so horrible?" Elly asked out of her own hurt, not caring about her friend's feelings. "Get drunk or something? Is that what you're so ashamed of? Why? It's not the first time, after all."

Laura stopped and faced Elly. "You must be the only person in Franklin who doesn't know what happened. Honestly, you're so dumb that I can't stand to look at you! You don't see what goes on right in front of your eyes—you just moon around and talk about Garbo and Willa Cather's books and all that junk."

Elly felt as if all her skin was being scraped off her bones, bit by bit. "You can't mean it—you!"

"Don't let it bother you, what she says," Margot said. "Please. Let's go to the store."

Elly turned on her cousin. "What do you know? She was my best friend." Then she clapped her hand over her mouth. "Ugh!" She had said it—*was*. The difference had been made.

They stood, irresolute, at the top of the hill. Elly thought that if she went away from Laura, it would mark the end of their friendship—and over such a small thing! Perhaps she had been too dramatic in Angelo's; she had seen disbelief in Laura's face. Still, Laura was upset. Tentatively, Elly smiled and waited for an answering smile.

Laura turned away. "It's no use, Elly. Some things you don't understand . . ."

"Try me," Elly said breathlessly.

"I wish . . . I wish I could," Laura said. "But it's my whole life, and I don't want to explain it. O.K. I couldn't see what you were talking about in there—I thought it sounded plain silly—that's the way it is. And you can't see me, either. So what's the use?"

Elly thought, *I won't plead*. But she did say, "I thought I *did* understand."

Laura shrugged. Her eyes seemed larger and darker than ever, and they looked right through Elly, right through Franklin. She simply was not here any longer. "I don't think we have to rehearse together any more, do you? Now that we're not doing the scene. The play—that's no problem. *If* you decide to stay in it, that is. But I guess you will, now that you've had your big moment."

She picked her way carefully up the crumbling stone steps to the Green and scuffed across the grass to her house. Elly stood watching until she opened the door and went in. Then she stared at the empty space.

"In the locker room," Margot said, and Elly jumped

at her voice, "the girls were talking of this, what her father did. He drank too much when she and her mother were away, then he attacked one of the girls at the school. So he must go at once, there is a big scandal, and Miss Fox keeps on the mother only because she is a relative."

"Attacked?" Elly asked. "But how? What do you mean? Then why is she mad at me?"

"Sometimes," Margot said, "you *are* impossible. Attacked—in her bed. You know what I mean? To rape her. I do not know if he did or not."

"Oh," Elly said. "Why didn't I know? Maybe I do dream too much—Pop calls me moony sometimes. Did I just miss the talk?" She had been thinking all day of her own decision.

"How should I know? I am only a poor relation . . ."

"Oh, stop that, why don't you? For God's sake! I feel awful enough as it is—you know that. I plain didn't know—*you* know how Mama keeps such things away from us."

"Yes," Margot said. "I know."

"And then I went and made such a fool of myself to Mrs. Wilbur." Elly shivered in the sun. "How will I go back there tomorrow?"

Margot turned to walk back down the steps to the alley behind the store. "Yes, that was stupid of you, blowing off so much emotion. If you had asked me, I would say to you, absolutely no."

Elly had to agree. She followed Margot down the steps, aware of the emptiness on the Green behind her, of the final closing of Laura's door, of the hesitation in the center of the coming of spring. Why had she ever imagined such a scene? Why plunged into it? "I *was* stupid," she admitted, "but . . ." then she stopped.

What difference did it make? She was burning to hear the details about Laura's father, but Margot did not know them. How awful! How thrilling! How romantic! How stupid she was again! Her thoughts ran rapidly from one mood to another; no longer could she linger in the one she wished and daydream the hours away. "Oh, I'm going to miss Laura!"

Margot turned around. "You'll get used to it," she said briefly.

Lilac bushes tumbled over the backs of the board fences along the alleyway. Pale buds were forming at the tops of the stalks laden with green leaves. There was no way of escape from the enchantment of the coming season, of cutting oneself off from the promise it held out.

"Why don't we finish our homework fast and practice the play?" Margot suggested. "I can use some help." She leaned her shoulder against the door to the back room of the store and stood quietly for a moment.

Elly guessed what she was thinking about. "When your father comes . . ." she said, touching her cousin's arm.

Margot pulled the arm away. "He will not come," she said bleakly. "I dream about him and Uncle Leo, and they are moving further and further away from us all the time."

Elly shook her head. "Don't say that. It's not true. I'm sure it's not true." Before they went in, she pulled one cluster of the new buds off the lilac bush at the back door. "Nice," she said, sniffing, and Margot agreed.

12

"I WOULD RATHER not know almost," Aunt Anna said, waving the letter around the hospital room. "Letters! And to wait. To know nothing." Her shoulders slumped.

"Two months is not such a long time," Pop said gently. "Not for you," he added. "For Michael, yes. Believe me, *now* I know what it means, waiting."

"I've asked Henry Kocinski's younger boy, Witold, to put in the vegetables," Mama said. "Two dollars a day. The earth is sweet now."

Pop nodded. "These flowers are beautiful, Sonya." He spoke very quietly.

"In springtime, in springtime, the only pretty ring time, when birds do sing . . ." Elly sang under her breath, and stretched.

"Yermolay does good," Mama said. "To tell the truth, I will be happy to have back the store to myself, though. Business is not bad . . ."

Pop put up a hand. "I trust you, my dear—let it be. How is Freda, does she write?"

A smile dimpled Mama's cheeks. "Ho! She writes like she is on vacation instead of working so hard."

"And then what will I have?" Aunt Anna asked in a

low voice. "It is no secret, surely, that we were not so happy before, so what shall I have now?"

"Sweet lovers love the spring," Elly sang to herself.

"You have turned out to be quite a cook," Pop teased his sister. "Upholding the honor of our family."

Aunt Anna had no sense of humor. "I do what I must," she said stiffly. "I do not hear complaints."

Elly drummed her fingers on the table. "Hot in here."

"So open the window," Pop said. "Won't kill me." Everything he said was gentle. "Nothing can kill me now."

Mama leaned forward. "Leo, take it easy!"

"*You* need the rest," Pop said, and the doctor came in, whistling, and beckoned Mama to come with him.

"To pay the bill, no doubt," Pop said. "Elly, find me tomorrow something to read, if you please. *Anthony Adverse!* Fah! Take it back to the library with you."

"I send up some Goethe," Aunt Anna said. "More than anyone he sustains," and she went on praising him while Pop met Elly's eyes with his, and they smiled at each other.

"That is very fine," Pop said gravely, "except I do not read German any more; it has gone clear out of my head. No. Mmm, what do I want?" He sighed. "That is the trouble with the life we lead—I can no longer read like when I was young. A café sitter. How we read and talked! Something political. Ask Phil to help you."

"Cafés," Elly repeated, half-dreaming. "Shakespeare? You could borrow my copy. *Gone With the Wind?*"

Pop shook his head. "I'm not up to either of them. Maybe when I come home. Thank God for the radio. And the Rotary." The Rotary Club had given the radio to him. "I hear everything. Even Toscanini on Sunday. Did you hear?"

"Mmm," Elly said. "Beethoven. Plenty of Beethoven. Come home? When?"

"Like with Michael, I will come when I come. So tell me how you are doing in school. Where's Phil? His cold gone?"

"Sure. Went to the movies with Margot," Elly said, and quickly added, "Quinny's taking me tomorrow. *Drums Along the Mohawk*." She fiddled with her skirt, pleating and unpleating the material. She didn't want to talk about school any more; what could she say? "I'm passing, if that's what you mean."

Pop's eyes twinkled. "Your mother told me about Laura. It's hard to lose a good friend. Very hard. I won't bore you with *my* memories . . . you know, I've been thinking a lot, lying here. And you wouldn't listen."

Elly shrugged. Her hair flew out from the tortoise shell band. "What's so awful is that she's still *here*—in the play, in my classes, everything. And, well . . . we talk to each other, but it's as if we had a glass wall between us. It's bad. I can't explain."

"You did very well," Pop said, and waited.

"It was the same," Aunt Anna said, "with Margot's friend Gudrum. She could not be with Margot . . . her parents would not allow. She still wished it, but her parents . . . ! So to break it off, she was cruel, especially since she did not want to do it."

"That is twice as hard," Pop agreed.

"I miss Laura," Elly said mournfully. "We had such perfect understanding—I thought. Phil and I used to be like that—remember, Pop?—then *he* changed. I wish . . . no, I don't, I guess I don't wish anything to change. That's wrong." She fumbled for the words to express what was in her mind. "I'm glad I changed—I was pretty awful in the winter, wasn't I?"

Pop grinned at her. "You were."

She blushed. "I'd like not to remember. Oh, Pop, I feel so bad sometimes, and I feel even worse complaining to you, but here I am doing it."

"Anna, do you remember your misery at this age, eh?"

"Leo, what nonsense!" she said sharply. "The trouble is these children have nothing more important to think about these days. We had to work!"

"Naturally. How right you are!" Pop said with a solemn face. Behind his hand, he winked at Elly.

It was remarkable how much better she felt. Pop had a soothing effect on all of them; how they missed him! "I dreamed about Laura and me walking and talking, and today we were reading Shelley's poetry in English class . . . I had been *waiting* for that . . . and it was no good, we weren't going to talk about it. Ever!" True, she had Quinny, and she smiled at the thought. Quinny wasn't the same, though. He liked her—and her skin tingled—which was good. But she felt vaguely ashamed of him, with his sloppy speech and frank disinterest in books. Oh, she was ashamed of herself for her feelings. They didn't go away, however. Quinny and Shelley! She giggled. She didn't want to talk about Quinny.

Or about Mrs. Wilbur, who treated her with cool courtesy, never referring to the scene in Angelo's, never inviting her back to the restaurant, coming down hard on her whenever she made a mistake. The two weeks that had passed seemed like two years. To her surprise, she didn't mind very much; she deserved the reproach. When she was a small child and disobedient, Mama made her sit in a chair placed in the middle of the parlor and feel the sting of remorse in silence and isolation. And, oh, she did, she did! And felt all the better for it afterwards. Cleansed.

Each day she sharpened her performance, discovered things about Penny Sycamore, that foolish, trivial woman who nevertheless turned out to have quite a deep interior life. Mrs. Wilbur said that was the secret of good acting, to understand that every character had this life, even though it was not shown on the stage, so that every gesture and speech that *was* shown was attached to a long life of its own and should come out of that life. Yes. Slowly, very slowly, Elly was beginning to see what she meant.

"Leo," Mama said briskly, coming in again, "we must go. The movies will be out, and Phil will drive us home. Poor boy, he works too hard, and he worries so about the college." She lifted her hands, let them fall helplessly, then leaned over to kiss Pop. "The doctor is pleased. Soon. Soon."

"The longest word in the language," Pop said. "So what else did he say? It was a long conversation to say he was pleased. He didn't, by any chance, mention the bill?"

"We have money for the bill, Leo, don't worry. I put the rent from the flat into the bank—the Cummings people are good tenants, praise God—and paid the mortgage from our profits, so we manage. And already the Kocinskis pay me fifty dollars to cut our hay this summer. They are so glad to have the cows, and without the cows, we do not need the hay!" Mama reflected. "I should have done this long ago. For two dollars a week he will sell us what we need—milk, butter, cottage cheese, sour cream—and I told him the store would take the rest."

"You know something, Sonya," Pop said, "you like to be a woman of business. I see that now. It's something to think about." He patted her hand. "There is nothing you cannot do well once you start."

Mama blushed. "That's why I'm a millionaire," she said, smiling. "Good night, Leo, until tomorrow. *Spahkoynee nochee.*"

The darkness outside the hospital was still new and had not yet settled down comfortably around the trees and houses. Mama spoke slowly, telling them that Pop could come home as soon as they found a place to live in town, the farm was too far away, especially without a telephone, and he could not be left alone all day.

Elly started to say something, but Mama wasn't through. "Anna is there . . . and I could put a phone in . . ." She talked more to herself than to them, murmuring of the advantages of the farm, how Pop could walk all around the land, and, "after all, the bedroom and bath are downstairs," and Elly and Aunt Anna said nothing. "He will have to be very quiet, of course. The doctor says in town is better, he can walk to the store and work for a few hours, he must work—this is a young doctor, he has good ideas—he says without work, Leo will fall apart. But how? Shall I do it my way instead?"

Aunt Anna interrupted to point out how hard the farm work was and how very isolated the house, but Mama cut her off. "I am so tired. I am so very tired! It is too much!" she said to the night. "Tomorrow I will think again."

The echo of Mama's words stayed in Elly's ears all the way home in the packed car while Phil talked about the movie, and she made another big decision, hoping it would not be as foolish as the one she had made at Easter. To be certain, she talked to Margot when they were in bed that night. "It might take only an hour or so; we wouldn't miss much school. I'm sure they wouldn't say anything if we were late just once. It would take such a weight off Mama, don't you think?"

"Why should he talk to *you?* In Germany this would be quite impossible!"

"I don't know," Elly admitted. "But we could try, couldn't we? I mean, this is Connecticut."

"Not we," Margot said. "You."

"O.K. You'll hold my hand, though, won't you?"

"Since you ask so nicely, then I do it," Margot said.

Elly didn't fall asleep for a long time. She kept imagining the houses in town they could rent, with big rooms and modern kitchens. She imagined new furniture, even though she knew very well they would not have any, and she imagined a new Elly Josephs moving in those rooms with straight hair and a slim figure and no more problems.

Strange, how the tension between her and Margot had gone. No. Not gone. There. Accepted. When she had been able to *see* Margot . . . giving up her dreams had been so hard . . . still, she was happy to have her cousin to talk to . . . it was all different . . . almost four months . . . seems longer, how easily we get used to things . . . like Pop so ill . . . what did Phil think of Margot . . . must ask him for some math help . . . there would be a gleaming white tile bathroom . . . tomato sauce and coffee at Angelo's . . . Mussolini . . . poor Spain . . .

And she was asleep.

"I'm pure, plain scared," Elly admitted the next morning as they waited for Mr. McGuire to come into his realty office. "I shouldn't be. I've known Mr. McGuire all my life, not well, of course, but still . . . and Rob is in the play," she rambled on.

"Sssh," Margot said. "You are talking too much."

Margot was right. Elly looked out the plate glass window to Upper Main Street and concentrated on the people going by. Nine-thirty. Soon her English class would be over. Would Mrs. Marshall say anything about her absence? Maybe not. Where was Mr. McGuire? The secretary said he was on his way. She tried to study her French but couldn't concentrate. Margot was absorbed in her history book; how could she?

When he finally came, Mr. McGuire made it easy for them, inviting them into his office. "Sit down, always glad to meet frends of Rob's. How's the play going? What d'you think of him? Nice boy, eh? We're going to see if we can't get this business rolling so he can come in with me. Wants to go to college. Waste of time if you ask me. I can name you half-a-dozen fellas in this town alone fell apart in '33 even with college. Well! What do you need me for, little ladies? Want to sell some tickets to your play?"

"No," Elly said. "I want to ask you some questions if I can. I don't know anything about it, really, but . . ." and she took a deep breath, "do you know our farm?"

" 'Course I do. Know every piece of property within twenty miles of Franklin. On all sides. How's your old man? Coming along, is he? Jeez, I was sorry to hear of it —you tell him to take care, won't you?"

"He's much better, thanks. Mr. McGuire, if we sold our farm, how much money could we get for it?"

"You asking me to handle it?"

"I don't know yet." She paused, then plunged wildly ahead. "My mother sent me."

Margot looked startled, raised her eyebrows, then shrugged, and let her eyes wander all over the office. "Told Sonya years ago to give up that place. She works too hard, stuck way out there. Not fair to Leo, either. Well, I can't give you a firm answer, you understand. Depends on a lot of factors. How much cash you need? Willing to subdivide? Sell animals and farm equipment with land or separately at an auction? And so on and so forth. How much land you got?"

Elly started to say she didn't know, but he waved her silent, called in his secretary, and had her look it up. "Keep careful records. Can't afford to let anything go in this business. Three hundred acres. Not bad. You got a creek and a pond, meadow, woodland, garden. Listen, honey, let me think about it and give Sonya a call."

"No, please don't do that! I mean, she's got so much on her mind right now with the store and my father, I don't think she'd even pay attention. Could I come by after school tomorrow, and you'd write it all down for me, the possibilities and the money? Just to give us an idea."

"Sure, sure," he said. "And then what'd you do?"

"That's the second part," Elly said triumphantly. "You could help us there, too. We'd buy in town, a nice house with a big garden for Mama and plenty of room for us and . . ." She drifted off into a half-reverie. "Like in Yankeetown."

There was a long silence. Mr. McGuire coughed, *harrumph, harrumph,* and turned away to stare out the window that gave onto a dirty alley. "You really thinking of Yankeetown?" he finally asked.

Elly was scared again. "Is it . . . is it too expensive? I have no idea . . . maybe I was wrong . . ."

"You'd get plenty more for your land than you'd need to pay down for a house; that's good land you've got. All a question of finding the right buyer. Might take a little time, but things are picking up. Once we get that Roosevelt out of the way, get someone like Taft in office, we'll do right good again. No, it's not that, sweetheart. You wouldn't want to live in Yankeetown."

"Oh, but I do," Elly assured him. "I don't know about Mama . . ."

He paid no attention. "We'll fix you up with a nice house on the Green, maybe, near school, near the store. Or where we live, over in Woodmont, it's a new section, finest construction. Harvey Meyer lives there; your Dad knows him. Meyer's Men's Shop. Fine man. Doctor Bierenberg up at the hospital just bought there. Through this office, in fact. Both of 'em."

Again the silence spread. Elly would not give up her dream of a large clapboard house lapped by wide lawns under an arch of maples and elms. Woodmont was raw, it was nothing compared to Yankeetown!

"Aha," Margot said softly. "Thank you so much, Mr. McGuire. Elly, what he is saying is Jews cannot buy houses in Yankeetown."

Elly turned to stare at her cousin in the silence that followed.

"That's about the size of it," Mr. McGuire said uncomfortably. "Not to mislead you, it's damn hard for a Catholic. I wouldn't consider it myself. Be with my own kind, where I'm wanted. Know what I mean? Now we're trying to keep Woodmont open to all."

"But I don't *want* to live in Woodmont," Elly said desperately.

"Can't see why. We're pretty careful there, understand? Too many Frenchies, who'd want to live next to *them?* Not that *I'd* mind, sold two houses to 'em, one to young Dupré at the sawmill, he's got a government contract, wanted to move up. I say more power to 'em. But by and large, you got to be careful. Everyone knows *your* father, Elly, he's a right guy; Harvey's the best; Bierenberg, hell, he's a *doctor.* Still and all, who knows the next guy to come along, what he'd be like. Get my point? Woodmont's the place of the future in this town, a little bit of everyone all mixed up. Like America. Who needs Yankeetown? What d'you say?"

Elly's cheeks burned. "I say it's awful! *Awful!*" She wanted to add, *But we're not even Jews, not really,* then she remembered Margot sitting next to her and what Margot had said about that not making any difference at all in Germany, so she bit her lip in silence.

"That's as may be, little lady, but it's the way life is. Especially when you're in business. Ask your Dad. Tell him I was asking for him, hope to see him around here real soon. Spring'll set him up right, wait and see if it doesn't. Polly!" he called out to his secretary, "put 'em down for . . . what time? . . . 4:30 tomorrow afternoon. Josephs. Thanks for coming—glad you thought of us first."

"What you want," Margot pointed out as they walked along the street, "is to sell the farm. Buy in town. Have money for Phil's college. Keep that in mind." She couldn't resist adding, "Remember before I begin to school?"

Elly's cheeks burned. "Honestly, Margot, I didn't think there *was* any problem! And I've lived here all my life!"

Margot was amused. "Didn't you really know before? I think you are only trying to make me comfortable when I see how you and Phil are not so liked. And others. Didn't you know why?"

"Let's have a soda before we go back to school. I'll

blow up, I swear I will! Sure, I know why they didn't like us, the snobs; we were too smart for them."

"Because you were smart Jews," Margot said carefully. "I will have again a coke."

Elly flipped through the pages of *Modern Screen* in the drugstore. Remain calm, she told herself, the days of screaming are over. "Ginger Rogers and Fred Astaire. Hmm." She replaced the magazine on the rack. "Do you really think that's the reason, Margot? There's Mama, of course—oh, how could they? *Everyone* loves Mama!" But then, Mama wasn't Jewish. What did that make *her?*

"Well, you are asking the wrong person. What did we think in Germany? That we were Germans! And we were wrong. So, why ask me?"

Elly shuddered. "It's not the same thing," she insisted.

Margot agreed. "Otherwise, we wouldn't be here. And we *are* here, not so? I even begin to like it." She looked closely at Elly. "Calmer?"

"A little," Elly admitted. "But every time I think about it—! Don't want Jews! Did you hear him? Mr. McGuire, I mean. Taft for president! I'll have to tell Phil about this. But not Mama. Taft!"

Margot was puzzled. "Tell me, please, what is all this?" She combed her hair back from her face. "Must wash it tonight. Spanish politics, I know, and German, and even impossible French, but who is this Taft?"

"A Republican," said Elly. "It's a long story. Forget it. Let me pay. Hi, Mr. Plotkin. Two cokes."

"You like the Shakespeare?" he asked, giving her the change. "Four more copies still in stock. This is not a town for Shakespeare, I'm afraid. Give my regards to your papa."

"I can't believe it." Elly raged on once they were outside again. She squinted into the sun. "Phil *won't* get into Yale, like he says. But why? Golly." She shook her head in confusion. "I never thought it would touch me!"

All the way to school, she kept wondering about the mystery presented to her for consideration, and she was no further to the end of it when she walked into the lunch room than she had been down at the drugstore. She stood with her cousin in the doorway and looked at the students eating lunch, kids she had gone to school with and known for ten years, and she looked at them differently. Hardly any of them were Jews. And the others? Were they like the people in Yankeetown? What was the matter with Jews? With her? With Phil? How were they Jewish? She had never thought of herself as anything at all, and she liked it that way. And Pop? Plenty was the matter with Aunt Anna, but that was *her*, Anna Blum, and she would be the same no matter what she was. And Margot? How was she not German?

She caught Quinny's eye, and they went to eat at his table. Did Quinny feel that way? He was taking her out. His parents? She could never ask. How friendly they were! But it was Mama they knew. What did they *really* think?

She lifted her carton of milk in a toast to her cousin, who had known it all and in the worst possible way. "To Margot," she said, "for deserving it." It was her apology for everything.

And Margot understood. "Yes," she said, "two is better than one, no matter what."

"I'll drink to that!" Quinny said, moving his leg up against hers under the table and running his hand over her kneecap.

She pulled her leg away, then let it move against his once again, enjoying the quiver from the touch that went all the way up to her spine. The bruise on her spirit was still there behind the talk and laughter; it would not so easily disappear. At the same time, she wanted to be close to Quinny for more than the comfort he gave. She wanted that quiver to come back and touch her body further and deeper.

13

"FIRST RUN-THROUGH next week," Mrs. Wilbur said that afternoon, and panic reigned. "You're nowhere near ready for the dress rehearsal—I've never had so much trouble with a play before! Ready to do Act Three in some kind of order?"

Lines were forgotten, cues dropped, actions performed with clumsy hilarity. Laura played badly, self-consciously, barely looking at the others, including Rob, who walked through his part of Tony with dull determination. Mrs. Wilbur stared at her shrewdly a few times, but said nothing. Margot whispered. When reminded to speak louder, she looked startled, raised her voice at once, then let it fade away again.

Fueled by her anger and her desire to win Mrs. Wilbur's full forgiveness, Elly forgot nothing, rescued the other members of the cast and gave a stunning performance. She knew it at the time—and she knew that the others sensed it, too. She was in complete control. It was wonderful! The words came, as if she had made them up herself. The gestures came. The right kind of Penny Sycamore voice came. The rhythm came and sustained her to the end. Gone from her mind were Yankeetown and

Woodmont, gone her misery and depression, gone the break with Laura. It was as if she had gathered herself together for a leap, jumped, then soared high, trying her wings and discovering that they would indeed keep her up. When she finished, she was breathless with exhaustion.

Mrs. Wilbur did not speak. She didn't have to. Elly walked off the stage and kept on walking into the dressing room, where she closed the door behind her, and when she was certain she was alone, hugged herself, made faces at herself in the mirror, and waltzed madly around the room in a delirium of joy. She had done it! She had not fallen apart, she had used everything, she had pulled it together!

When the other girls came in for their books, she went out into the hall, not wanting to talk, wanting to keep this hour to herself for as long as she could. There was nothing to say, anyway. How could you talk about such completion? You could only do it and try to remember for yourself, then hope and work to do it again.

Laura passed her, head down, and still she sat, whistling an offkey version of "Stardust." In twos and threes the others drifted out. Quinny stopped to tell her he was right proud of her, and she smiled at him, but no, she didn't want to go walking on the palisades by the river. Not today. Next week? Certainly.

Where was Margot? She wandered back to the auditorium, not wanting Mrs. Wilbur to see her hanging around and imagine that she was waiting for a compliment. No, that would only spoil everything. Ten minutes more, and still no Margot. Where had she gone?

The door to Mrs. Wilbur's office was ajar. Voices inside. Margot. Had Mrs. Wilbur come down especially hard on her? She had remembered her lines, been no more inept than anyone else.

"I cannot," Margot was saying. "I am very sorry I cannot continue. I think I shall lose my voice, my throat goes tight." Right then she began to rasp.

"That's a darn shame!" Mrs. Wilbur said. "I won't pretend you showed a great deal of talent—that would be a lie. But you did well, you know."

"Yvonne Audier will do well, too," Margot said. "She knows the part, so I do not think I'm letting you down. I have tried . . ."

"Umm. Of course, it's not a big part—thank heavens! A juicy one, yes. Important, yes. But Yvonne can do it. Not as well as you, I'll say that. She'll be happy for the chance, though." There was a long pause, and Elly started to move away, only to hesitate when she heard Mrs. Wilbur say, "I think you've not had an easy time of it."

Margot laughed. "I have allowed myself to follow Elly, which was a mistake."

"Ah!" said Mrs. Wilbur. "Elly is an entirely different matter. She has great possibilities—if she can discipline herself. Who knows? I wouldn't dare predict. But I've been around theatre people a lot, in New York, in summer stock--I don't just vegetate in Franklin all year round—and Elly's got what it takes in temperament. What she'll do with it . . . well! Without the temperament, though, you can't do much. It's the beginning of everything."

Elly had been planning to interrupt, to make some noise to alert them, then knock on the door and walk in, commiserate with Margot, go back to the store with her cousin. Impossible to do now. She backed quietly away, hiding in the wings, exultant. She had the temperament! What else would they say?

"I have the more careful temperament," Margot added. "There is no wildness in me!"

"Listen!" Mrs. Wilbur said, "I'd like to hear more, I *do* wish you would tell me a little about yourself. Probably the last chance, eh? What a lovely face you have! May I invite you to Angelo's?"

Elly fled. Backstage, down the corridor, out the heavy side door. Don't let it bang. Surely she would just keep on flying. She had the temperament!

The sun shone obliquely between the walls of old buildings to light her way down the cobbled path and brick steps to the Green, where she turned off and went into the library, still stepping softly, as if she were cradling a basket of eggs on her head. So Margot couldn't do it! Immediately that thought went, to be replaced by another—*she* had the temperament, the talent!

The library smelled of wood polish and paper. Phil, behind the circulation desk, went on stamping books and gave her a big smile that spread across his homely face. She saw him as if for the first time and knew how much, rock-bottom, she loved him.

Almost empty, the reading room smelled musty, as if it had been put away in mothballs for the winter. She dropped her books on a table and went to the ladies' room. No one was there. Good! Working slowly, she washed her face, scrubbing and scrubbing at it until all the powder and lipstick were off. Then she brushed her hair and pulled it back from her face, letting it fall in its stiff, crinkly layers down her back. Must get it cut, it will never fall silkily like Margot's. Or Laura's. Laura! If only . . . if only she were here!

Very seriously, Elly studied her naked face, recoiling at first from its customary look, the look she called ugly. Her forehead was good, not too narrow or too broad. She slid her glasses up on her head. Eyes: good color, a rippling brown, the color of rocks in a stream bed when water percolated over them. But too small. And too myopic; how weak they looked without the shield of her glasses! Nose: far too big and assertive, it gave her face distinction, yet at the same time unbalanced the face and drew attention from her cheekbones, which were nice and high, if a trifle too broad—a visible legacy from Mama and Baba. Still, none of it was irreparable; one needed a strong face for the stage, although she would never make it on the screen without a complete remodeling. It was the lower part of her face that she could not be at home with—a chin too pointy, a thick lower lip oddly married to a thin, slightly crooked upper lip, and uneven teeth speckled with too many fillings.

And these features spoiled the unity of her face, turned it into something far below beautiful. She moved as close to the mirror as she could and studied her pores, the contours of her jaw, the whorls in her ears. Her heart beat fast, as if she were playing a jumping game, and the words that dinned inside her head were, *This is me, this is me.* She rubbed the palms of her hands gently over her cheeks, relishing the meeting of flesh with flesh, both of it hers.

The brown-tiled room behind her was blocked out; all she could see was her enlarged face as if in a camera close-up. She would never again forget what she looked like. This face would have to do, she would have to shine her talent through it and transform it without the help of white teeth or regular lips, and this she would manage

—she vowed it, listening nervously for the door to open because she was more than half-aware of the foolishness of her romantic notions, but not yet ready to discard them.

She left her skin bare and tied her hair smoothly back, parting it in the center and pinning it behind her ears, and went forth into the reading room. All the rest of the afternoon, while the sun made tufts of light dance on the panelled walls, she sat and read, curling her feet around the rungs of the chair in excitement when some especially marvelous page traveled from her eyes along her spine down to her toes. She read Edna St. Vincent Millay's poetry and Keats's and sighed for the wonder of being alive. Although she was hungry, she would not stop for a snack, feeling thinner with each unanswered rumble of her stomach.

She did not think of her family at all, only of the words on the page in front of her and how they expressed what she had done in her acting this afternoon, some mysterious transcendence of ordinary life, which did not escape from that life but shed upon it a bright light of transfiguration.

At times her body tingled as it had when Quinny touched her. How very confusing! But not to be escaped from or dreamed away. She was past that now—forever, she hoped. And why not? Today had been such a good day! She stretched and went on reading.

At six o'clock, when Phil tapped her on the arm, offering to walk home with her, she was startled and trembled with the force of her emotions. The long twilight that eased itself around them was rich with possibilities, too many to grasp. "Spring, spring!" she cried out, twirling around on the cobblestones and feeling foolish, a great big lunk of a girl acting like a ninny, but she had to do it, anyway.

"Getting like me," Phil said. "Not much to say for yourself."

She nodded. "Margot quit the play. I overheard her talking to Mrs. Wilbur."

"Umm, I told her to. She was making herself sick over it, trying to be like you."

"Me? Oh, I don't believe *that!* She never let on—not one word! Why didn't she even hint? She acted as if she could hardly stand me—I mean, I didn't know what to say to her, she was so . . . well, you know . . . distant. In the beginning, at least," she had to add. "It's true, she's better now. But to be like me? Hunh! I wouldn't mind *looking* like her. Don't you think she's beautiful?"

"She's all right," Phil said. "Basically, she's no different from the other girls. She's interested in going along without thinking much or *doing* anything. Probably get married, sew, have kids, worry about 'em. In the beginning I thought, with her experiences, she'd be more interesting, but you know, all she wanted was to stay in her school in Germany, stay with her friends, have her father home—she had no other thoughts about it. Nothing political at all!" he continued disgustedly. "Now she's here, and she's gotten over being unhappy, so she settles down to sewing clothes and going to the movies."

"With you," Elly pointed out. She did not think her brother's analysis at all correct, but then, he didn't notice people very much. On the other hand, Margot surely didn't tell him all her thoughts; no girl would be that frank with a boy.

Phil grinned. "With me. I don't want to give the impression that I find her unattractive. Far from it. I like girls. If only they could be more serious."

"Ho! When you say that, you mean about science."

"Well, why not?" he asked. "There's always Madame Curie. I wouldn't mind a marriage like that one. Yes, I'd like that." He paused, flushing. "Well . . . I'm just talking. Excuse, please."

Elly saw that Phil was afraid to make a fool of himself and had cut back on his dreams for fear that they could not be realized. It didn't seem fair when he worked so hard that he should not even allow himself to dream, and she wished that their life could be easier for his sake. For a long time she had been taking it for granted that, because he was so brilliant, he didn't suffer as much as she did, he was something above it all; and he added to that belief by his remoteness and refusal to admit that his feelings even existed. No matter what he said, Margot *had* been good for him, she had allowed him to open up a little in an uncomplicated way, even if that meant he felt more keenly than ever the narrowness of their life in this town and on the farm.

"When you go to college," she assured him, "you'll meet plenty of serious girls. Why, you'll be a godsend to them—they'll flock around you like birds, waiting to meet this celebrated person who actually *likes* smart girls!"

"If I go—! And which college? I'm supposed to hear about the science awards by the end of April—and here it is, the end of April, with no word yet. Gets to me just a little."

"You've already said yes to Columbia, haven't you? I thought it was all settled. And you'll live with that friend of Mama's, Madame—what's her name?"

"Poplavsky. True. But a hundred dollar scholarship won't see me very far, will it? And the Poplavsky lady wants to get paid for her room, even if she *is* a friend of Mama's. Not to mention that I've gotten into the habit of eating."

Selling the farm would bring in enough money, she thought again—and at that moment remembered in a flash what had happened in Mr. McGuire's office that morning and had been wiped out of her mind by the rehearsal. She wanted to tell Phil about it, was already sorting out the words in her mind—and here they were at the store. Mama had already closed up, and she and a subdued Margot were waiting to go home to dinner. Later. It would keep.

Still, she thought of it all the way home, fighting down her anger at herself, at Mr. McGuire, at God, and at Mama, who acted as if love were enough. "Ah, me," she sighed. "Hey, the blackberries are coming out on the hedges! Saturday I'll ride Sasha down here—want to come along, Margot?"

"Shall I be able to ride?" Phil had been teaching her, overcoming her timidity, but she was comfortable only on the level fields within sight of the house. "Besides, you will not be talking to me when you find out that I gave up on the play. Oh, it is not for me!"

Elly tried to look surprised and ask the right questions, not giving away what she had heard earlier. "As long as there's an understudy . . ."

"Oh, your Mrs. Wilbur was very nice about it—Yvonne Audier will play the part. It is not much, anyway."

"She won't be as good as you," Elly said.

Margot laughed. "So Mrs. Wilbur said, too. It is all the compliment I want on my acting, believe me. Enough! Next time I design the costumes or something. I was foolish, and now I am happy it is all over."

Amen, Elly said silently; Margot's last words could apply to her as well. "Riding Masha's nothing to be afraid of—I'll be along. And we can pick blackberries. I've never seen them out this early—we're in for a long, hot summer." She groaned. There would be nothing to do on the farm; she absolutely *had* to talk to Mama seriously about moving. Right away. And there was the whole business of what Mr. McGuire had said to be gone through. Might as well begin.

Again she had no opportunity. They slowed down for the mailbox, Mama pulled out the letters—one from Baba in New Jersey, one from the Immigration and Rescue Service, and one from the Connecticut Board of Education for Phil—and everything gave way to the exquisite excitement of the mail as they pounded pell-mell into the house, waving the envelopes like flags. Elly didn't even mind waiting.

14

AUNT ANNA'S DINNER grew cold on the stove. Mama tucked Baba's letter into her pocket to read later. A warm and tender breeze blew across the fields into the house through the open kitchen door.

"Why bother to write this?" Aunt Anna asked.

Phil read his letter again. "Second prize."

"What does this tell me?" Aunt Anna complained. "By this time I need more."

"Wait!" Phil exclaimed. "Here's something else!"

Mama read Aunt Anna's letter aloud. "*Confirm release one hundred men International Red Cross Germany*. Ah, this is a copy of a telegram . . . I see. *Names not confirmed. Information to follow*. But my dear, they wouldn't send this to you if they didn't think Michael was one of them! Maybe they know but aren't sure. Yes, I'm convinced that's the case. God be praised!" She read it over. "Nothing else. No dates."

"That is just what I am saying," Aunt Anna exclaimed. "When? I have waited so long I cannot imagine him any longer—yes, that is the truth. To go through such things in life once is enough but . . ."

"Read this, Ma," Phil said. But he didn't hand over

the letters before he studied them once more.

"This is for me two times," Aunt Anna continued. "Yes! In 1916, before we are being married, Michael is missing for three months in the war. In the East." She shook her head. "Now it comes back to me many times, how I felt. Who knows if it was for the best? It could have ended then." She unfolded the letter again, muttering to herself.

"I do not understand this," Mama said to Phil.

"What?" Elly asked. "Second prize—what does it mean? How much?"

"Two hundred and fifty dollars," Phil said. "Not five hundred . . ."

Margot clapped her hands.

"But you do not need five hundred," Mama protested. "We have for you one hundred and fifty still saved, and with your scholarship and the money you are earning, why, you will manage for this year."

"I still don't understand what the second prize means," Elly repeated.

Phil told them he had submitted two projects for the science award, and the easier one had received second prize. "Naturally. You see, it was nothing, just a proposed curriculum for a new kind of high school physics and astronomy course with materials that the kids could make themselves—I made samples, of course. Not very good telescopes—what you'd expect—but at least they could learn by doing it. It wasn't very hard to do—you know most of the high schools in Connecticut don't have any modern science courses at all? Mr. Tischler told me. He gave me the idea, actually."

Mr. Tischler was the head of the science department at school, an elderly man who had studied in Germany, contracted tuberculosis, and been forced to give up his dreams of an academic career for a quiet life in a northern climate.

"I hope they don't put it in our school until I'm finished," Elly said. "I'd flunk it for sure!"

"Mutti, let me write a letter for you to the Red Cross," Margot said. She had changed from her school clothes to a sports outfit she had designed and made—a bright blue skirt buttoned down the front over a one-piece playsuit in blue and white stripes—and she looked cool and fresh.

"No, it is better to wait. Believe me. It is then possible to hope, and I live on hope."

"The other project," Phil said slowly, "I can't explain to you. It had to do with measuring light rays given off by certain stars. An interesting problem."

"You mean like the spectrum?" Margot asked.

"Something like . . . huh, how'd *you* know?"

"A guess," she assured him. "I love to look into prisms."

"Well, anyway, I had some ideas and worked them up. Tischler helped me, of course; poor man, he's way behind now on the work being done in the field."

Elly helped Aunt Anna dish out the food—roast chicken, beet salad, mashed potatoes, creamed peas. Aunt Anna's food was just as fattening as Mama's and not even as good. "I should think *that* would have won, wouldn't you?"

Phil showed them the second letter. "This was an extra," he said quietly, but it was obvious he was enormously pleased. It was from one of the scientists on the selection committee, a physics professor at Yale. He too found the problem interesting, approved of the direction Phil was taking in his investigations, and urged him to continue. He had voted for this project for first prize because of the elegant simplicity of the indicated experiment. However, his colleagues had pointed out to him that the proposed solution betrayed a weakness in its mathematics, and indeed this was the case. He himself was not deterred by this, however, considering the youth of the scientist and the boldness of his attack. The mathematical deficit would be repaired in college. No less than the great Einstein himself found mathematics a problem! The professor closed by inviting Phil to visit him for further discussion of his work and for any help he could give at the start of what he hoped would be a brilliant career.

"This," said Mama, "is better than the prize." She prayed a very short Grace. "Now tell me more while we eat. And we must tell Leo right away tomorrow—we shall call the hospital from the store."

For the first time in many months Phil was relaxed and gay. He leaned back in his chair, let his long legs sprawl under the table, and imitated the librarians for them, catching and slightly exaggerating their mannerisms. When he was a child—a long time ago, Elly thought—he would imitate his teachers for her when she had been too young to go to school, but that gaiety and zest had gradually disappeared, swallowed up in his desire to learn, to know, to work hard enough to overcome what he knew were the disadvantages of a small high school with a poor laboratory. Since Pop's heart attack, when he had taken on so much extra work, he barely spoke to them at all. "No, I won't do Tischler," he said, laughing. "Not him. He's a grand old man, Tischler. Do you know that old fellow translates physics articles from the German for me? Hey, Margot, when will you do that?"

"When we first came here," Mama said, "sixteen years

ago, he was supposed to be dying from his tuberculosis! Then someone told Leo he had been dying this way for twenty years before that. He must be almost ready to retire—65 or close to it."

Margot laughed with Elly but ate very little and finally gave up altogether. "I wish all the time had passed," she whispered. "I agree with you, Mutti, this waiting is impossible. I think I shall finish my dress if that is all right, Aunt Sonya. Then I can start on that one for Elly in the checked gingham."

"Shall I write?" Aunt Anna asked. "Oh, I am so happy to think I shall speak German again! And Michael will need me, I will not be any longer his pretty doll." Then her voice dropped. "If he is to come. If."

Mama reassured her. "They would not write to you if he were not alive. As for the rest—why imagine? What will be, will be, Anna, and the imagination adds nothing, takes away nothing."

"Mama, you are wrong!" Elly said, surprising even herself with her vehemence.

"Hah! What do you know, miss?" Mama said. "Come, help me clear up here—Phil, dear, you *will* do the chores?—so I can read Mamushka's letter." She turned again to Elly. "The imagination is the home of much that is bad. It makes us discontented with what we have and to long for other things."

"Brilliant scientist slops hogs," Phil said, going out. "Waters goats, mucks out barn. Read all about it!"

"Exactly!" Elly said triumphantly to her mother. "That's why imagination is *good!* Listen, Mama, I *must* talk to you."

"Shah, let me read your Baba's letter first. Go, put the food away . . . and don't ask me about leftovers, Elly, you know what to do by now!"

Mama was thoughtful while she washed the dishes, humming to herself and staring out at the pale green fields of spring.

"What did Baba say? Is she well?" Elly asked.

"Eh? Oh, yes, her cough is entirely gone. So I did right not to let her know about Leo, have her come rushing back here . . . Get a dry towel, please! Still, how upset she will be when she finds out! She will think I treat her like a child, keeping such a serious thing from her." Mama shook her head vigorously. "I only can do what I think is right." She appealed to Elly.

Elly was still angry over her mother's remarks on imagination. "We all told you to write," she said, biting her lip. "But I don't suppose it makes any difference now. When does she say she's coming back?"

"She doesn't," Mama said after a long silence. "Here, I'll help with these glasses. She says they have twenty-five people from Germany; they all insist soon war will begin. Dear God, when will it end, this fighting? They have lost everything." She lapsed into silence again, and in silence they finished the dishes. "You will walk with me?" Mama then asked. "You have no homework? I am tired, but to walk in these fields . . . I feel new again." She patted her hair and folded her apron. "This is the bad time of day for me without Leo. Come!"

"Oh, Mama, the farm can't make that much difference!" All Elly saw was the untidy rear yard, the pool of dishwater flung to one side, the rusty clothes drier, broken bits of flowerpots, tools waiting to be repaired.

"You, too? I think your Baba does not wish to come back. She does not say this openly, but I can feel it."

"Well, why not? Mama, there's nothing to do here!

I've been trying and trying to tell you, and you won't listen!"

"Look here, the beans are starting. You are right, this will be a long and hot summer. Sunday I'll put in the poles. And set out the tomato plants—this year I want to make green tomato relish for the County Fair. You are so unhappy at the farm? Truly? Oh, I can remember other times . . ."

Elly remembered them, too. Walks through the meadows and woods, horseback riding, romping with Jump, the collie, before he died, the blaze of autumn leaves, sledding on the snowy hills, reading by the kitchen fire in the winter with the smell of fresh baking all around her. . . .

"Mama," she said, stuttering a little, "there was more, too. How hard you worked!"

"But I wanted . . ."

"And Pop—the long drive. In winter he never even *saw* the sun! And Phil—he *hates* the chores as much as I do—ugh! that filthy barn! And somebody always has to be home for the animals. That's not much fun for us, I'll tell you that!"

"But you never said a word to me!" Mama protested.

"Oh, Mama, we did! You wouldn't listen—it was our age or the heat or the cold or something. You hated to think we just didn't like it, that's all. How long the summers were! Why do you think I had no friends? All the kids in town played with each other all summer, and I was stuck out here!"

"I did not think a child could ever be unhappy on a farm," Mama said thoughtfully. "Why in the cities parents *pay* to send their children to farms! For me, this was my life's dream, to bring my children up so."

"For you."

Mama pointed out that they had not been so isolated. All during the summers friends had come from New York to visit and talk and would do so again this year if Pop were well. "Oh, those discussions, do you remember them?" Mama's face lit up. "Leo's friends! They would talk the moon down from the sky!"

They were walking uphill now into the dank woodland that lay between their last field and the long upland slope to the mountains west of them. "Let's walk up to the brook and see if the trout are jumping," Mama added.

Elly followed. How could she make Mama understand? After what Mama had said about imagination—that still rankled—she did not think she could. "I remember all right." She touched her mother lightly on the shoulder. "It wasn't awfully interesting to me," she said in a lower voice. "Only the presents sometimes. You had so much food to prepare . . ." She let her words trail off. There was no way Mama could see the difference, see what guests were like to a child who was always in the way.

"I thought I was doing the right thing," Mama said.

Elly took a deep breath, then burst out, "The right thing? Oh, Mama, all you did was shut us up away from so much! Why didn't you let us find out about life?"

"Life? What about life?" Mama was bewildered. They walked more slowly now, bending back the overhanging branches and stepping over dead limbs on the rough track. "Plenty of wood here for the stove."

Elly flung out the first word that came to her. "Love! You brought us up to think that only love mattered, nothing else. And you didn't let us understand—oh, Mama, I went to see Mr. McGuire today—I was going to do it all alone and surprise you . . ."

"Surprise? What?" Mama stood dead still, facing Elly, little red spots glowing on her cheeks.

"Well, just wait a minute, won't you? I went to see him, Margot came, too, and he told us Jews couldn't live in Yankeetown, why didn't you let me know that? I made a fool of myself. I never even thought we were Jewish! How can you stand it?"

"Who would want to live in Yankeetown, anyway?" Mama asked.

"That's what Mr. McGuire said. As if I were crazy. I'll tell you who—I want to, Mama, me, me, Elly Josephs! *I* want to!"

"Nonsense," Mama said firmly. "Look, the beavers have built a dam on the brook—watch out for the water here!"

"The fish, whatever happened to the fish?" Elly cried out. The brook was only a thin, muddy trickle surrounded by swampy ground. "Let's pull it down, shall we? Ugh, the mud!"

They used dead tree branches to knock away enough of the beavers' lodge so that water could flow through a side channel, although they could not budge the strong central underpinnings and knew that the beavers would build the dam up again.

"Everything changes," Elly said. "Next year we'll have a pond instead of a brook. Why is it nonsense, Mama? We'd have heating and a modern kitchen," she went on dreamily, "and no barn smells, and the yards are big enough for you to have a real garden, anyway . . . I could have my friends over . . . Aunt Anna would like it better, too, and Margot . . . imagine, the change for them . . ."

Mama snorted. "I'm imagining! So what? They came from death to life, and it's not enough? And Yankeetown is something to cry over?"

"Maybe not that," Elly admitted. "But Mama, why can't Jews move there? Isn't that like Germany? Why didn't you ever do anything? You never even told me!"

"Truly, I don't know what to say." Mama sighed. "Yes, I tried to keep this from you and Phil. Leo too said I was wrong. I could not believe this would go on. I could not! Even when Phil said he could not go to this college or that, I thought this is not so in America, he was not serious. In Russia, yes. In Germany, yes."

"Yes," Elly said. "But yes, here, too." And all the pain and confusion came flooding back.

"And then, too, I wonder," Mama went on, talking almost to herself, "how is it you are Jewish? This I do not understand. Not by the mother, surely, which is the way Jews count it." She gazed away over the treetops to the mountains. "You liked the Easter service, no?"

"What difference does *that* make? Mama, what people think seems to be enough!"

"I don't know," Mama said. "It is too much for me to understand. When I married Leo, I was told . . . then I did not believe, either. I should have had you baptized as babies. I did not for Leo's sake. When you grew up, I thought, you would choose—and he agreed—I did not doubt you would wish *yes* to Christ." They began to walk again side by side. "Tell me, is it so wrong to wish to keep from evil those you love? Is it? We are tearing down the beavers' lodge to rescue some trout—shall I not rescue my children?"

"Oh, Mama, I'm not talking about rescue! I was so hurt. And Margot was there. She was cold to it, as if she did not feel, but I knew she was afraid."

"Poor child, after so much other trouble. What else did Lou McGuire say? That he had to do business with everyone?"

Elly scuffed along a narrow track bordered on both

sides by tall flowering grasses. She picked a stalk and tickled her nose. "He said Catholics can't buy in Yankeetown, either." Mama nodded. "He recommended that we buy in Woodmont. You see, I was trying . . ."

"Buy what?" Mama asked. "A house? But how? I do not much like Woodmont, either. They are building there a private pool. For myself, I like best to live among the Italians."

"What's the matter with a private pool?" Elly asked, and then, before Mama could answer, she plunged on: "I thought I'd get all the information for you without saying a word and when you saw it right in front of you, you'd agree. It's the only way. Pop could come home—I miss him!"

"I miss him even more than you," Mama said grimly.

"He was going to talk to you—before he got sick—about selling the farm . . ."

"To *sell* the farm!" Mama exclaimed. "No, I did not think this—ever. I was thinking to rent for a short time in town, to have the Kocinskis or the Mullers on the other side rent the land here . . . we must have a place for Michael when he comes, he will be ill . . ."

Elly scuffed her shoes in the dust. What was the use? Mama would never understand. "It's no use, Mama, staying on. Not for any of us. Don't you see? This way we'd have some money, it would be easier. . . ."

All at once Mama was crying. "I thought in the end you would come to be like me and love the farm. Was that so wrong?" They came down out of the wood again to skirt the fuzzy green field. Elly went down the path first, pausing for Mama to lean against her. "Understand? You talk about understand! Do you understand me? Leo is almost dead, I am working until I am sick, I think about money and the animals and Phil and you and Anna and Margot and is Michael coming soon; I think how shall I pay this bill and that one and will the food come—and all this goes around in my head, and I am dizzy and I think of my mamushka, so I write a happy letter when I am so tired I cannot see to make the words and forget my Russian. And Leo . . . I feel *his* pain in *my* heart! Tell me, then, what shall I do? From a stone, you do not squeeze blood. Look at me! Am I a stone? Where will you find the blood you want?"

Elly turned away, trembling. She was embarrassed to be shown her mother's weakness, and afraid, too. Mothers should be strong; who could she depend on if not Mama? Aunt Anna had fallen apart and left Margot to take over too much responsibility, but Mama would never do that. "Mama," she said softly, "don't get so upset. Please! Listen. I told Mr. McGuire I'd see him tomorrow, anyway. You don't want to come, do you?"

Mama shook her head. "What have I to do with that? Leo never said one word to me. I know nothing of any move."

Elly fought against any disappointment in her father; after all, he had been ill. "I'll do it myself, then, just get the information. Then we could find a place to live in for a few months, couldn't we? That's all. So Pop could come home . . ." Deliberately, she damped down her enthusiasm, did not go off into her vision of how the house would look. This was more serious now; she had to do what she was only pretending to do earlier—help find a place to live. Could she do it? A chicken hawk flew up in a spiral from a clump of hedges nearby, circled above their heads, then held steady in the updrafts, dipping and swooping with an easy grace. Maybe they should stay on the farm, as Mama said, put in a telephone, and manage this way. "I think I could do it."

"Who else is there?" Mama asked with a faint smile. "I must stay in the store like in a prison . . ."

"I didn't know you didn't like the store!" Elly exclaimed naively, then clapped her hand over her mouth, but too late.

"Ah, if you thought about it, you would see."

"Yes, well . . . Mama—Pop doesn't like the farm—still, we live here."

"You know absolutely nothing about it, Elly!" Mama said, as angry as Elly had ever seen her. "You think I am wrong to keep you from so much—yes, I begin to agree with you on that! But you don't talk about yourself, always with your head in a book, mooning around—Leo calls you Moony for this!—never interested to help, to learn!"

"Mama, I'm trying! I've got to do it my own way. Can't I find us a place?"

"How do I know what you can do? You never even try, only for yourself! What's wonderful about that? And then you come to me and ask such a reasonable thing—that I give up all my life and what it means and go quietly to live inside the skin of another's life. Hah! That is all."

"No, Mama, I don't want that. Truly." Then Elly began to wonder. Maybe she did. The trouble with acting so much was that she couldn't be quite sure. No! She certainly didn't want anything that would make Mama as unhappy as she had been on this walk. "I don't."

Mama went down the narrow path around the corner of the barn to the kitchen, lingering for a moment at the open door of the barn where the animals were set for the night, snuffling and stamping. The sun was setting behind the pine woods; long lines of pink and purple light spread like fingers over the meadow and the weathered boards of the house. "Don't you? Still, it comes to the same thing in the end. What can I say? Do it. But not in Yankeetown!"

Elly laughed shakily. "I won't even try."

"And not to worry Leo with this, either."

"Doesn't Pop *know?* Oh, Mama . . ."

"What do you take us for? Why did he agree with me to live on a farm? He felt it even more! But he would not see that it could happen in America, he thought always it was the exception. And it is!" Mama asserted.

Elly shrugged. "I'm confused . . . I feel, oh, I don't know—how does it touch me? I don't feel that I'm anything at all. I *like* it that way, do you see? But others . . ."

"They don't leave you alone," Mama said grimly. "That's why you need a family, don't you forget that. Where would Anna and Margot be now, do you think, without your father to help them?"

"It worries me," Elly admitted. "They didn't think they were Jews, did they? And now—it's not fair! It's scary." She stopped; why worry Mama with something like that now?

"God alone knows what is fair," Mama said, putting her arm around Elly. "So we leave it to Him, eh?"

"Meanwhile, shall I go to see Mr. McGuire? Truly?"

"The decision is yours," Mama said. "You wanted it." Again, a faint smile touched her lips.

"Did I? I suppose I did," Elly agreed. She sat down on the large flat stone that was the kitchen doorstep, hugging her knees to her chest. "Wow! Look at the sunset! I think I'll stay out here until it gets dark."

"Once upon a time," Mama said, "you were afraid of the dark. Then I showed you how to play with the shadows the lamp made."

"I'm not afraid of the *dark* any more, not that," Elly said, and left the rest of the sentence dangling. Mama went in. The noises of night rose around Elly, the last music of birds settling in, the chirr of cicadas, and the night came and swallowed her up as she sat with the lights of the house at her back. No use being afraid of the dark. Suppose Mama couldn't light the lamp and play with the shadows? Well, then, she'd have to do it herself. She was old enough not to be scared, and if she were scared, why, she'd do it anyway. Only it wouldn't be quite as easy as she had imagined.

She dreamed and drowsed until a sound at her back made her jump. Mama stood in the kitchen doorway, smiling down on her. "Better get some sleep, you got a busy day tomorrow. Phil and Margot are playing parcheesi. They ask you to join them."

"Right." She hated to leave the night behind, yet it was with a sense of relief that she walked into the comfortable old kitchen glowing with light.

15

ONCE MAMA HAD given up, had put the decision into Elly's hands, she wanted nothing more than speed. Hurry, hurry! Make a decision, move quickly! Then Pop would be home. Soon, soon! Uncle Michael was on his way. How? When? No one knew yet, but Mama had a feeling. They could not wait until the play was over; it was precious time lost. Who knew what would happen in May or June? No, Mama wanted to be settled by May 1st.

May Day, the international workers' holiday, Pop remarked with a smile when Mama told him of their plans. Elly's plans, really. And Pop gave her *such* a smile! He was sitting up in bed for a few hours a day, still pasty white though, and eager to be in the sun. Yes, yes, she would hurry. How? How? There were rehearsals, homework, the long hours in the classroom, shifting restlessly on the seat as the sun grew and spread outside to cover the town and the river and the woods beyond with the shining warmth of spring and the day, unfolded all around her. Wasted, wasted, she thought, swelling with impatience, watching the sun climb up to the meridian, then begin its descent.

When? How? Mama had done it, given her the power of decision. Her head whirled with the possibilities; what if she failed? And she *was* on her own. Margot had gone back with her to Mr. McGuire's office while she explained what they wanted and listened to him insist that renting a place for a few months was impossible and expensive and pointless besides. Elly nodded and agreed and trembled and continued to say that they needed something temporary and maybe, yes, maybe, if . . .

Mr. McGuire shrugged and temporized and agreed to work up some possible listings for her by Saturday, and did she think that Sonya would actually agree to sell the farm? He doubted it, but then, things changed, didn't they, and who knew?

Who indeed? Margot said that she had had enough of his two-cent philosophizing and had decided, now that she was no longer in the play, to take the school bus to the farm after school, stay there on Saturdays, and keep her mother company. In the shadow of her father's coming—always *if, if, if*—she was moving away again from Elly and Phil, back to her mother, to pick up the threads of their old family life, however they could.

In the end, however, Elly did not go house-hunting alone. On Saturday, Rob McGuire was waiting in his father's office, dangling a bunch of keys, and Laura was with him, looking somehow smaller and older, belonging very much to herself for all that she allowed Rob to hold her hand. *Can't do it,* Elly told herself. *Impossible.* Then they ran into Quinny Fry on the corner of Upper Main and Algonquin. "Hey, I was just going down to the store for you, Elly. Guess what? Two Andy Hardy films down at Loew's. Want to see them? Say yes! I've hardly seen you at all the last coupla weeks."

When Elly told him what she had to do, he agreed at once to go along and help. "Why, if you're in town, there'll be plenty of Saturdays at the movies, right? Lead the way, Rob!"

Rob had his father's car to drive. "What do you mean, can I?" he replied, when Quinny kidded him. "Huh! My dad's been letting me drive since I was twelve. Pretty good, eh, Laura?"

Laura smiled at him and said nothing. She did not look at Elly; there was a space between them filled with tension that Elly still could not cope with. When she was eight, she had broken her arm; long after the bone healed and the cast was cut off, she felt monitory twinges that reminded her of the break. So it was now.

"You gonna take over your dad's business?" Quinny asked, as Rob escorted them around town, flourishing the keys.

"Maybe. *He* wants it. I'd kinda like to try a year of college at least. He says no. My mom's talking to him."

"You're nuts! Isn't he, Elly?" Quinny said. "With a good deal like this, why bother with college?"

"There's the insurance agency, too," Rob said. "I guess if you had to put it in dollars and cents, my dad's one of the biggest men around here." He squeezed Laura's hand, and she gave him another wan smile.

Quinny nodded solemnly. "You could do worse," he said.

No one remarked on the difference between the McGuires and the Frys; Elly wasn't certain if Quinny even minded. How dull he was! And how strange that when he kissed her, she could forget his dullness and kiss him back again with a warmth that made her flush slightly even in the remembrance. "Oh, lord," she exclaimed, "I would *die* stuck in this little town."

Quinny laughed comfortably at her. "You'll think different one of these days."

They had not realized how difficult finding the right

place would be. No stairs. Enough rooms. Convenient location. A big yard. And—not too expensive. Rob drove them to sections of town they had not even known about. Not to Yankeetown.

How drab much of Franklin was! How dull! She would *never* change her mind about it! Rob showed them one house crouching in the shadows of the Connecticut Thread Company, a pinched-looking place with cheap green shingles, a steep roof, enormous porch, and six dark and chilly rooms without a single closet, and with a lean-to kitchen worse than the one on the farm. And in the French-Canadian quarter a wooden house badly in need of paint with a deep but narrow yard in back that ended on a cut over the railroad tracks with a privy off to one side.

Elly had a headache. The old houses around the Green looked better and better. How about them?

Rob shook his head. "Too many stairs. Too many repairs. Naw, no one wants those places but artists and antique dealers and people like that. Don't know how we'll sell *your* place, Laura, when *your* tenant moves out!"

"Oh, you could sell anything to anyone," Laura said nastily. "Yourself to me, for instance. A born salesman."

Quinny chuckled in the awkward silence.

"Going down to the World's Fair, now it's open?" Rob asked casually. "I'll probably see it in June, once school's out."

"That's nothing," Laura assured him, "we'll be living in New York by then, and I'll go as often as I like. So there, Mr. McGuire!"

"Good, I'll stay with you when I come," he replied, unperturbed.

"So it's true then?" Elly asked quietly.

Laura nodded. "Certain as anything with my parents.

They don't ask *me*, you know." Her hands pleated the edges of a dirty handkerchief.

They stopped for lunch at an Italian grocery in the north end of town. Rob had money from his father to treat them to those long grinders, which made them stink afterwards of onion, garlic, and spiced salami. Good, yes, but how eager Elly was to keep looking! Suppose they could find nothing suitable? Well, they *had* to!

"Let's go! Ready?" she urged them on.

"Now, if you could have something upstairs," Rob said, around mouthfuls of the sandwich, "we've got some nice flats over the stores here. Big and sunny. Cheap. You know, like yours. Hey, why don't you . . ."

"We've got tenants. Good ones," she said glumly.

"Well, we'll find *them* a place, how's that?"

Elly laughed. "Rob, you really will be successful in the business!"

"Yeah, well, let's get back to it. I got only three, four places left," Rob said. "Let's try this one. It's a little more than your mom said she could pay, but if you take the whole house, you'd have great space. Dad's got his secret little mark on the card—see that yellow dot?—means it's a really good deal, don't haggle about price. Seventy-five dollars a month for both flats, heat included."

"Two flats?" Seventy-five dollars? Oh, Rob, we couldn't afford that!"

"Sure you could, Elly, it's just a matter of thinking differently. What do you get for the place over the store? Twenty-five a month? Put it to the rent here. Figure what it's costing for your dad in the hospital . . . you charging rent for the farm? You could get twenty-five for it easy."

"Mama wouldn't do that," Elly said firmly. "The Kocinskis are taking care of the place for us."

"Of course, they are," he argued, "but they're getting the use of it, too, see? The milk, the eggs, the equipment, and so on. Anyway, come and see it. I think you'll change your tune. The owner wants to sell soon, but meanwhile, he'll rent it out."

"Goody-goody mama," Laura whispered. "Can't. Won't. Doesn't."

"Hey!" Elly exclaimed, "you don't have to do that. Gee, if I . . ."

"Know I don't have to," Laura said wearily. "Do it, anyway. Don't ask me why. Like father, like daughter."

Rob began to sing, "Don't ask me whyyyy, 'cause I will cryyyy . . ." He turned to grin at them. "Great, eh? Trouble with you girls is you take everything too seriously."

"True," Laura murmured. Elly thought she was playing a part badly.

The house was on a back street, a lane that Elly had never noticed, though it opened off Wilson Road just behind the town junior high. Showed what a country girl she was! Of course, she had gone to the county consolidated junior high over in Washington, a village the other side of the farm.

At the end of the lane, before it twisted uphill to join Putney Street, which went through the French-Canadian neighborhood, three groups of red-brick, semi-detached houses had been put up about fifteen years ago. These were two-family houses, Rob told them, for rent to teachers or mill foremen or maybe skilled craftsmen, people ready to move out of flats but unable to buy homes. His father had been managing them all along and keeping them up, even when they had been vacant for long periods during the worst of the Depression, and that was why they still looked so good, primly fronting the street behind narrow hedges and pocket-handkerchief yards.

"Let's see the back first," he said, leading them down the drive that separated one double house from the next. "Look at this!"

Out of habit, Elly turned to ask Laura's opinion, then looked away from the misery on the girl's sallow face, misery that made her forget all Laura's sharp words.

Rob was right to be proud. There was no way to tell from the street, but the rear gardens, although narrow, stretched far back behind the houses to end in the rough woods of a small wild patch high on the hill above them. There would be room for Mama's vegetables here and flowers besides. Rob showed them the garden shed and the wide paved space off the back porch where laundry lines could be put up. "This is a real solid place," he said, rapping the concrete steps of the back porch.

The house smelled of fresh paint and floor varnish. How spacious it seemed in its emptiness! They ran around crazily, enjoying the booms of their feet on the bare floors and the echoing booms that sounded up and down the stairs. "See, one flat's not going to be big enough for all of you; you'd need two, and at thirty-seven-fifty each, that makes seventy-five."

"I wish you wouldn't keep mentioning the rent," Elly said. "You're spoiling my fun."

For she *was* pleased. The kitchen was smaller than Mama would like, but completely modern—white and gleaming with its porcelain stove standing on high legs and a refrigerator, not an ice box, a white sink instead of the slate one they had at the farm, and white, glass-fronted dish cupboards. The linoleum was blue and white squares, matching the colors of the walls and cabinets. No dining room, but a small breakfast room and a porch opening off the kitchen. And there was a white-tiled bathroom, a large living room, and three bedrooms, a big one for Mama and Pop, and two smaller ones at the front of the house.

Upstairs was the same except that the kitchen was red and white. There were plenty of closets and a dry cellar. Pop could stay in bed and be part of the family, since the big bedroom opened right off the living room.

"Heat!" Elly said, "steam heat. What luxury! And we'd be living in town—oh, I can hardly believe it!"

"No furniture," Laura said.

Elly would not be deterred. They *would* do it! The place was perfect for Pop. And when Uncle Michael came, why, there would be the entire upstairs for privacy. Why not? From the breakfast room at the back, Mama could look out on gardens and woods almost as if she were still in the country. Once again Elly admired the bare, clean rooms. Shades on the windows. Doors on the closets. Shiny wooden floors. The tiled bathroom. It smelled of city life, whereas the farmhouse was just that —an old farmhouse.

"You'll be downright rich," Quinny said admiringly. "I'll help you move. It'd be a privilege."

"We'll manage," Elly insisted. "Mama can always find something in the way of furniture. Isn't it beautiful, beautiful?" And she twirled around once again on the bare floor. No use wondering what Mama would think about the rent; she'd find out sooner or later. But this was the place for them!

Laura walked around slowly, moving apart from them. "It's so *bourgeois*, don't you think?"

"Oh, come off it," Elly said, stung. "What's so hot about the way *you* live?"

Laura shrugged. "Isn't that what you wanted? I

thought so. Artist's life and all . . . Better stay in the farmhouse for that! Hide in the country. Why not? Franklin's not so much."

Elly listened to the sadness in Laura's voice more than to the sharpness of her words. "Well," she said kindly, "you're leaving this hick town, anyway. Who knows when I'll go after you? New York, here we come!" Her efforts at humor fell flat; there was too much unhappiness to overcome.

Laura walked through the living room into one of the small bedrooms, her feet tapping on the floor, and Elly followed her. They stood together by the front window, Laura playing with a fancy shade pull. "No, I don't want to leave at all," she said fiercely, and looked away from Elly out to the quiet street. "I'd like to spend the rest of my life here, hidden away on some street like this where no one would ever find me at all. I'd keep birds, maybe, lots of birds, and have a big overgrown garden, like the sleeping beauty, and I'd hide there. You'd have to find me—only you wouldn't. I'd make sure of that!"

Rob came up behind them. "Darn tooting I wouldn't, if you were such a nut."

Laura flushed and went quickly away to wait in the yard.

"Interested?" Rob asked. "I swear, I don't understand women!"

"I'll tell my mother right now," Elly said, feeling the excitement take over. "We've got to have it—no question."

Quinny lingered to gaze at the brickwork. "Coupla years, I'll have a place like this for my family, see if I don't. Hey, Elly, I meant it, we'll help you move, the whole lot of us. Tell your Ma for me. Sorry we can't make the movies—next week for sure!"

Rob held the car door open, but Laura turned her

back on him. "I think Elly and I'll walk back together. Nice day. Thanks, anyway, Rob. See you tonight."

Laura led a puzzled Elly across and halfway down the street, then turned abruptly into a narrow alley, almost hidden by overhanging trees that met to form a canopy over their heads. "You won't believe this," she told Elly, "but if you come down this way, look where you end up!"

A flight of crumbling stone steps at the end of the alley took them down to another alley, this one running between the movie theatre and the small brick medical building on Upper Main, only two blocks above the grocery store. Elly *couldn't* believe it; how had she not noticed this before? Then she could see; from the sidewalk in front of the theatre, the upper alley was invisible. All she could see was the arching thicket of green, a secret bower in the heart of Franklin.

"Let's go back up," Laura suggested, and they did, lingering under the greenery in the cool dampness of the steps, walking slowly along the pebbly surface of the alley, scuffing their feet on the dirt growing through the cracks in the old paving. "I found it a few weeks ago," Laura said.

"And *this* is the place you meant when you said you'd like to be hidden!"

Laura responded with her old glow of pleasure. "How did you guess? I've been walking around a lot by myself these past few weeks. Isn't it beautiful? You can forget the rest of the world up here. And dream . . ."

Laura's silence gave Elly a chance to fight her embarrassment; how difficult it was to speak of feelings growing inside of you! Mama would plant her tomato seeds in the cold frame and not move them outside until they had put up sturdy little shoots that could stand the chilly night air. Maybe her thoughts were ready now to be spoken without withering; but, oh, how hard!

"I'm glad for you that you're going—New York is going to be . . . well, in a way, you know, I envy you, living there. It's where I'm going to end up once I finish school." She laughed shakily. "I don't let myself think of it too much because what good would it do—you know what I mean?"

"None of it bears thinking about," Laura said. "I'm stuck, too. Where can I go? One thing," she said bitterly, "I'll never forgive him—both of them, really. Why doesn't Glenna leave? She did it once and we had such a good time together! But she loves him more than she loves me!"

Elly thought about that. "Well, naturally," she remarked and saw Laura's face close up. "All along," she continued, "I've thought that my mother didn't love me enough—she wouldn't do what I wanted, you know. I'm not so sure now. I wish she didn't care so much. I don't need it any more, not the same way."

"It's different with *you*," Laura said; then, "I don't want to talk about it any more. As if there were anything *to* say!" After a time, she asked, "Hey, what do you think about *Gone With the Wind*? I can't wait for it to open, can you?"

Elly ignored that. "Will you write to me from New York?" she asked.

"If you want," Laura said indifferently. She plucked a leaf from a tangled morning glory vine and tore it into smaller and smaller pieces. "If you're not too busy with your exciting life to answer." They walked together through the alley to the road and down the steep street to the Green.

"Please!" Elly said. "You *know* I'll miss you. Next

year in school will be awful—no you, Phil in college. Me alone."

"I feel very sorry for you," Laura said with weak sarcasm.

And after that, there was nothing more to say. This time when Laura crossed the Green to go to her house, Elly did not turn to watch her. She had too much to tell Mama about tomorrow and next week, too much to look forward to. If Laura wrote . . . well, she would see. Right now, she had to hurry back to the present. If she did not think too much, maybe the pain would go away.

"Good! I am glad you are back," Mama said, gesturing to the store crowded with customers. "Find anything? Yes?" Mama beamed. "Here is an apron." And Elly had to wait on customers the rest of the afternoon, writing long orders, figuring prices, and making change until her head buzzed.

"I found a big place," Elly said, carrying ten pounds of butter from the big freezer in the cellar.

"Good. Go see if we have more cartons of Ralston cereal downstairs. Tell me later."

Later meant six o'clock when the store closed, and Elly had been up and down the stairs two dozen times. A few people were still waiting in the store, so that it was 6:30 before they could sit down in the back room, leaving the last orders for Phil to pack and deliver before they went home to dinner. "And I hope a good one—Anna spoke of sauerbraten—for I am truly exhausted," Mama said. "You still losing weight?"

"Ten pounds," Elly said proudly. "But not on sauerbraten, Mama!"

"On hard work," Mama said. "What did you find? Shall I call Lou McGuire now and tell him *yes?*"

When Elly finished describing the house, Mama sat

with her head in her hands. "Seventy-five dollars! Are you crazy?"

"Mama, what could I do? There wasn't anything else. Not a thing! Can't we manage it at all? I mean, there's the rent from the flat upstairs . . ."

Mama's cheeks flamed. "Yes, and there is the mortgage we must pay on this building—fifty-five dollars a month. With the flat renting for twenty-five and the garage for five, we must pay here only twenty-five, which we can do. Oh, why do I tell you all of this when you do so stupid a thing! We have also the heat and gas and electricity and taxes. Still, that we can manage. And the farm is only taxes. But seventy-five dollars! I shall be ill!"

Elly also felt sick. "Couldn't the Kocinskis pay rent?"

"What do *you* know about such matters? No, they could not afford to live on the farm then at all. Electricity they pay, and for the wood. No more. There was nothing else?"

Elly described the other houses, and Mama shook her head. "This seventy-five dollars, it includes the heat and utilities?"

"Only the heat, Mama. You should see it—it's perfect for Pop, he's certain to get well . . ." Oh, why couldn't all go well and Mama be pleased! This was the first time she had done anything like this on her own, and she wanted to triumph quite directly over all the annoying obstacles of the real world.

Mama went over to the New Testament she kept on the dresser and opened it without looking. Her finger searched for a spot; then she read what it marked. "Look at the birds of the air; they do not sow and reap and store in barns, yet your heavenly Father feeds them." She paused. "Oho! You make fun of me for doing this, yet look and see!" She had changed utterly. Elly could not credit the broad, smiling face her mother had put on. "It all comes out right for you. We will do it. I am wrong to worry so. I will tell Lou McGuire that we shall stay there until the end of August. We can pay until then—four months—then we shall see."

"You mean we'll move back to the farm then?"

"I mean nothing," Mama said firmly. "Tomorrow will take care of itself. Each day has its own troubles."

"Mama," Elly said, laughing, "you sound like an apostle yourself."

"It is no more than common sense, and I am shamed that I needed the Bible to remind me. Four months is something. Anna shall need her own place when Michael comes here. That is a fine thing. You did well."

Elly had not imagined she could ever feel pleased with such an ordinary experience as finding a place to live; in her dreams, joy always came from extraordinary happenings and romantic events. She fought to free herself from what she and Laura had once called the tyranny of the mundane so that she might embrace more fully the life of art—not now, to be sure, but in the future. To her surprise, however, she was delighted with the house, with her mother's praise, with the thought of living a most ordinary life with her father once more at home. How much more complicated than her imagination life had become!

16

BY SUNDAY EVENING they were settled in the house. More or less settled. "Camping out," Phil called it when Elly complained about the sparsely furnished rooms. But what could they do? Phil's furniture had come from the farm to fill his room, and Mama and Pop's furniture filled theirs. Elly had her bed, dresser, and bookcase in her tiny room, nothing more; and the living room furniture had to come from the back room of the store, all broken down and falling apart. Mama bought a breakfast set, six plain pine chairs and a matching table, and that was all.

Upstairs was even more barren. Furniture from Aunt Anna's room at the farm was spaced out to fill the big bedroom and the living room, and Margot had a bed plus an old dresser and table Mama had found in the back room of Mr. Fry's carpentry shop. Albert and Krystyna Kocinski, who would stay at the farm and care for the animals and garden, needed the rest of the furniture, for they had just been married, had nothing of their own, and blessed Mama a thousand times for this godsend.

They all ate downstairs because there were not enough

dishes or pots to equip two kitchens. When Uncle Michael came, the refugee committee would provide some money for dishes and linens, but not until then. Regulations. Meanwhile . . . neither Aunt Anna nor Margot had any money of their own and were growing increasingly upset about living on what they called "charity," but which Mama called "sharing."

They had all pulled together after Pop's heart attack; now that he was recuperating, petty quarrels and bad temper appeared again, and Aunt Anna's tension crackled in the air as the time for Uncle Michael's anticipated release came closer.

Mama praised the light, the space, the garden, the heat, and the bathroom. Aunt Anna allowed that, properly furnished, the house would be tolerable, but certainly not like this. Even the farmhouse was better—quaint at least! All Elly could see was the emptiness of the rooms, the signs of poverty all around them. How out of place what furnishings they did have looked in such a fine house!

"If this is the practical life," she said, putting the freshly-washed dishes away, "I don't want any part of it."

"Benisons on thee, o child of wisdom," Phil said, clattering with the pots. "There *is* something killing to the spirit about it, no doubt of *that*. But weren't you all agog just last week?"

"Well, yes. But . . ." She could not explain. "I thought it would be different; I thought *I* would be different. It was what I wanted!" Was it only in imagination that such changes could be believed? How hard it would be to bring her dreams into this resistant world and make them live!

And she had no one to talk to about them.

"You want too much, you will break your heart over life," Pop said to her the first evening he was home, resting whitely in the big bed, the bedroom door open to the living room. Elly ran to hug him; she had to keep touching him to make sure he was really here again. He pinched her cheek and said he was proud of her, but to please remember she had seventy more years to live and not to use up all her energy at once.

Phil was preoccupied with his graduation. He was to be valedictorian, and that meant a speech. "Stand up and talk," he grumbled. "Can't do it. Waste of time, talk."

He wouldn't let Elly help but turned to Margot for the job of listening, first to his ideas, then to the speech itself. "Criticize, criticize," he urged. Elly couldn't imagine her cousin would ever do any such thing; no wonder Phil had chosen her! And neither of them, of course, had any time for Elly.

So she kept everything in. School and home were a blur. Let Margot shut herself up with Phil; let them both study and triumph; let the World's Fair open and Roosevelt give another Fireside Chat; let the Connecticut Textile factory add another shift when it won a government contract to make army uniforms; let spring ripen in the town all around her. She rejoiced, but at a distance. She *lived* from 3 to 5:30 each school afternoon on the stage and in Angelo's afterward with Mrs. Wilbur. It was only ten more days until opening night.

She *saw* all that happened around her, saw with incredible clarity that made her wonder where she had been before, but it all took place at one remove, as if she were watching it on the screen and would walk out of the dark when the show was over.

She went with Quinny through the town, intoxicated

by the spring twilight. Jack-in-the-pulpit and hepatica bloomed on the meadows high above the river; and thickly clustered birds sang spring songs over their heads. Quinny could identify these birds with an ease that astonished her, could even imitate their calls, but could not understand anything she was thinking. How nice he was! But not for her. She could just barely pretend to him; how could she pretend to herself?

"I define myself by opposition," she wrote in her neglected journal, and liked the look of those uncompromising words.

Once, walking with Quinny on the palisades above the river, she saw Laura and Rob, half-hidden by a clump of shrubbery, lying on the ground in each other's arms, eyes closed, lost in some private world of flesh that excluded everyone else.

Quinny had seen, too; he chuckled and pulled her closer to him. She pulled away, then stopped, relaxed, and leaned closer, willing him to put his arm around her and warming under the pressure when he did. But she would not let him walk her off the path into the tangle of undergrowth on the side. Not now. His tongue nuzzled behind her ear; she fitted her body against his, and waited for him to sweep her hair up and kiss her neck.

Little shivers went all the way down her spine, and she clenched her feet inside her shoes as they walked out again into the sunlight away from the trees. And she blushed, not for Laura's actions, but for her own thoughts.

The time would pass, had to pass, and all would be well, you'll see, Mama repeated, not only to Elly, but also to Aunt Anna, to Pop restless in bed, to Phil with his concern over his speech, to all of them when the news came over the radio of Germany's rush toward war, of threats against Danzig and the Polish Corridor, of French shilly-shallying and English dithering.

Maybe. And the play, too, will be the best ever, Mama insisted.

Maybe. There was no point in trying to engage Mama in a serious conversation. Detachment helped Elly see that. Better to agree and withdraw.

She stretched herself out to the fullest each day as the play swiftly came together, flow and movement folding in and out of each other, the pace picking up, even the weak actors being gathered into its spirit as the lines flew back and forth, actually sounding funny. Mrs. Wilbur timed them with a stopwatch and was merciless in her criticism. How many things one had to remember!

"Elly, your hands! Will you *please* think about your hands? If God had meant them to hang like potatoes on a string, he'd have given you potatoes. Penny Sycamore's hands—think!"

The others laughed. Elly had never thought about hands before. Or about the way an older woman would turn her head on her neck, not like the quick, unthinking way of a young girl who never had a backache in her life. Mrs. Wilbur was relentless, especially toward Elly and Laura. After a time she left the others alone unless they did something astoundingly wrong.

"So it bothers you," she said to Elly, pushing aside the coffee cups at Angelo's and lighting a cigarette. "It is supposed to. And it works, you must admit that. You are getting better and better."

"But the others . . ."

Mrs. Wilbur waved her away. "The others. Now, what would help them? Rebirth. Nothing less. I work with what I have. They will learn to walk, not shuffle, talk, not mumble, keep their heads up and their eyes focused, which will be a remarkable accomplishment for some of them, and that will be all. Enough for this play. What can I do? Quinny is a nice boy"—and she gave Elly a sharp, shrewd look—"I would not hurt his feelings for the world. He's certainly no actor, though! Look at the girls—Rosalie, Frances, Susan, Marcia—in three years they'll all be married and having babies, you can feel this domestic thickness in them even now, and they are the best I could get. After Laura and you."

"O.K., then. I see it. Only, it's so hard. You see, what I'm trying to do . . . well, it's this way." And Elly spoke hesitantly of what she had noticed, that everything disappointing and confusing and fragmentary in her life became whole and clear on the stage. "Laura says that Georgia isn't like *Gone With the Wind* at all. But you see, that's wrong, isn't it, if art is an escape? Mama says that art for art's sake is wrong, we shouldn't try to escape from life but confront it and live it and change it if we can. She says that's what Tolstoy did. Although I can't see it in *Anna Karenina,*" Elly added in a lower voice. "It's so awful that Anna had to die that way—it doesn't seem right, does it?"

"I thought the same when I was younger—about poor Anna, I mean. Don't you see? If Tolstoy let her live, he would be doing just what you said, escaping from life. It had to be that way. Anna had closed all the roads to life; there was only death left." Mrs. Wilbur shuddered. "In a way Anna was lucky. Some people die slowly, so slowly that you don't even *know* they're dead." She sighed and leaned back. "I love this place. Silly of me, isn't it?"

"Why did you *really* leave New York?" Elly asked in a whisper.

Mrs. Wilbur heard but did not answer. "You are

right, Elly, to find this wholeness in art that life doesn't give. That's one of the reasons you're so good already. It's what art does, you know, takes all the bits and pieces of life and makes them whole again to hand back to life—don't forget that, and you won't have to worry about art for art's sake. We hand it *back* to life—to show a way of wholeness, even if it's only inside the person, whoever you are. That's something, too."

"But how?" Elly pressed. "I'm all in pieces myself, yet . . ."

Mrs. Wilbur laughed. "Yes, that's the mystery." She spoke so softly that Elly could barely hear her. "I wasn't good enough. That's why I left New York."

In the long silence between them, Elly forgave her teacher everything. And her mother, too. How could she forgive the one without the other? There was no way.

"I must go home to dinner," Mrs. Wilbur said gently. "My husband does not like me to be late. And no doubt you must go home, too. Your parents will be worried—how good that your father is home again! First, though, I have something for you, a little gift. I wanted to wait until the play was done, then I thought it wouldn't be right to give you something . . . and I couldn't wait. It's a book. I just finished reading it, and I know it's right for you."

She handed over the neatly-wrapped package that she took out of her shopping bag, and Elly tore off the wrappings, uncaring. *Of Lena Geyer* by Marcia Davenport.

"It's a new book about an opera singer. Based on Alma Gluck, no doubt. Marcia Davenport's mother. Like opera?"

"I don't know much about it," Elly admitted. "We listen on Saturday afternoons."

"Oh, yes. Milton Cross and Texaco. There's more, you

know. Well, the book is about you, too. Maybe. If you work hard and keep your desire." She cleared her throat. "And one more thing."

Elly could barely bring herself to close the tantalizing pages.

"Look at it later, all right?" Mrs. Wilbur said. "And listen to me for a second, if you will. This summer I've been asked to run the drama program at Willimantic State Teachers College. Teachers from all over Connecticut come for summer work, and there's going to be a course in drama for the high school student. I've been asked to give it."

"Wow! Aren't you flattered?"

"A little. A very little. What I've decided is to put on an actual play, something a bit more difficult, and have them work on it from start to finish—costumes, scenery, music—everything. I've picked the play. *Twelfth Night.* Do you know it?"

"If music be the food of love, play on," Elly said, and paused. "She never told her love, but . . . with a green and yellow melancholy she sat like patience on a monument, smiling at grief."

"Bravo! It's a lovely play. What I want to know from you is this: could you be my production assistant for the summer. You'd get some valuable professional experience. How old are you? Sixteen?"

"Not until September 3rd," Elly said, barely breathing.

"Fifteen? Never mind, you'll do. I'd let you understudy Olivia, so you could learn the part, otherwise you'd be my girl-of-all-work. Hard work. I'm warning you. Oh, yes, you'd be paid. Ten dollars a week for six weeks."

"Sixty dollars!"

"Six weeks. Eight hours a day. I'd take you with me to

Willimantic and back every day. Your mother wasn't counting on your assistance this summer in the store, was she?"

"No," Elly said. "Yes. It'll be all right. Oh, yes. Of course! Gosh! My first job in the theatre. It's real, isn't it?" *Remember,* she told herself, *remember what this is like.*

Mrs. Wilbur retreated from her enthusiasm. "My dear, I must run. Let's see what you think at the *end* of the summer." As they crossed from dimness to soft light, she said casually, "Pity Laura's leaving. I could have arranged something for her, too. Hysterical, but talented. You work well together."

"I'll miss her," Elly said flatly. Had Mrs. Wilbur not noticed the absolute blankness between them? Or had noticed yet chosen to speak this way? People were a wonder!

"She'll miss you more. You're tough." That was the closest Mrs. Wilbur would ever come to apologizing for her anger when Elly tried to withdraw from the play. The matter was closed between them.

And something new was beginning. Elly walked slowly home. To the new house. The clock in front of Benker's Jewelry Store said six o'clock. The bells from St. Joseph's Church rang out the hour. Cling clang cling clang cling clang. The world was astonishing, shooting sparks off all around her. She walked down the hill from Angelo's in a wordless daze, clutching the exciting new book and her joy; her face shone so that people on the street smiled back at her in delight. She did not even see them as she moved through the spring twilight that blossomed around her.

The furnishings of the home toward which she was moving suddenly mattered less than the stage settings for

Twelfth Night, already taking shape in her mind. Hey nonny, nonny! She wanted the *people* in that house, she needed them, she had to share her news. When she was small, she would dash off the school bus and run full tilt into the kitchen to share with Mama all the exciting happenings of her school day, and reliving them in talk had been a double pleasure, recreating them in the words she would carefully search for as she chewed happily on a slice of Baba's fresh bread and drank a glass of foaming milk. Not for a long time had she rushed to Mama with that kind of excitement; today she felt the imperious need again. She could keep silent no longer.

"Am I late?" she called out, letting the kitchen door slam behind her. "Dinner over?" No one was at the table crammed into one corner of the kitchen. "Where is everyone?"

"In here!" Mama called.

They were all together in the big bedroom, gathered around Pop; Aunt Anna was chattering away in German, and Elly was surprised at how much she understood of it. Her head was still filled with *her* news, filled to bursting, yet she had to listen.

Uncle Michael was free! Actually released! It had happened! She noticed everything at once—Pop's rosy color, Mama's wide smile, Aunt Anna's fluttering hands, Margot's transformed face. Phil hung back; how could he share any more than she could? Uncle Michael was an unknown man, no more real to them than a figure in a story, and his sufferings were even less real, since the imagination had nothing to work on. So her rejoicing could not be spontaneous; rather it was an effort of the will, forced.

Pop waved the telegram over his head like a flag of triumph and beckoned her to enter the magic circle.

RELEASE FORTYTWO CONFIRMED BLUM STOCKHOLM ADVISE ARRIVE NEW YORK.

So few words for so much happiness!

And right in front of Elly another Margot was showing herself from moment to moment, meeting Mama's eyes and Pop's smile head-on instead of with her usual downward glance, taking deep breaths as if some weight in her chest had been released, and allowing herself to exult openly in whatever the future might bring. "I too shall now have a home," she whispered to Elly. Then she smiled, dimpling. "What kind I do not know, that is true—but a home!"

Elly thought back to that first night, when Margot had set the photograph of her father on the empty dresser top and spoken of him with such fierceness. "I am happy for you," Elly said, able to speak simply now. "Very happy." Yet she was not sure how she herself would feel awaiting the coming of the man with the stern face and narrow lips. Still, he was Margot's father!

Aunt Anna too was changed; the marks of tension on her face had been replaced by the slack skin of an aging woman; in her case, it was an improvement. Her hands were looser, her legs no longer drawn tight, as if she were prepared to welcome at least a little life once more.

And Elly could feel their happiness—she really could. Who could not? Yet, she felt her own little happiness more. Even as she acknowledged this to herself and admitted shame for it, she knew again a leap of joy at the thought—a summer job—for she worked up to the supreme moment slowly—a paying job, a job in the theatre!

"How long?" Aunt Anna asked. "Two more weeks? One? I cannot face this . . . what will he be like? What has happened to him?"

"It will be all right," Mama assured her, "all right. Hasn't everything gone well so far? Prayers . . ."

Aunt Anna turned on Mama exactly as she had in those first winter weeks. "Prayers! Nonsense, if you ask me, Sonya! All right? What has gone all right? By rights we should be living in our beautiful apartment in Berlin with our things around us and no separation. And not being charity relatives with emptiness only where should be a future. How shall Michael come back? Do you know? Then why speak?"

There it was again, the old conflict, breaking out even at this time. Pop said, "Anna, the worst is over. Free! *This* is the miracle! Believe me when I say this, for I know."

"I wonder about the future," Margot murmured. "So fast it comes."

"Sounds like my speech," Phil said, grinning.

"I'm thinking about the immediate future," Elly said. "I'm starving!"

She offered to make the meal, wanting time to let her excitement flower in her. They were camped here like gypsies, finding things in the kitchen was impossible, and dinner was more like a supper with leftover cold meat, fried eggs, and bread. Still, it was all right, it would do; no one cared to be reminded right now of ordinary life and how it would go on, so any meal would be eaten with no attention paid to it. She herself didn't care as long as it was food.

"Time to eat!" she called three times before she was heard. Excitement bubbled over and across Mama's prayer of thanksgiving; talk never stopped; there was a constant flow of movement and gesture that made the scene seem to Elly like one in a movie.

Yes! That was it—why she herself was happy and part

of it. This was the scene she had been imagining and waiting for ever since she knew the Blums were coming, and now it had happened, and everything was going to be all right.

She waited for the talk to die down; then, with the dessert, she took a deep breath and told them her news.

PART THREE

Waiting Days

17

"REMEMBER WHEN I WAS little, Baba?" Elly said. "And I'd sit close to you and put my head in your lap, and you'd talk to me very softly or sing those old songs? I always felt safe. Remember when I had measles?"

"Go ahead," Baba urged. "Nobody is here only us and"—her voice fell—"I promise I will not tell."

So Elly sat on the floor by the chair, her legs doubled under her, and put her head on her grandmother's lap. Bright May sunlight flowed through the polished windows onto the bare floor and lit up the lilacs drenching the room with the fragile odor of spring.

"I'm glad you're back, I missed you."

Her grandmother put down the sweater she was knitting. "Really so? Then how come you only once wrote to me, eh, tell me that, little kitten?"

"Only once? I don't believe it! Must have been more."

Baba shook her head. "One time only. You were so excited about this summer job."

Elly blushed. "But I was thinking of you, I really was. And loving the Shakespeare book."

"Then good. You did not need to write. Especially now that I know what months you were living through.

At your age it is natural to think of yourself only . . . and to be the one to find Leo . . . such a shock! No, it is Sonya I do not understand—to treat *me* like a child, not to let me know! And if he had died . . . well! That is the way she has always been, my daughter—makes up her mind and sticks to it no matter what!"

"Baba, do you think Pop was right to go to New York with the others? I'm worried about him."

"He was right," her grandmother said firmly. "It is like a vacation for them. Phil will watch out for him. Oh, I am *glad* this boy is going off to college, I do not like to see such a young boy working so hard to look like an old man."

"Mama says *she* worked hard when she was young."

Baba chuckled. "Your mama does not always remember exactly. It has been a long time with her. She remembers as she wishes. As do we all. Do you want some tea?"

"Oh, don't move, Baba, it's so comfortable here. I'll have to get up soon and change but not now . . . it's funny to think that Mama is your daughter." Elly stretched and sighed.

"Why funny? Only now she treats me as if I were *her* daughter, too. Not to write, not to say one word to me these months. Impossible to think of!"

"She didn't want you to worry. Besides, she knew you were happy at Green Branch." How lame these excuses sounded! "Aren't people strange?"

"True, I am happy there. It is so good to hear Russian spoken all the time! But I would have come back. Do you know that when you are a baby I came on a visit to help out your mother with you so she could run the farm? And stayed for fourteen years! Too long a time. I will not do that again."

"I thought you liked staying with us, I thought you always meant to. Mama said . . ."

"Yes, your mama said. Sonya was always a very strong girl, she would have her own way. Like you."

"Oho! Mama should hear you say that! She thinks I'm some kind of nut, nothing like her at all!"

"Well," Baba said mildly, "what makes you think it was different for me and Sonya than it is for her and you? When Sonya wished to marry Leo, she threw in my face all my ideas and Green Branch Farm and all the possible men there for her to marry . . . God be praised, it turned out well, Leo is a good man . . ."

"The best," Elly murmured.

". . . but what she wanted was to get away from me, live her own life. And I myself? Do you think my parents were happy when I went from home to follow Tolstoy and teach in village schools? Can you imagine the scandal? First I cut off my long hair, it was a sign of our emancipation, the short hair instead of long and heavy braids. Then I worked side by side with strange men. Who could tell what awful things would happen? And that was only the beginning. The czars—first Alexander, then Nicholas—did not wish for peasants to be educated, and right enough for their purposes. Did not wish for young ladies and gentlemen from universities to go into villages and see how peasants live. Did not wish Count Tolstoy to leave Orthodoxy for its emptiness and service to Caesar!"

Her voice rang out as she spoke, and Elly could almost, but not quite, imagine her grandmother young again.

"They begged, they pleaded with me, my parents," Baba said. "So what did I do? I married your grandfather," and she crossed herself, "and went my own way. Never did I ask help from them, not even when he was in 1905 killed by Cossacks and I was with Sonya alone in the world and afraid of Siberia. God be praised, I did not go to Siberia but to New Jersey, and thus I am here —my rebellion all old as I am myself now, and still not sorry I did not listen but went my own way."

"It's hard for me to think of you as young," Elly admitted.

"How will you be actress if you do not think yourself inside others?"

"I thought you didn't want me to be an actress," Elly said, rising to her feet and wriggling to stretch her stiff muscles.

"Nor do I. For me it is wasteful way to spend life. But I do not tell you what to do, only to do it well always. What is the time?"

"Five o'clock. I'll have to be going soon." Elly's palms were clammy. "Oh, Baba, I wish they were all here—opening night of all times! I've been looking forward to this so long, and Uncle Michael's boat had to come in the same day—and Mama didn't even hesitate, did you know that? And then everyone else left, too . . ."

"Come, walk with me in the garden, we'll see what is growing this warm and sunny day. They will be back for the last night, Elly, you know that."

"Yes, but . . . it's not the way I planned!"

"Look at the cabbage starting already there. See! And carrot tops. Sonya is a magic gardener, she has the gift. Shall I pick some asparagus for supper? Asparagus maybe, and an omelette to make something light for your stomach?"

Elly nodded.

"You know, darling, you should not try to force the future, to lay upon it plans here, plans there, this must be, that must be. Come down this way, here is beautiful asparagus—pull from here. Gently! Let the future come to you, it will surely come. The strawberries will be out soon, it is so warm; I must net them so we do not feed only the birds, but also ourselves."

"Do *you* want to go back to the farm, Baba?"

"I will help Sonya this summer; she must have some help, so much is clear. Then I will return to Green Branch no matter what you do. I was wrong all these years to stay here . . ."

"But we love you!" Elly protested.

"Mmm. Of course, you love me—and I you! But I am here only a little alive, big pieces of me are put away. At Green Branch I am all alive, it is a joy to wake up each morning, to be with others like myself. I am not strong enough, you see, not such a big person, to carry my faith like a flag into the world outside with no support. There are such, like saints, heroes of God. This is not me. I need to be with others in community. It takes me sixty-six years to find this out. So you see, there is hope yet for all of us. Come, come now . . ."

"Oh, I hate to go in, it's so beautiful out. Did you *ever* see such weather!"

"Then why are your hands so cold?" Baba teased.

"The play. The play," Elly groaned. "Suddenly, I'm freezing."

When they went indoors, the phone was ringing. "It is good that finally Sonya gives in and has a telephone."

"In case Pop needs it," Elly said. "Hello!"

It was Mathilda Fry inviting them to supper. "You two shouldn't be by yourselves on such a big night. Coming?"

Baba nodded yes and pointed to the asparagus.

"We'll be right over—with fresh-picked asparagus," Elly said.

They walked slowly up and down the hilly cobbled streets from the house to the Frys' flat near the hospital;

and while they walked, Elly told her grandmother all that she wanted to know about the bitter months behind them, reliving, in the warm spring sunlight those snowy winter days. Baba had arrived in Franklin only three days ago in answer to Sonya's desperate summons to stay with Elly while the rest of them went to New York to meet Uncle Michael.

At first Phil was to stay home, but the librarian agreed that he needed a holiday, and he was eager to see Columbia University and the room he would rent from Mama's friend. Elly refused to stay anywhere else but home, even if she had to stay alone. That was too much, to tear her away from the peace of her own room at the very time she would be acting in the play. She *would* stay alone.

Suddenly, she longed for her grandmother. So Baba was called, and Elly was happy despite the abandonment she felt now and again when she reminded herself that the others would not be watching her. "Good thing Margot gave up the Grand Duchess role."

"I worry about the store," Baba said. "You think that Mr. Cummings is honest?"

Elly shrugged. "He was awfully grateful for the chance."

"Well, maybe then is all right. He would not, you think, risk this chance to fool with the money?"

"He's very nice. Pop says they're good tenants."

It was Mr. Cummings who had moved into the flat above the grocery store in April with his pale, quiet little wife and three small children. They had almost no furniture and were embarrassingly grateful for the material Mama had given Mrs. Cummings for curtains and bedspreads. Mr. Cummings had a job at the depot unloading freight trains, but two weeks ago he had strained his back, and the railroad had laid him off. He figured it would take about five years for his claim to be processed, and he was desperate. The little wife sat upstairs in exhausted despair, and the babies cried all day.

When Pop heard about it, he suggested that Mr. Cummings clerk in the store and do the delivering in exchange for the flat and food. For the time being. They would see about a salary later on. And what better time to begin than now, when they had to be in New York to greet Uncle Michael?

Pop said nothing, but Elly remembered what Mama had told her about the rent from the flat going to the mortgage, and she wondered how her parents would manage the mortgage and the rent on this house besides. Surely they couldn't. And this meant they would have to go back to the farm. Which wasn't so bad now that she would be spending six weeks with Mrs. Wilbur in Willimantic. Maybe Baba was right, and you should simply wait for the future to come and bring its special gifts to you.

"I'm so glad to be away from the store," Elly said.

"Phil, too. I am happy he is not burdened, such a brilliant boy, with a grocery store on his mind."

Whenever anyone talked about Phil's brilliance, Elly was stung by a large prickle of envy. She did not even *want* what he did; why then did she grudge it to him? Well, she would try not to, especially tonight of all nights.

"The big night at last," Quinny said, hugging Elly at the door of the flat. "Nervous? Excited?"

"A little." She drew back from him.

"Aw, don't be such a prig! I'll be glad to get it over with, to tell you the truth. Too bad your folks're away."

"Don't mention that, Quinny, do you hear? Don't mention that at all!"

Nervously, he apologized. When Mrs. Fry wrapped

Elly in a big hug and asked if she wasn't just as pleased as punch that her Pa was well enough to make the trip to New York, Elly had to be polite. It took the cream off her evening. Quinny's sister Paula giggled at the excitement and wished she could be in a play some day. His brother Virgil ate in silence, shoveling the food into his mouth, then grabbing his jacket and rushing down the stairs. "Softball game," Mr. Fry said apologetically. "Gas station fellas against lumberyard team."

Mrs. Fry was what is known as a good, plain cook. Once more Elly saw how much she depended on Mama and had inherited her standards, for Mama's meals were much better, and Elly felt a trifle cheated eating the meat loaf, mashed potatoes, and stewed tomatoes, which Mrs. Fry served up as her festive meal. The signature of a company dinner was the dessert—a layer cake with pink coconut frosting. "Don't make these fancy cakes much any more, somehow the heart's gone out of me for them."

Baba, who daily made bread, pies, coffee cakes and desserts, nodded in agreement and looked sharply at Elly, who only bobbed her head in silence. The windows were open, and warm breezes drifted through from the river. Quinny was talking about going out on the river soon for fish. They wouldn't mind having some fresh trout to eat, or bass, maybe—there was nothing like it.

"But best of all is frying it in camp right after you catch it—pop! into the hot pan, sizzle, turn it over, and it's the tastiest food you can find anywhere in the world. Right, Pa?"

Quinny's face positively shone with joy. For the first time he looked handsome to Elly. They would go to the cast party together; he had already whispered that into her ear. "I'm taking the *star!*"

She sighed. Clearly, she would not be as sharp as a tack for the play; sharp as a sponge, more likely. She knew that professionals always came through, but she did not feel terribly professional. Even after she and Quinny called for Laura and Rob and the four of them walked solemnly up the steep hill to the school, she felt cold and indifferent, pursued by a desire for solitude. Yet, if they had left her alone, she would have been frightened, with that queer, nameless panic that had attacked her in the nights of her childhood, so much more terrifying for being rootless and unnamed.

All during the final instructions and make-up time, she felt this spreading, shapeless blob of fear invading her insides while her skin stayed cold, and she forced herself to speak slowly and quietly in a very mimicry of unconcern. It was too late to pull out now; she would have to go through with it and fail, the humiliation eating her up alive. The other members of the cast were wavering outlines with mouths in them, mouths from which words came to which she responded. Laura squeezed her hand. Quinny squeezed her arm. She rubbed her hands and her arm, rubbing, rubbing, gazing into space, noticing how chipped the paint was on the backstage area and the corridors, wondering why it wasn't painted, rubbing her arm, rubbing her hand. Why did everyone have to *touch* her?

Mrs. Wilbur passed among them, a frown on her face and her hair awry, pinning them into costumes, reminding them of special bits of business, restraining her own exasperation, although her hands clenched and unclenched in a cockeyed rhythm and she kept twisting her mouth from side to side, unknowing. "What a time! Every year I vow never again—and here we are! Laura, let me see your dress. Beautiful! You know, I couldn't really see you as Alice in the beginning, she seemed so much more . . . *ingenue*. You've made her an interesting part. Very interesting. Elly! No, my dear, I think we've got to do something more with your hair. A hair net! Who has a hair net? Oh, I don't care what kind! Here we go! Now, look at yourself—don't you look deliciously frumpy?"

Seeing her strange face in the mirror, Elly did laugh, had to laugh, and slowly, the fear crumbled into little pieces inside her, weighing down her arms and legs but leaving her torso free. That's just what she did look like, deliciously frumpy. At the very last minute she stuck a pencil through her hair net into her hair, the picture of a writing genius without enough time for neatness.

From far off a bell rang. A knock sounded. A voice was heard. It was calling her name. It was saying, "Telegram for Miss Elly Josephs." And a yellow envelope was thrust into her hand. Yellow paper unfolded. ALL THE BEST DEAR CHILD LOVE YOU CONFIDENT YOUR TRIUMPH MAMA POP. What beautiful words! She read them again. And again. And tucked the telegram in the side of the mirror. Like a star. The little pieces of fear were crushed now into a powder and scattered unpredictably here and there. At least she would manage to make the stage, remember her lines, not fall entirely apart.

"Can't stand the tension," Quinny groaned, pacing back and forth outside the dressing room. "Never again, believe me. Don't know how you stand it—look at you, calm as a cucumber."

"Ooh, Elly, shall we make it, isn't it splendid? I feel like marble and ice."

"Laura." Enabled by the excitement of the moment to cross the barriers, the girls clung together. "You are beautiful," Elly said. "Oh, you are beautiful."

"I don't feel like anything at all. Glenna's here—Owen's gone already, wouldn't, couldn't stay." Then in a changed voice, "Good luck!"

And then Elly had to go on stage because she was there when the curtain went up, typing away at a play in an unusually cluttered corner of the cluttered set that represented the Vanderhof living room. At least she wouldn't have to walk out on the stage! Mrs. Wilbur, in the wings, patted her as she went past. Now what? Remember! She adjusted her hair net, pushed her glasses down on her nose, stroked the cats who were to sit on the manuscript, tried the typewriter keys in silent pantomime. Then she relaxed and sagged in her chair, looking around the room, feeling herself into it so that she became the kind of person who would live in such a room in unconcerned happiness. There was candy in the empty skull on her desk.

An unmistakable creak. With agonizing slowness the curtain went up. Elly was alone on the stage. She typed one word, then stopped and frowned. She read what she had written, which was nothing more than *oh oh oh oh*. Typed again. Thought. The cats played around her on the table. Somewhere out there was an audience. Don't think of it. Hello, cats. They stayed nicely where they were because catnip had been hidden in the slightly opened desk drawer. She reached into the skull for a piece of candy and chewed it thoughtfully, studying her page. And the first light gusts of laughter reached her. She typed again, faster and faster, finished the sheet, whipped it out of the typewriter, lifted a cat, and put the sheet on the pile, set the cat down again. More laughter, robust this time.

Then Rosalie Albana came on as Essie in her ballet slippers, leaping through the doorway to more laughter. And spoke the first lines of the play: "My, that kitchen's hot." Could she be heard? Yes, there was more laughter. Elly's throat was dry. She coughed slightly before answering, "What, Essie?" And they were under way at last.

By the time the curtain went down briefly at the end of the first scene, the audience was with them all the way; laughter was followed by sharp clapping. After the short second scene was over and the curtain dropped for intermission, they ran around backstage hugging each other and shouting for joy.

As the curtain rose on Act Two, with Martha Hunsley lounging around the stage as the drunken actress, Gay Wellington, the laughter burst out at them, enormously jovial and appreciative. They were lifted up on it and leaped lightly through the action, playing to each other and not forgetting very many lines.

Elly too was lifted by the acclaim; at the same time, she was aware that this was not her best performance. She had done better at the final dress rehearsal. It was nothing that anyone else would notice, except possibly Mrs. Wilbur. Still, the edge was off, she was a split second behind, she had to *think* too much instead of reacting smoothly.

Quinny was marvelous as Paul, the best he had ever been. Laura was good, too, possibly a bit hysterical and tight, but that was right for the part of Alice; it added some depth to that silly role.

The trouble for Elly had begun during the second scene of Act One when she was offstage, with time to think that in all the audience out front only her grandmother belonged to her. That was a mistake. She repaired it well enough, but the crack showed through. And she knew it.

At the end they all sat around the dining table while

Rheba and Donald brought in the blintzes to the uproarious laughter of the audience. The curtain fell. What winks and squeezes and hugs! Rob McGuire danced a jig, then grabbed Laura and kissed her. Quinny kissed Elly. The curtain lifted, and they bowed, the entire cast forming one long line. How many there had been! Then the backstage crews joined them, hustled on by Mrs. Wilbur, and the applause grew. The line melted away after the curtain fell, and when it rose again, only Laura and Rob bowed, then scooted off into the wings left, while Elly and Quinny ran on from the right wings, bowed, stepped back, and welcomed Henry Bushey, who had played Grandpa Vanderhof so well. The applause was intoxicating. Elly raised her eyes from the footlights to the audience and felt herself melting into it. She wasn't afraid any longer, either of those people out there or of herself up here inside her skin. She could have jumped the footlights out to them, kissing and being kissed.

"Oh, my goodness, how wonderful!" Rosalie Albana called, once the curtain was down for good.

There was a great sorting out. Much shouting. Much kissing.

"Hey, that's my cold cream!"

"Close the door, stupid, I'm changing my clothes!"

"Anyone seen my shoes? I'm not going home in those dumb ballet slippers!"

"Weren't we just grand? Weren't we the greatest? Now, tell me true. Can't wait for tomorrow night."

"We oughta do this for the King and Queen of England when they come here next month. What d'you think?"

Elly stared at her strange face in the ugly, unshadowed glare of the dressing room mirrors. She kept wanting to fall asleep, as if something deep inside her were dragging her down into a peaceful exhaustion. Her hands lay in her lap, too heavy to move. The jar of cold cream on the dressing table was miles away. From time to time she and Laura looked at each other across the din, then looked away; otherwise, their faces gave no clue to their inner elation. So this was what it felt like. So heavy. So tired. A sense of ending.

"The King and Queen! Who cares about them?"

"I do! Three cheers for the idea!"

"Three cheers for Mrs. Wilbur!"

"It didn't go too badly after all, did it, children?" Mrs. Wilbur said mildly, standing quietly in the midst of the throng. Sweat dripped from her red face. "I didn't think we could pull it all together, but we did. Tomorrow night, remember, same time, same place. Now why don't you all go home to bed?"

A great chorus of shouts answered her. There was a cast party at Rob McGuire's house, and she knew it. "Coming?" Rob asked her.

"Oh, for a moment. I'll look in on my way home." She crossed the girls' dressing room to the mirrors. "Very fine, Laura. You made something of that part. Hard to do. What happened, Elly, after the first scene?"

Elly shrugged. "You noticed. I slipped a little. A verv little."

"Ah, you knew? Well, good then. It was nothing. A tiny bit."

"I lost my pacing."

"You came back fine, though. That's what a professional is—give a good performance, no matter what. How about *Twelfth Night* for next year if it goes well this summer?"

"Oh, how can you think of next year?" Martha Hunsley gasped. "I can't think at all."

The parents drifted backstage, a good-humored, jostling crowd. "By George, I've got to hand it to you," Mr. McGuire told Mrs. Wilbur, "giving us something to laugh at like this. Just what we needed."

"The right medicine," Mr. Plotkin agreed. "The kids'll eat it up tomorrow. Nothing like some fun in bad times."

"I saw it on Broadway," Mr. Hall, the English teacher, said, "and these kids ran 'em out of the ballpark, let me tell you."

"No comparison," his wife agreed.

"Why don't they all stop talking?" Elly murmured to Laura. Didn't they see it was the *performances* that counted, not all the talk afterwards?

Baba enfolded Elly in a warm, quick hug. "You were really good, my little one. Believe me, when you were on stage, no one looked at the other actors. I saw!"

"Don't you think you're just a tiny bit prejudiced?" Elly teased, but she was happy. "How do I look with this make-up on? I hate to take it off."

"For a young girl is not suitable," her grandmother said seriously. "Have a good time at this party. Not too late come home, mind. I'll be waiting up to hear all your talk. You have a way home? Someone will take you? Then fine. I see you later."

"My babies, my lambs!" Glenna trilled. "To think that this is what you were cooking up all those hours in that little room! Someday they'll put a plaque up on our house, see if they don't. Two great actresses worked together here in their youth. Two!"

"Don't overdo it, Glenna," Laura whispered. "People are looking at us." She was miserable again, and again a stranger to Elly.

Finally, they made their way out into the dark town, singing noisily as they piled into cars for the trip across the river to the McGuire house in Woodmont. The cool spring night gathered them in with all their happiness. Elly let her tiredness and separateness slip from her like a costume and would not, *would not*, allow herself to feel apart from those around her. How beautiful the night was! She would be part of this celebration.

In the back seat of Rob's car, Quinny pushed her into a corner and kissed her hard on the lips. She felt herself grow warm and then hot as her body relaxed after the long hours of tension, and her arms went up around his neck to hold him close. His face scratched her cheek, she pulled back for a moment, then looked at him, smiled at what she saw, leaned into his body, her leg pressed tightly against his, and they clung together in the darkness, feeling their hearts beat together as the spring night blossomed around them.

18

“UNCLE MICHAEL, Uncle Michael, Uncle Michael,” Elly grumbled to herself, shading her eyes from the sun. “Two weeks, and I'm tired of him already.” She waited just as eagerly as he did for the magic letter from the refugee committee that would tell of success in finding him a job while he studied to pass the medical board examinations.

“So I realize/when a lovely flame dies/smoke gets in your eyes,” Margot crooned, vamping the song a little, her eyes sparkling with mischief.

“Hear, hear!” Phil said, clapping, stretching out his long legs on the grass.

Uncle Michael could not believe what he was hearing. He sputtered and shook his head. “Barbarism,” he finally said in his thick accent.

Phil, Margot, and Elly laughed. Uncle Michael sputtered some more, this time in German.

Three languages were being spoken alternately or at the same time, conversations were started but never finished, interruptions in turn became new, incompleted conversations, and all the details of ordinary life were pushed to the background until Uncle Michael had caught up on six months of missed time.

He had to spend extra hours in bed and eat many small meals each day; between meals, he sipped slowly at a glass of milk and smoked cigarettes with his eyes half-closed and an inward smile of bliss on his face.

It was not that Elly had expected a genial uncle; Margot's photograph and the remarks she and her mother had passed made quite clear the nature of the man. But she was still not prepared—none of them was prepared—for the stiffness and even harshness that was revealed at once. The camps had not broken Uncle Michael; rather, they had stripped away only the flesh to reveal the bone beneath, and it was a hard, enduring bone indeed.

"Is this what he's really like?" Elly had asked Margot.

But Margot wouldn't answer. She smiled and turned away with cryptic words. "It's all in the way you look at him. Of course, in Germany it was different. He was a *doctor!*"

Elly thought of their family physician, Dr. Bierenberg, a plump and rumpled man whose office was in a wing of his house and who frequently greeted them while he was eating a sandwich he had fetched from the kitchen, and tried to make sense of the idea that a doctor was supposed to behave with such insistent sternness; it was impossible. "If you say so," she said, unconvinced.

"What do you expect?" Phil said to her. "Margot doesn't want to rat on her father! If you ask me, I think she's disappointed, too, after the way she built him up."

"So you don't like him, either!" Elly said. "I feel ashamed."

Phil grinned widely at her. "Don't. Who could like him? Besides, why should you? He doesn't like *us*. Roll with it, kid, roll with it."

Of course, she reflected, it was easier for Phil to say that. He was seldom home, and when he was, he worked in his room on the speech he was to give as valedictorian. When Uncle Michael heard about that, he unbent as much as he could, gave Phil a frosty smile, and offered to help him develop his ideas.

"I do not think," he said, "it is so easy to think in America as it was in Germany when I was a young man. That was the whole purpose of our education. Here, it is all fun and games."

"Boy! Instant expert!" Elly muttered.

Phil declined the help in his slow German, and when Uncle Michael criticized his accent, he ducked his head and said to the room in general, "Well, I hope my accent in German isn't as bad as a German accent in English," and a flush slowly spread over Uncle Michael's face.

After that, he said less to them directly, and it was easier to stay out of his way. And Margot clung to Elly, presenting a bland, unruffled manner to the adults, yet finding things to do which took her out of the house as much as possible.

Today was Memorial Day, and the sun shone upon it. In the garden they could hear the distant sounds of band music—a trumpet toot, a drum roll—as the Franklin American Legion Post prepared to lead off the parade. Down through the center of town they would march, past St. Joseph's and beyond the hospital to the old military cemetery tucked away against the side of a hill. Here two dozen men killed in the Civil War had been buried long ago when the graveyard was far out in the country along a dusty road from town, and gradually it was filled with veterans of that war and the Spanish-American War, and most recently, World War I, "the war to make the world safe for democracy," as President Wilson had called it. When Pop repeated that to Uncle Michael, he was greeted with harsh mockery.

The mayor, Mr. Buckle, would make a speech, and there would be free doughnuts and lemonade in the Parish Hall of the First Congregational Church and a fried chicken picnic lunch for a quarter. And balloons and bunting. And a baseball game later in the afternoon on the high school field. And in the evening a band concert in Livingstone Park across the Ibanaki River.

Sitting in the remote and leafy garden, Elly could predict exactly what would happen, for the events of Memorial Day, like those of July 4th, were fixed, still points in a turning world; tampering with them was unthinkable. Every year they cheered the parade—once or twice Phil and Elly had marched in it—listened to the mayor's speech—and in election years to the remarks of their congressman—munched doughnuts and sipped lemonade, but eaten food brought from home, gone to do the chores instead of watching the baseball game, then driven back to town in the velvety evening to sit on a blanket near the bandstand and listen to the marches that rose into the sweet night air.

They would not be going to the festivities today. Uncle Michael didn't want to go, didn't feel up to it, didn't understand all this fuss, did not hesitate to hold over them the full weight of his suffering.

"But why can't *we* go, Mama?"

"Elly, he is a guest. He has been . . ."

"Yes, I know all about it. Great suffering. Unimaginable suffering. So O.K., I can't imagine it."

Mama looked grave. "It is not anything to make light of. He will not speak much of it, but we have heard at the refugee offices some of the stories . . ."

And indeed they were horrible. To begin with, there was the fine blue tattoo on Uncle Michael's arm, a number that would never come out, the number that had been his identity during those six months, for names were never used by the guards, only numbers barked out with deliberate insolence. Upon that number depended the meager rations of watery soup, dry bread, weak coffee, and rotten potatoes; depended the assignment of a narrow board sleeping shelf with a wafer-thin pallet and a single worn blanket; depended the inmate's connection with the entire world outside the camp, a world that he gradually lost hold of as days and weeks and months passed of a monotonous existence, broken only by bouts of more extreme terror and the solitary, anonymous deaths of others that reminded you of your own end if once you relaxed your steadily weakening grip on life.

"Some held on. Some did not," Uncle Michael said. "You could not tell who would be the stronger until you saw. I believed I could hold for one year surely. And then I did not know. So I kept to this idea of one year. And needed only six months."

Only six months was easy to say. What it meant came out as they talked the long twilight evenings away, sitting on the back porch or in the garden as the flowers bloomed around them in a thousand signs of life's renewal. There were pitchers of iced tea and small cookies flavored with cardamom. Uncle Michael did not care for the food, he admitted that at once. "Of course, I am in no position to be critical, I must to eat, and so I shall." And he bowed to Baba for her efforts, he drank a quart of milk each day and never refused ice cream. "But you will see when the time is come that I am once more strong, I shall show what it is to eat the fine foods as the French cook. Eh, Anna, you will do this for me? In Berlin we had Dorothea to cook, and excellent she was, too. Remember? How often in the camp I thought of those meals!"

For once Aunt Anna spoke sharply, her eyes averted from her husband's pallid face. "Fah, Michael! There is no use to talk of such things—cooks! French food! And where will this refugee committee send us? In all of this country, believe me, you shall not find what Dorothea cooked for us. When she must leave last spring . . ."

"Last spring . . ." Uncle Michael said, then also fell silent.

Last spring was for the Blums a lifetime away, marked by the terror of the summer and autumn, the jagged separations of the winter, and the new life of this year, but they tried to return to it with words that could not travel over the barriers of time. They would seek to summon up the flowering lindens on the streets or the suntanned crowds in the Grunewald, the German words lying heavily in the air between them.

Then, in the middle of a sentence, all would crack, and Uncle Michael would speak very quietly, mostly in German, about autumn and winter and spring in the camps, about the mud and the cold and the utter desolation of the surrounding heath, which chilled the heart. "We are the peat bog soldiers," he intoned, mocking his own solemnity, forbidding any other mockery.

And when spring came in the camps, the pain was even more unbearable as the inmates felt the contrast between their own exhaustion and filth and the sudden lushness of the season, yes, even on the heath, as birds returned in great flocks and tiny flowers blossomed, half-hidden in the thick grass. Day followed day, and the sun rose higher in the sky, and the hours of light lengthened, and their despair grew despite the bravest efforts to fight it, until the Red Cross representative had come with the thinnest possible shred of hope and . . .

"And now you are here, God be praised," Mama said.

Uncle Michael was surprised. He was not used to being interrupted, especially by a woman. "I will not forget," he said.

"Of course not," Mama assured him. "But now is a better time, a time for growing strong again, and for thinking of the future."

"It is out of my hands," Uncle Michael said with a resignation clearly false to his temperament, raising his hands and letting them drop again. They were amazingly thin; all of him was gaunt, his shaven head almost skeletal; yet, despite this, he looked cool and elegant in the white linen suit he had contrived to find in Stockholm, and which he wore with long-sleeved white shirts and sober ties.

How rumpled Pop looked next to him, Elly thought, and yet how much more comfortable, how human! He too had lost weight, his face had aged and was marked with lines, although his round stomach remained, and he looked like some tranquil Buddha, leaning back in his deck chair, listening, nodding his head, and talking occasionally in a low voice that almost always had a hint of humor in it.

He would not yield to anyone in his own house; at the same time, he would not be drawn into arguments or discussions on all the laws Uncle Michael was laying down for the proper way to do this, that, and the other thing. Mama expostulated, Baba shook her head, Aunt Anna alternately sulked or responded with exaggerated agreement, but Pop only listened, nodded, and remarked that,

"Yes, of course, that was true, but on the other hand . . ." and let his words trail off into a comfortable silence.

Uncle Michael went on, of course. He went on and on and on! He did not like the house, for one thing. No, it was not the lack of furniture that disturbed him nor the shabbiness of what they did have, for he pointed out to them that Europeans were not so in love with newness or with endless consumption as Americans. No, he did not like the absence of a formal dining room! "It is perhaps charming to eat *al fresco* for a holiday, or even when one is young and finds a certain charm in being *déshabillé*. But then there is the necessity for understanding good manners at table and the proper respect to be shown to food, and this comes only from a dining room."

Then he reminisced about the dining room in his apartment, the polished mahogany furniture, the linen cloths and silver serving dishes, the Rosenthal china and silver cutlery for twelve, and Elly listened with mixed feelings—distaste for the stuffy formality she imagined, astonishment at the richness of the possessions, and wonder that anyone who had been through the experience of a concentration camp should still evoke with such love these same lost possessions. What difference did they make anyway?

"Well," Pop said one evening, as they walked down to the drugstore for the *Boston Globe*, "he hasn't had the benefit of your mother's teachings. You complain, oh, how you complain, but there you are! Not much attached to such things—and good for you, too! You would not believe how much misery can come into the human life through love of silver or jewelry or diamonds, even of sofas or rugs! As if there were not anyway enough unhappiness simply from other people!"

Of course, Mama and Pop told her not to criticize, and of course, she would not have, anyway. One did not criticize even the most obvious pomposities of a man who had, after all, survived an experience that killed many others. This manner had served its purposes. Nevertheless, there was no way to control one's thoughts. Where did such a man fit in?

More interesting, however, than any exchange of opinions Elly could have had with her parents were the conversations with Margot that had gone on whenever they were together from the first day she had returned from New York with her father and an entirely different look on her face.

She was abstracted and answered only, "Yes, yes, yes, it was wonderful, what do you expect?" to all of Elly's questions about New York. She seemed more interested in the play than in her father and had fought him bitterly when he railed against her attending it instead of remaining with him.

"Shock," Phil said.

"Delayed reaction, poor child," said Baba.

Both true. But it was more than that.

"He thinks I should not wear lipstick," Margot said to Elly one day as they walked home from school.

"He thinks school uniforms look better," she remarked another day at lunch.

"He does not approve of boys and girls to go to school together," she said to no one in particular in the garden one evening, taking advantage of her father's poor understanding of English to mock him to his face. The deceptive mildness of her tone fooled the other adults as well, who were not really listening to any subdued conversational murmurs but were enjoying the oncoming night in the peace that follows a full day's work.

"He most certainly does not approve that boys and girls should go places together," Margot announced as she walked with Phil, and Elly with Quinny, high above the river after coming out of the Saturday matinee at the movie theatre. "He thinks I am studying in the library, which is a fit occupation for a young girl."

Margot had said no more at the time, and the four of them walked on that day and many others whenever they had time from school and work, talking more about the future that was rushing rapidly toward them than about parents who were, in any case, fading gradually into the background they would call "childhood." She should not, Margot told Elly, say one word against her father after what he had suffered, except that she was afraid she would never get free of him if she did not fight.

The song Margot was singing in the garden that Memorial Day afternoon was part of the fight. "You do not like these kind of songs?" she asked her father. "They are good, I think, and maybe I shall become a singer rather than a dress designer."

Uncle Michael leaned back in his chair and put his long, thin fingers over his closed eyes. "This will be an endless tragedy, America . . . I do not like what it is doing to these children. Let me tell you, it was not like this in Germany!"

Aunt Anna spoke up. "Oh, Michael, it was so in Berlin, you said this yourself, from the breakdown of the war, the children were no more like the parents, and all was mixed up. Such drug takers he saw in the clinic you would not believe—mere children, too! And the girls with diseases . . ."

Here Uncle Michael sat up abruptly and stopped her with a stiff gesture, pointing to Elly and Margot. "Not with the children here, Anna, shame on you!"

Aunt Anna flushed but did not give up. "You will see, Michael, once we are settled in a big city with a proper school for Margot, you will see this differently. It is what I have been waiting for, this move."

Uncle Michael was no longer listening, he was talking, in a mixture of harshly-accented English and swift German, of the proper relations between parent and child.

Margot got up and beckoned Elly to come with her. "Shall we see the parade, anyway? We do not need them with us!"

Elly was afraid of her uncle, afraid of his cold eyes and heavy voice, afraid of the authority his suffering had given him, which she couldn't match, afraid also of her strong dislike of him, which seemed to her to be her fault, since any reasonable person would warm toward an uncle who had lost everything and come through unbroken, almost a hero.

So she hesitated to interrupt Uncle Michael to tell Mama they were going. We're not children, after all, she reminded herself, feeling very small and weak. A few minutes passed, she shifted from foot to foot, the sounds of band music grew louder and closer, tree leaves cast delicately moving shadows across the grass, and birds darted down from the sky to rest briefly in the branches. To waste such a day!

"Mama, listen," she said loudly, watching Uncle Michael stop talking to stare at her in astonishment. Pop winked. "It's all right with you, isn't it, if Margot and I go to see the parade? Could we eat the chicken dinner this time? Just once?"

"I'll go, too," Phil said, getting up. "I've got money to pay for everything."

Mama worried about the quality of the food until Pop said, "Sonya let them go and have a good time, why don't you? Maybe we'll join you later. I should walk, the doctor said, not lie all day in a chair. Go, enjoy!"

Uncle Michael started to say something again; they did not wait to hear what it was. "Probably I am not to go," Margot said. "He does not understand how it is in America."

"Welcome to the new patriot!" Phil said, taking her hand, and they pelted downhill past the shops to the place where the parade was assembling, ready to march off across town. "You deserve a balloon."

The parade was irresistible with its drums and trumpets and uniforms and flags, fire engines and police cars leading sections, then Boy Scouts, Girl Scouts, Campfire Girls, American Legion posts, Masons, Eastern Stars, Daughters of Job, Rotarians, and Elks all marching, bands from St. Joseph's High School and the Shriners from Newchester to supplement the Legion band and the one from New Franklin High, and decorated floats from all the area schools. The sun sparkled on the instruments, and the flags whipped in the light wind that blew down from the mountains over the river.

Quinny joined them, proud of the float his father and brother had made, a log cabin representing Abraham Lincoln's birthplace. Riding on it, dressed in old clothes with a stick-on beard and swinging a hatchet over a split rail fence was Virgil Fry, playing Lincoln, and they applauded lustily when the float swung into view.

They ran along at the tail of the parade to the cemetery, now an irregular ragged field surrounded by low wooden bungalows and thick shade trees that transformed the summer streets into cool green lanes. And while the mayor spoke from a platform decorated with bunting about sacrifice and war and gallant young men, they chased around the tumble-down gravestones, tickling each other with tall dry grasses, before stretching out under a huge oak that had been old when the first stone was set up in 1861.

The words that spoke of bravery and death and freedom came from far away across the rows of chairs set up for the spectators, across the marchers and band members sprawled on the sloping meadow, and across the broken rows of graves with their worn headstones that marked the burial places of Civil War soldiers and veterans.

"Ah, don't listen," Elly said, rolling over to lie on her back and stare up at the cloudless sky. The flags of the color guard folded in on themselves and out again in the light breeze that rippled the tree tops and lifted small curls of hair above the girls' heads.

"How long ago it seems!" Elly said. "And yet it wasn't really, was it? Seventy-four years . . ."

"Twenty-five since the World War began," Phil said.

They walked through the cemetery looking at the dates on the gravestones. So many young men killed in 1862 or 1863 or 1864, aged eighteen or nineteen or twenty or even, in one case, aged sixteen, with the familiar crossed sword and rifle of the Connecticut Volunteers carved on the stone. And the more recent graves from 1917 or 1918—only a few of those—relatives of people in town they all knew.

"In Europe," Margot said, "there are miles and miles

of cemeteries, you would not believe how many, and in each of them are rows and rows of white crosses, more than anyone could count, all from the World War, until you grow dizzy and think there will be no end to the dead, and who is possibly left to be living. My mother had a brother who was killed in 1915."

"Fighting for Germany?" Quinny asked. "Well, then . . . !"

"It was his country," Margot said simply. "To fight for any country is stupid, I think, but not for one more than another. I should not fight."

"Like Mama," Elly said. "She's a pacifist. Baba, too. Not Pop. He thinks you've got to fight injustice—like what happened to your father, you know. They used to argue about it a lot before you came. About Spain, too. Now . . ."

"I do not think I am a pacifist," Margot said. "Only it is stupid to fight. For anything."

"Depends," Quinny said. "Wouldn't go to war for nothing. Hah, not me! Wouldn't catch me enlisting in any army—friend of Virgil's over Newchester way just went off and did it—but I guess I'd go for this country. My pa was in the Navy back in the World War, looking out for German submarines—pow! Never saw a single one, though."

"No difference what you think," Phil said, "or what the mayor says,"—the mayor had now arrived at his peroration and was shouting to the winds that America would never again join the wars of Europe—"we'll be at war soon enough and Quinny, you'll go and I'll go, and that's the way it will be. Let's get something to eat."

Rob drifted over to them as they sat on the lawn in front of the First Congregational Church, digging into the dinner piled on their plates—fried chicken, cole slaw, potato salad, pickles, and biscuits—and listening to Phil analyze the European situation. "Laura left this morning," Rob announced at once. "Her mother couldn't even wait for the parade," he complained. "Can't figure some people out. Did you see me driving my dad's car?" And Elly felt the only pang of the day, watching that whole friendship slide into the remembered past when she wanted to keep it in the throbbing present.

How quickly everything was lost! The play was over and done with, the waiting for Uncle Michael had been packed away into limbo, the time before Margot lived with them might never have been. And this day, too, was going before it was grasped, the bunting taken down, the speeches forgotten, the church lawn littered with cups and plates and chicken bones.

Leaving Phil and Margot behind, Elly led Quinny up to the Green, hoping for a last glimpse of the life that had been lived in the Fitzgerald house, a last look at Laura's room. The door was open onto rooms barren of furniture with dust mice rolling on the wooden floors; only the lingering smell of turpentine and oil paints suggested the presence of the vanished family.

"Who's there?"

They jumped at the sound of the voice. "Friends," Elly called back, and a thin woman with gray hair piled untidily on top of her head came bounding down the stairs, her hand held out.

"Why, hello, you're my first visitors. I'm trying to clean up the studio—oil painters leave simply a tremendous mess behind—then I'll tackle the kitchen. You don't know anybody willing to help, for money, naturally," and then she took a breath. "I'm Lia Temorio. Just Lia."

"I'll help," Quinny said. "How much?"

"The weaver?" Elly asked.

"Fifty cents an hour suit? Yes, how'd you know? Thought I was anonymous here, want a cup of tea, wait a minute, kitchen's thick with grease, come on in, no place to sit, thinking of building a brick patio out back, might have plenty of work, furniture's due here in two days."

"Laura told me," Elly explained, fascinated at once by the vitality of this woman.

"I'd help with the patio, too," Quinny volunteered. "I could lay as many bricks as you wanted."

When the tea was ready, Lia led them out the back door. "Mind sitting on the step? Let me show you," and sketched out, with her words and her hand gesturing in the air, her ideas for a patio and fenced garden. "Yes, I'm going to live here forever, exactly what I want, train service to New York and Boston, gorgeous scenery, don't you think, place to earn my bread—awful girl's school, my goodness, I hope you don't go there, my dear, do you?—still they pay for my teaching, beautiful old house, fine studio, walk everywhere, good for the health, away from the city . . ."

"I thought you were only renting," Elly broke in, "and maybe Laura would come back." Hadn't Laura intimated as much?

Then Margot and Phil came to the door, called out, were answered, and found themselves on the back steps, mostly listening, but sometimes talking, and after only a few minutes Lia had discovered that she could buy her groceries right down the hill at Pop's store, that Margot was interested in fabrics not as a weaver but as a designer, and that Elly had been Laura's friend.

"Goodness, I almost forgot, she left something for you, now where did I put it, don't go, be right back." And sure enough, she had returned in a moment with a flat wrapped package she placed in Elly's hand. "Open it, we're all dying to see what's in it, can't wait to open parcels myself."

It was Laura's diary, all written in, with a note saying only, "To the other half of me," and Elly almost cried, began to shake, wouldn't open it, felt separated from the people looking curiously at her. She would have to live through all of it again! "Thank you," she whispered, and "Come eat with us tonight," she invited, and without even closing the door behind her, Lia came, linking arms with Quinny and Phil, until Quinny dropped out to help dismantle the family float.

Margot did a little dance on the brick walk before the house, giggling at her clumsy steps. "I think I like being an American," she said, "I really do."

"Surprised at yourself?" Phil asked.

"Astonished!" Margot assured him. "In Germany it is impossible I should meet all these different people; I would be," and she hunched her shoulders, "all locked in to what my father believes is right. Poor Vatti," she added. "What he has suffered shall count for nothing; it will be an embarrassment."

Naturally, Lia had to hear the entire story as they walked home through the narrow, twisting streets, and she exclaimed all the while over the charm of these picturesque lanes and alleys, yet listened, her head cocked to one side like a bird's, clucking over the details of the camps and applauding at the end.

"You are a veritable hero," she announced to Uncle Michael once the introductions were completed, but he brushed her off with a rudeness that took Elly's breath away and brought Pop to his feet in a sudden swift movement. Lia had no existence for him; it was Margot he shouted at, and more than Margot, he screamed with fury at Elly and Phil, the German words poured out of him in a thick stream, his hands gripped each other until the knuckles whitened, and the impeccable surface he had presented to them collapsed in a moment.

And what was he raging about? Difficult to understand from the German words that came spouting out from his twisted mouth. But he began with the specific complaint that Margot had gone out without asking his permission, had been gone all day, had left him when she knew . . . and abruptly he switched to an attack on Elly's manners, her unwillingness to help with the housework, her assumption of independence, the way she spoke to her parents, her bad influence on Margot. And Phil—how would anyone imagine him as a scientist with that ungainly walk, those offhand manners? And he and Margot were together far too often, this was not the way of a true gentleman.

Aunt Anna tried to pull him down, Mama rushed up to plead with him, to no purpose. He wiped his face, coughed hoarsely, then launched once more into his impassioned harangue, the bitterness and harshness swelling in his voice until he was almost choked with his own fury.

Margot, shaken, whitened and reached for Elly's hand; she did not answer back nor did she retreat, as Elly was tempted to do, edging back to the porch steps by a series of imperceptible motions.

"Impossible!" Uncle Michael cried out. "There is nothing in this for me! For me!" And he tapped at his chest with his clenched hands. He refused to believe that this was all happening to him, that he had been pulled out of his comfortable life, thrust into a filthy prison camp for no reason at all, there was no justice in the world, no justice at all. And then, when he had been freed, what had it been for? No, he would not live his life out in this alien land where at every turn the customs outraged him and where his own child was being torn from him by the vulgar habits he had so carefully protected her from. Then his tone changed. "Margot," he said softly, "don't you remember how it was between us? The music . . . your skating lessons . . . the summers in the mountains . . ." He conjured up, brokenly, a lost world that still had meaning for him, a world of glittering restaurants and private lessons, of fur coats and hot house flowers, and the great sadness that came from his words as they fell without resonance into the spring garden was the sign of how lost indeed the world was to everyone but him.

Margot went up to him at the end, and all she could offer was pity as she told him, "What is impossible is you, if you do not understand. Lost is lost."

"You did not always believe this yourself," Pop reminded her. And only then did she turn away, crying.

Aunt Anna gabbled like a goose in German, explaining, imploring, exhorting. With a weary gesture, Uncle Michael pushed her away and lay back in his chair, eyes closed, muttering. "Is it so difficult a thing to ask one's father for permission to go out?"

Then, as if she had not been brushed aside before, Lia firmly went up to him. "To ask anyone else for permission to go to a parade is absolutely demeaning," she said, "and if you were yourself, you would see this, I am sure.

It is what you have been through, you are a veritable hero, of course you are upset, but you would not wish to drive away whom you love, I am sure you would not," leaning forward to hold Uncle Michael's wrist and bend her head close to his.

Watching her, Elly fell in love. She could not stop looking at Lia, sitting on the edge of her chair, gesturing widely with her bony hands and nodding her head so vigorously that her loosely piled gray hair kept tumbling down. Without looking, she would pin it up again, each time more untidily than before. She gave the rest of them time to recover.

Elly and Margot helped prepare the meal and set the table on the porch. Mama stood looking out at the garden for a minute. "I never thought to see Michael actually human. But, you know, Anna says he was never another way. Poor man. Get out the borscht from the refrigerator, please."

"And isn't she so full of life?" Elly enthused to Margot; and that was it, Lia represented all that was life-enhancing, while Uncle Michael was the other way, someone wedded to rules and laws, which stood between a person and his own experience. She set the table without feeling ashamed of their Woolworth dishes and unmatched flatware; it no longer seemed important. The food, too, was life-enhancing, prepared with joy—brimming bowls of borscht with dabs of sour cream floating in them, the great loaf of dark bread, the platter of cold meat, and the dish of pungent goat's milk cheese surrounded by slices of onions and scallions.

"How happy I am!" she thought as they assembled around the table on the screened porch. She had seated herself across from Lia, the better to observe the weaver, and blushed when Lia caught her steady gaze and winked.

"You will see, Dr. Blum," the weaver said, "that you will be reborn, it should happen to everyone, don't you agree with me, it is a gift, goodness, am I right?" And she looked around the table at each of them in turn. Yes, everyone knew what she was talking about.

Pop spoke of his heart attack, and Baba of her trip to America, and Mama of moving to the farm. Aunt Anna remembered leaving home and marrying, leaving Berlin, being afraid almost to death, and coming now into some new life whose outlines she could not yet see. Elly thought again of the play and of her summer job that would be starting soon in Willimantic. What would it be like?

A kind of peace settled over the table. They could hear the band music clearly through the soft night air filled with thousands of tiny stars floating above their heads. Not that anyone could forget Uncle Michael's words.

Elly and Margot walked Lia home, and Margot spoke of how she would have to fight—this was only the beginning—and worst of all, she did love her father; he was right, they had shared so much together.

"All he asked," said Lia, "was for you to give up your own life. Not so much—to him. Everything for you."

They paused to look down across town to where the band was playing in the park. Rows of small lights twinkled among the thick-branched trees, and the music of a Strauss waltz rose to meet them. "I shall go on my way now," Lia said. "Thank you for inviting me. This has been a splendid evening, too many like it would kill me, do you wonder why I live alone? There are too many people who want a piece of you, yes, we all fight these same battles, maybe we win, I don't know, good luck, come by whenever I'm not working, fare forward!" She waited.

"Nothing to say?"

Elly shook her head. She was content merely to watch and listen to Lia. How easy it had been to know her! Maybe Margot was right, and this was America; then hooray for it!

19

THE FIRST DAY there had been awkwardness between them during the long car ride from Franklin up and down the roller coaster road winding through the hills and passing right in front of the Josephs' farm on its way to Willimantic. After Mrs. Wilbur explained what she expected Elly to do and Elly croaked a nervous answer, there was no more to say. Elly stared at the dusty day already putting on its July glare before the sun was visible behind the pine trees.

A few hesitant stabs at conversation had been disastrous; what had they in common but the play? The drama teacher, it turned out, was a Republican of no uncertain views, an enemy of British political and French cultural influence, and much agitated by the growing power in Connecticut of what she called the Romish Church. She could not bring herself to mention Roosevelt's name at all. This was said in ten minutes and left a long and uncomfortable silence, which Elly could not fill. She was puzzled by the two people who lived inside Mrs. Wilbur's skin: the narrow, corseted dentist's wife, and the woman flushed with enthusiasm over her work and generous with her friendship.

It was that second Agnes Wilbur who came to life as soon as they entered the white frame house that served as the drama department, and she began at once to draw the dozen or so ill-at-ease teachers into her plans for the summer's work. "No need to waste time, we've got too little of it, anyway. Elly's my assistant, she'll handle all the details, we've got *plenty* to concentrate on."

Elly's first job was to make coffee for everyone. While she waited for it to perk, she explored the ramshackle house with theatre posters taped to its yellowing walls and closets crammed full of costumes and props. Her work was absolutely at the bottom; nevertheless, she cherished it, at least during the early weeks. She was to make sure there was always lots of coffee, wash the cups, empty ashtrays, get the sandwiches for lunch, clean up after rehearsals, keep track of the scripts, and make certain any changes were incorporated in all of them, make a listing of costumes and props needed for *Twelfth Night*, and in general, anticipate Mrs. Wilbur's wants and needs. Later, when rehearsals began, she would feed cues and take the parts of any of the cast who were absent.

She ran around town looking for restaurants and laundries; she checked the catalogs of the town and college libraries and made arrangements to borrow the necessary books, then loan them out to the students; she ran upstairs and down and washed endless cups with an alacrity she had never shown at home; and every minute was precious to her. This was *the theatre*.

There was so much to talk about on the ride home! Mrs. Wilbur lamented the stiffness of the teachers who were her pupils and admitted that high school students were looser, more imaginative, far easier to work with. She pointed out the deficiencies of each person, her remarks without malice, yet so accurate that Elly, who thought her powers of observation quite sharp, was dismayed by all she had missed of nuance and gesture.

It was a shock each day at four o'clock to open the door at home into another world—Baba in her crisp housedress making supper in the hot kitchen, Uncle Michael in his immaculate white suit reading Goethe on the porch, his elegant legs crossed, the fingers of one hand twitching, Aunt Anna struggling with her English grammar book. Even the smell of the two houses was different: the drama department was coffee and grease-paint and musty old clothes; while home was soapsuds and linoleum and chocolate and potatoes. In Willimantic, everyone ran about frantically; here all was somnolent, as if no one had moved since morning.

Of course, they had moved. Mama and Pop were at the store, where Pop could work until one if he then walked slowly home to take an afternoon nap. When Elly came home, he was generally in the garden, stretched out in a deck chair, humming to himself. Phil was working in the library and Margot was—

Well, that was the rub and the reason why, after two weeks, Elly became dissatisfied with the work she had looked forward to with such enormous expectations. Margot was almost always to be found at Lia's house.

Elly was restless for other reasons. "It's basically so boring!" she told Lia one afternoon, as the three of them sat on the back step drinking strong tea from thick pottery mugs made by an English friend of Lia's.

"The patio will soon be finished, your friend Quinny is doing a good job, or so it seems, I must send him home at three, he comes at seven, imagine! Outdoor furniture and yes, an umbrella, too, don't you think so, Margot? Then we won't have to sit on the back step any more."

They didn't mind. The yard was shaded by two old

plane trees and a thick wall of lilac bushes, their leaves a juicy green. Even in the July heat it was cool and fresh. A puff of wind twisted gently through the papery leaves of a clump of birches at the far end of the yard and made a rustling sound in the ivy. The stone step was chilly beneath them.

Lia had completely transformed the house, painting the rooms stark white and staining the floors dark brown. The walls held large, bright abstract pictures of a kind Elly had never seen before, although, to her mortification, Margot knew of Kandinsky and Mondrian. And Klee. "Who are they?" Elly had asked, and Lia tossed a book to her, but it was in German, and besides, she had no time to read it. Stupid pictures!

"It eats up your whole life," Elly complained. "Sitting around, repeating, rehearsing, then in the evening I've got to go over all sorts of stuff for the next day, and there's no time for anything else."

Anything else. What more did she want? Didn't she have what she had wished for—a job in the theatre? Not much of a job, to be sure, and hardly in the theatre, yet it was a start. What was wrong? She was disturbed by her own restlessness. It was the same as the move to town, which she had yearned for with such passion. What had changed? Living in town, she still wished for something more, without knowing what she wanted. It was a problem, no doubt about it, and she was a little ashamed of herself for her inability to rest happily with what she had. It seemed to her a flaw, a defect in character, that only she had. All around her people were reasonably content; at least, she *thought* they were, by and large. Had anyone else ever had such feelings of dissatisfaction? What was wrong with her?

The questions itched at her like so many mosquito

bites; scratching brought no answers. But she knew she wanted one thing, to see more of Lia. And how was that to be arranged? She had only these few minutes every afternoon to be in Lia's house. Margot was there all day, learning how to weave, working on the smaller of the two looms Lia had set up in the spacious studio. Laura's old room was now a storeroom, crammed full of bundled wool, pieces of looms, cans and bottles and tubes and packages of dye, and great pots for the dyeing. The kitchen had been transformed, hung with copper saucepans and black iron skillets, smelling of fresh herbs and the yogurt Lia made for herself. She said that she lived on yogurt, salads, soups, fruits and nuts, and tea.

There was very little furniture in the dining and living rooms, but that little had been made by another friend of Lia's, a cabinetmaker who built very simple pieces whose wood surfaces shone like silk—a light table, four chairs and a dresser in the dining room, a low table, a pair of rocking chairs, and a bench piled high with pillows in the living room. Lia had woven rugs for the floors and curtains for the windows.

However, she really lived in the studio, her narrow bed tucked into a corner and covered with a blanket she had woven, books piled on shelves and heaped on the floor, her clothes in an antique chest, and more pillows—enormous ones—covered with weaving done by Lia's students, tossed on the floor for lounging and reading.

Elly had a precious few minutes to find a book while Lia went over the day's work with Margot, explaining what went wrong, introducing new ways of weaving, comparing one technique or fabric with another. She couldn't help listening while she leafed idly through books that would have gripped her at any other time, but now couldn't compete with the scene, so painful for her, of Margot's and Lia's intimacy. That warm, bubbling voice of Margot's—when had she ever used it for Elly? All her reserve was gone as she talked to the older woman.

Not that Elly was at all interested in weaving; no, the truth of *that* was just as painful to recognize. It was another limitation, like her disinterest in mathematics or science or Mama's garden. What she desired, passionately desired, envied Margot for having until she was almost sick with jealousy, was the closeness.

So she complained about the tedious work in Willimantic, looking for attention and sympathy, sorting out her feelings as she talked. Margot looked at Elly absently, a half-smile on her tanned face, and flexed her tired fingers, leaning back against the clapboard house if they were outside or the white wall of the studio, speaking contentment with every line of her body.

"It's not the work I mind," Elly made clear, "but the uselessness of so much of it, because the cast is just dreadful! Do you know what I mean? These are teachers, and they can't remember lines, can't walk, can't sit still, can't speak. How will I ever be able to respect a teacher again? And Mrs. Wilbur goes over and over and over the same things." Elly sighed. "It's not what I imagined at all." Would anything be?

Lia laughed and put out a wrinkled, brown hand to touch Elly's knee. "That's the way it is," she admitted, "nothing's what we imagine it to be, isn't that the worst thing of all about growing up? *I* always found it to be, and so I carry my world with me on my back, like a snail or a turtle," and she gestured at the room, "and I play make-believe a lot. Now, tell me more about this dreadful day."

Yet, just as Elly believed she had Lia's attention focused fully on herself and her problems, Lia dismissed both of them and reminded Margot, "About ten tomorrow, I think." Once she said to Elly, "I like this girl very much. She can be silent for many hours. Much to think about, eh?"

Ah, that was rubbing it in! On the way home Elly said sourly, "Lia talks so much herself and so fast, what does she mean about being silent?"

Margot's face glowed. She too liked to talk about Lia. "Not when we're working. Then it's only to show me what to do. Even when we eat lunch. She puts some records on the gramophone—what do you say, phonograph? —German songs, mostly, and we eat quickly, which is not hard to do when it is maybe two slices of whole wheat bread with honey and an apple!"

Elly tried to make the lunches in Willimantic seem fascinating, lingering on the smell of coffee, the thick meat sandwiches, and the issues of *Theatre Arts* magazines she read with its articles that made her lose her appetite with excitement and envy. A few more pounds gone, and she would be almost as thin as Margot.

And yet . . . and yet . . . it was not enough. Her reports at home sounded increasingly hollow to her, and she pushed away Mama's and Pop's questions, only wanting to think about Lia.

It was better when rehearsals began during the third week, for she knew the play almost by heart, and increasingly Mrs. Wilbur turned to her to demonstrate how a line should be said or a movement completed. Coming home in the car, the teacher did not praise her, spoke very little, in fact; they were both exhausted from the heat in the house, barely kept at bay by two large fans, and Mrs. Wilbur was hoarse from five hours of talking. Words were not necessary, anyway; Elly could tell the difference.

Still, she was not satisfied. If only Laura were here to share it with! She had written to Laura and received no answer. Every night she reread a page or two in Laura's diary, nourishing herself on Laura's descriptions of her dramatic character, but that only pulled her back into the past, and the past was no use to her, it had swallowed its own tail.

Every Saturday she went to the movies with Quinny, then for an ice cream soda at the drugstore, and he was dear to her. More than dear. The truth was, she looked forward more and more to his kisses and embraces; even the remembrance of his hands cupping her face as they kissed could make her blush and grow warm. Yet she would no more tell him her thoughts than she would talk to a lamp post.

She tried keeping her own diary, then let it drop and took to spending her evenings on the porch, supposedly reading Granville-Barker's essays on Shakespeare's plays, which only confused her, so that she drifted into a reverie, swatting flies and listening to the desultory conversation of the adults in the garden. Too hot to sleep until late. Fans whirred, hoses sizzled over lawns, the sun abruptly dove into the great pool of night.

Baba left toward the end of July. She and Elly had been sharing the tiny middle bedroom for two months, an unhappy arrangement. "No person's fault," Baba said. "Just to tell me I must be on my way where I belong." She played a final game of pinochle with Pop, spent a day at the Tolstoy colony in Newchester, scrubbed the house, packed her small bag, and walked down to the station to wait for the evening train one

Thursday, surrounded by people who loved her. She was hot, and she was tired, and she had no advice to give anyone, she said.

"One word maybe," she added, and they all laughed. "Sonya, my dear, think carefully what you decide for the good of all. My blessing on each of you, yes, even you, Philip, you shall never be too tall to bend for your grandmother." She walked toward the platform. "Ten minutes. So soon. Will it be on time, Leo?" Elly walked with her. "Write to me if you like, I enjoy to hear from you. And if you want to come, come. For you there will be room."

"I'm sorry you're going."

Her grandmother pinched her cheek. "Nonsense! So much you have on your mind you float in a dream and do not see even the food you eat!" She put a folded bill into Elly's hand. "For your movie magazines," she whispered. "You have been so much better to your mother; I like that. She has much to decide, am I not right? Where to live." Her eyes twinkled. "Apparently a weighty problem, no matter what Jesus says about sparrows and lilies."

That's what the discussions in the garden had been about, which she had barely heard, so preoccupied was she with her own absorbing world. Decisions, changes, possibilities. Baba's leaving signalled a breaking up of their old way of life for good, and Phil the next to go. And the Blums. And then . . . ? What would happen to the three of them? To her?

"Why not stay right here?" she asked Pop. "Downstairs?"

"We don't want to make any decisions until Michael finds a place," Pop explained. "So don't press, all right?"

Press? *She* wasn't pressing—hadn't they noticed she

had changed? Now all the restlessness about moving was in the others—they were like birds perching on a nest and ready to fly.

Uncle Michael went to New York with Pop at the end of July, then Pop went back with Mama. Elly could not remember a time of such disorder; her life had always been surrounded with order, fields, good food, and clean clothes. Turning against this order to fight for something else, she had not realized how uncomfortable it would be to have what she wanted. She was finding out on all fronts what happened when your wishes came true. To come home at four o'clock full of *her* day, *her* news, and find no one home. No snack laid out. No supper prepared. And Margot at Lia's.

The heat clawed at her as she walked down the hill and up again to the Green, already disheveled after her quick shower and change of clothes, her mind on the problems of *Twelfth Night*. The play had been a mistake, Mrs. Wilbur admitted. A disaster. The teachers could not loosen up for the scenes between Toby Belch and Andrew Aguecheek. Impossible. And failure was making Mrs. Wilbur short-tempered. She snapped at Elly. That was bad enough. What was worse was sitting through the rehearsals day after day and listening to the play being torn to shreds, the beautiful lines hobbled, the humor destroyed, the joy leeched out of it.

"It's awful," she told Lia and Margot, "simply awful! And I can't get away."

"No," Lia agreed, "not at ten dollars a week and a commitment, but that's the way of the theatre, you know, it's not genius, genius all the way. You've got to love the theatre itself enough to survive, I've got friends like that, a trifle crazy—are you a trifle crazy, too?—they played with Eva LeGallienne in her old Civic Repertory . . ."

"Oh, I read about that in *Theatre Arts*!" Elly exclaimed.

Margot had seen Max Reinhardt's theatre. Lia had seen Louis Jouvet and the Pitöeffs in Paris. They talked about the Wagner Festival at Bayreuth and the Mozart Festival at Salzburg, impressions snapping back and forth between them in German and English. Elly had *read* about it all—God bless *Theatre Arts*!—yet how little the reading counted right now. When, when, when would she get out of here, move on? 1941! How to survive until then? The old malaise swept over her. Her hair twisted out of its band and curled damply around her face.

She groaned and rummaged for a book, dreaming of an austere theatre, a small theatre, that would look much like Lia's studio, the Elly Josephs Theatre, where she would present only the best plays with the best casts before a specially chosen audience and would not allow high school teachers in. Lia could weave the curtain . . .

She picked up the book because it was in French. She would show them what she could do!

She read: "*L'ancienne Comédie poursuit ses accords et divise ses idylles: Des Boulevards de tréteaux.*" Harder than she thought. Nevertheless, the pieces began to fit together. She looked at the cover. Rimbaud. "*Les Illuminations.*" "Look at this. Listen!"

She read with exaggerated emphasis: "Ancient comedy pursues its accords . . ."

"Harmonies," Lia interrupted.

". . . pursues its harmonies and divides its idylls:

Boulevards of . . . tréteaux. I don't know that word."

How much better she felt when neither Lia nor Margot knew it either!

"French dictionary around here somewhere in that pile, be careful, old book, falling apart, *there* it is!"

Elly read, "Trestle, stage. Boulevards of stages. How gorgeous!"

She was caught up in the next mysterious sentence, pronouncing it to herself in French, then struggling with the meaning. So many unfamiliar words! They beckoned her to follow, like a low, haunting sound from a deep wood. The exact translation wasn't enough; there was more to be grasped, more than she could imagine. She forgot *Twelfth Night* and Mrs. Wilbur's red face and the conversations between Lia and Margot. "Oh, how beautiful this is! And I don't even know what it means!" She laughed at herself.

"You want it? Take it," Lia said. "Tell you what. When's your work over? Middle of August. Well, I won't be here then, I'll be in Maine teaching at Skowhegan. September. Yes. Why don't you try to translate some of the poems, then we'll go over them together, see what we can come up with? You'll find this isn't like the theatre, you know, Elly. No groups, no company, no excuses—it all depends on you!"

She placed the thin book with its rumpled paper covers and ragged edges in Elly's hand, and Elly took it with Lia's warmth still on it and felt better able to cope with the supper preparations with that book as a talisman in her pocket.

"And this, too," Margot said, shoving a long white roll of heavy weaving toward Elly. "You must to help . . . must help . . . if you will. Oh, Lia, we thank you for this most magnificent gift!"

"What is it? Not a rug?" Elly asked, staggering with the weight of it. "We could use a rug."

"When we are home, you shall see," Margot teased, and they walked together with their ungainly burdens through the late afternoon heat haze that veiled trees, houses, and the sky.

"Hammocks!" Phil exclaimed after supper. "Now where did they come from?"

Lia had woven them, Margot said, years before, as part of a sample order for the Navy, and had come upon them when she moved. "They are a gift, she said, especially for you, Uncle Leo, for she likes so much your store."

It was not Pop who used either of them, however, once Phil had put them up, each one swung between a thick tree and the top of the fence, gleaming whitely like enormous moths as night came on. Elly rocked gently in one, the French book lying open on her stomach, and Margot lay in the other, head resting on her arms, both watching the stars glittering above them and the moon rising in the sky like a fingernail.

They talked about Lia, Margot speaking eagerly of how much she had learned about fabrics and even more, about the attitude one should take to work. "It is funny," Margot said, "that only when we are about to leave, I begin to see your mother better. But Lia has shown me how it is the attention we must pay to what we do that counts and not the effect or the glory, which is nothing to us, not part of us at all, only from others. And I was looking at your mother one day in the garden, then cooking, I don't know what, I do not much care for food, and I saw her absorption, like Lia's, and it all fell away, my dislike."

"Umm," Elly said, "very nice. But so moral. Isn't

there more? Isn't just *being* with Lia so . . . enriching? Do you think I want to be an actress for the glory? Oh, God! I thought I liked the *work* . . . and I don't know. Oh, listen to this: *J'ai embrassé l'aube d'été.* I have embraced the summer dawn. Isn't it beautiful?"

She settled into a comfortable position in the hammock. The scent of the nicotiana flowers overwhelmed her. Not to talk, not to think, not about tomorrow or life or moving. Or anything. Just to sway back and forth forever as the sun went down.

20

THE SECOND TRIP to New York had done it. "Wait until after the news, if you please," Uncle Michael said the day of his return, carefully washing his hands before supper. "After being once more in a grand city I feel here cut off from the world, not even a decent newspaper. Oh, such papers we had in Berlin!" He stared past the garden wall. "At least the radio news is a help, and this I shall not miss." He did speak a little of New York while they waited for seven o'clock, and a faint smile actually lingered on his face as he described the vitality of the streets and the excitement in the air. "No matter what, there is nothing like a great city."

According to the announcer, everything was peaceful, the summer was calm and hot all over Europe, President Roosevelt was vacationing at Hyde Park, Congress was in its summer recess; the only curious bit of news was the meeting of German Foreign Minister von Ribbentrop with Soviet Foreign Minister Molotov.

"Two rats at the same grain barrel," Phil said.

"May they bite each other's heads off," Pop added.

"This would be the end for millions," said Uncle Michael. His news was trivial next to that item, so casually dropped in as if it mattered not at all, when the world might be changed by it. In their bland summer unconcern, even the radio newscasters had failed him. A sport called baseball was far more important to them. Once more Uncle Michael summoned up the energy to condemn things American.

"Feel the electricity in the air," Aunt Anna said.

A sharp crackle of lightning flashed through the sky; another sizzled close to them. Static clogged the radio. Thunder sounded far over the mountains, and abruptly came closer. A wind sprang up swiftly to whip the tree branches left and right.

"The hammocks!"

"The windows!"

"Typical summer storm."

"Couldn't have come at a better time," Phil said.

Still the air hung thick and heavy, almost stifling them with its weight. A zigzag of lightning lit up the room, and the lights flickered.

"Better the kerosene lanterns we had at the farm," Mama said. "We had no worry in storms!"

"How dark it was on the farm," Elly said. "No, no, no! Electricity is better!"

"You never seemed afraid . . ." Mama started to say.

Uncle Michael drew in a deep breath. His fingers tapped on the table. Fresh coffee steamed in the cups. "This time something good has come in." He repeated it in German. "Already I do not believe it, I am turning into the refugee who expects only blows, and thinks all good fortune a lie. Nevertheless. There is such a place called Barnes Hospital, and it is in St. Louis. Yesterday in New York I am visiting a doctor, Friedrich Koch, who is at Mount Sinai Hospital, and he says this is a very good hospital and in St. Louis also is many German persons and a German community. Also a symphony, two universities, an art gallery, and many private schools. Then Leo is confirming all of this. So I have agreed to go there in September. And that is all I have to say."

A sigh of relief breathed into the room.

"Where shall we live? What shall we live on?" Aunt Anna wanted to know. "You never say, you never ask, you only tell. What shall we do? Is there an apartment for us? A school for Margot? *Mein Gott*, I cannot again pack up and leave for nothing, for nowhere; I am not even out of the house in six months more than a dozen times, I do not know anything."

And the rain beat down, drummed down, flooded down upon them, banging on the porch roof, pelting against the foliage, battering the windows, washing away grit and dust and heat, seeming to pull the clouds down with it.

Uncle Michael stared at his neat fingernails. "We shall have for a year one hundred dollars a month from the refugee committee I am to pay back when possible. And one hundred dollars a month from the hospital. I shall assist where it is not necessary to have a physician, in the clinic and the X-ray, while I study English and to pass the state medical exams. What is the state?"

"Missouri," Phil said. "Two hundred dollars a month? You'll get by, but not with much."

Mama calculated. "Ho! We have done it and more. Depends on the place you live. Margot already makes her own clothes for fall. Oh, you will manage, that is not bad."

"I have supported always my family in good style," Uncle Michael said stiffly, trying to hold on to his dignity, "so this shall be then enough."

"But to buy furniture," Aunt Anna said, "and linens, and dishes . . ."

"Anna, how important can all of that be now?" Pop

asked. "You have a future, that is no small thing these days—millions of people shall envy you, believe me. So you'll buy in Woolworth a set of dishes. It's more than you would have in a camp."

"For you this is easy to say, but . . ."

"Anna!" Uncle Michael said, and she subsided, sulking.

They would move in early September, he said. Less than a month from now. "And Sonya and Leo shall be happy to have us out of their lives, expense and all. This is no small thing they do."

Mama protested. Not Pop. He agreed with Uncle Michael.

The rain continued to pour down. With the windows closed, the house was stifling.

"I think St. Louis is pretty hot in the summer, too," Elly said.

Uncle Michael looked at her coldly. "Myself, I think a child has not an opinion on such matters as moving. Margot says nothing, which is as it should be. I have decided."

Elly turned away, hurt and furious. A person couldn't even make a simple remark in this house!

Margot looked up at her father, amusement written on her face, then let her long blond hair slide forward, partially obscuring her expression. She said nothing; nevertheless, her challenge was clear to see, and her father flushed.

When the rain stopped, she and Elly and Phil walked out into the dripping yard, brushing against leaves heavy with water and letting their bare feet sink down through the soaking grass into the mud. "St. Louis," she said. "Is it very far?"

"Halfway to California," Phil said. "You're not

scared, are you? After what you've been through?" He laced his fingers with hers.

"I thought there would be nothing here to hold me," Margot admitted. "From the first I thought only to get away." She laughed merrily. "With my father. Imagine!"

"Thank your lucky stars your father's got only two hundred a month," Phil said. "No private school for you. And he won't have time to keep after you, no matter what he thinks. Listen, kid, ride with it, that's my advice."

"At least you know where you're going," Elly said. "I still have to find out. Mama's said nothing at all about staying in town—oh, I'd *die* if we went back to the farm! Even Franklin'll be dull without anyone around."

"Except Lia," Margot said. "All yours."

"Except Lia."

No matter how exhausted she had been with those last desperate weeks of work on *Twelfth Night*, Elly had given a few minutes to that strange French book of poetry that did not rhyme or even fill the page in stanza form. She fought for each word and often enough found that the phrase or sentence still defeated her. "Brambles," she muttered, pushing her sweaty hair off her face as she opened the big French/English dictionary propped on her knees. "Like hacking a path through brambles." Pleased by the expression, she copied it into her journal. The page was spotted with corrections.

"Don't understand you one bit," Quinny said, as they walked out of the movies on Saturday, blinking in the bright sun. *Goodbye, Mr. Chips.* How romantic and how sad! How beautiful Greer Garson was! Elly's dreams of acting revived; forgotten the fiasco of *Twelfth Night*, forgotten the white-lipped rage of Mrs. Wilbur, forgotten her own doubts. How marvelous the world was!

"I think Greer Garson is my new favorite actress; isn't she wonderful? I can't get over her. Maybe the new *Modern Screen* will have something on her, let me look, okay?"

"There you go again, off on another one of your hayrides. I swear, you complained so much about this summer job I thought sure you'd be finished with that kind of nonsense now, and what do you do but get into something else. French poetry!" he said with deep scorn. "Now I ask you, what's that got to do with anything at all?"

"It's Lia's book."

"Great. I got nothing against her. I like her, in fact. Why shouldn't I? Earned almost two hundred dollars putting in her patio and fixing up the house. But do you really want to end up like her, a single lady living on nuts?"

Elly giggled in spite of herself. Then she had to protest. "That's not the way I see her at all!"

"Well, that's just what I'm saying about you, isn't it? But I can tell you, other folks in Franklin see her like I do, and you better believe it!"

"I do, oh, I do." No use saying any more. It was the same conversation they always had, and she rather looked forward to it and to their Saturdays at the movies to keep her from getting completely lost in the dark wood. There was always Quinny—and she did feel good about the way he continued to like her, no matter what he said. He noticed how thin she was and praised her clothes, and best of all, he was a real boyfriend who teased her and kissed her as often as he could.

He meant a lot to her; she plain *loved* the way they

walked down the street on Saturday, arms around each other, just like all the other kids. But it was Lia she had in mind whenever she thought about leaving Franklin and moving back to the farm. Something was in the air. Pop could drive again, and two or three times a week, he and Mama drove out after supper to look at it, coming back with the car full of fresh vegetables and Mama full of longing for the land.

"Mama, you can't stick me out on the farm again!" Elly cried.

"I am beginning to think Michael might be right about the opinions of children," Mama said. "You had all you wished this summer, and I said not one word to you about it even if you were no help at all in the house —none!" Then she softened. "The beavers have built their dam up again."

"Oh, damn the beavers!" Elly muttered. Which was no help at all.

Mama threatened to bar her from the room when Lou McGuire came to talk with them about the farm. At least he was coming.

"And at last!" she said to Pop one Sunday morning, as they ate a companionable breakfast over the *New York Times*. No one else was up and the morning was still damp and fresh.

"Well, it is your mother's decision," he remarked mildly.

Elly was disappointed in that. "But *you* are the one I'm counting on, Pop. Mama would stay on that farm forever!"

"You think so? Possibly. I am not able to do such hard work any longer. You think she does not know that?"

Elly cut in. "It should be *your* decision then!"

Pop sipped his coffee and a smile wrinkled his face. "It's Sonya's farm. Imagine you, my dear, if I told you what you should love or study or make of your life? Well, then, why should I tell your mother what to do?"

"Only it's different, don't you see? It's your life, too!"

"What's left of it," Pop said. "I don't like quarrels any more. Michael wears me out. Anna wears me out. You too start wearing me out. Sonya is very restful. Why shouldn't her choice be mine? To impose myself like Michael does—this is very distasteful to me. So I'm not much of an ally for you, am I?"

It was the first time she had been willing to admit a sign of weakness in her father. And weakness was what it was. She excused him—there had been the heart attack—and that was some comfort. Not enough. He had always been quiet, leaving the decisions to Mama, letting Mama discipline Elly and Phil while he received the fullness of their love. Yes, that was true, she could see it now; it was another step on her road of growing up, and she knew she would never be able to see him quite the same way again.

If Pop was not to be counted on, *she* would have to stay. Phil announced he was taking Margot to the movies that very night. "Look, Mama, if you want my opinion, I'll give it to you. I don't like the farm, it's too much work; I don't get any spiritual benefits from it, if that's what you call them; and I don't care. But I'm not going to be around much . . . who am I to say anything at all?"

Having given this speech, astonishingly long for him, he refused to say more and urged Margot out of the door with him the minute supper was over. Uncle Michael glared at them and muttered after they left. He and

Aunt Anna would sit in the kitchen and play pinochle. "Like servants," he said; no one rose to his bait. Mama sat alone reading the Gospels.

There was time for Elly to sit on the front steps and watch the day retreat against darkness, a little earlier now than last month. Although the heat still blistered each day, autumn was surely coming. Where would they be? The middle of August and still they rested in limbo.

There was time for the news. "Lou's going to be late, Sonya," Pop said. "As usual."

What there wasn't time for in the middle of this calm ending of an August day was the sudden shock, like an electric current, that the news delivered. Confirmation of the Nazi-Soviet Non-Agression Pact. Uncle Michael and Pop stared at the radio as if it were responsible for the treaty, not merely for the reporting.

"This is the war," Uncle Michael said, lapsing into German. "The others are trapped." He slumped, defeated, exhausted, pushed back from his positions of newly acquired strength.

Aunt Anna's little screams muted into cries of hysteria as she called the roll of their friends who were doomed. Beate Rosenthal, Bruno Frosch, the children—all the many children. The Rimskys, the Fragers, Martin Goslar and his Anni. It was the end. The end. *Das enden.* The German syllables clung to the ear.

And none of it seemed real. That was the worst of all.

"How we dreamed of socialism," Pop said softly. "So long ago. The revolution . . ."

"The revolution is a whore," Uncle Michael said, clipping off his words. "A diseased whore that spreads its disease to all who touch it."

Mama came out of her trance to say, "Such language!" and the bell sounded. Without waiting for an answer, Lou McGuire walked in, mopping his head and saying, "Sonya, would I take a drink? You bet I would!"

"Then it must be iced tea. You know we don't drink in this house, Lou. And you drink too much."

Mr. McGuire brushed off the news. "Ah, what's the war to us here? We had any sense, we'd stay clear out of it. Of course, with that loon in the White House, there's no telling . . ."

"Lou," Mama said firmly, "in this house, we do not speak of the President that way. And if *you* had any sense, you wouldn't do it, either. You don't seem to be suffering from him!"

Mr. McGuire laughed jovially. "Oh, I make out, Sonya, I make out. Can't say it's easy, though. How're you, Elly? Seen Rob lately? Just about persuaded him to come in with me—car of his own. Not bad, eh? Thank God that girl left town, worst possible girl for him."

Now Elly was angry. "Laura was my friend." She remembered Laura and Rob locked together in the woods—a picture burned on her mind. So what? "I miss her—why shouldn't Rob, now that he's stuck in this stupid town?" She felt panicky; how quickly life dumped itself on you! She didn't want to begin working right now, nor even next year. Poor Rob! So his father wouldn't let him go to college—what use was all that money then?

Mr. McGuire recovered quickly. "You're too sharp to be taken in by all that art nonsense," he assured Elly. "You're like your mother, good head on your shoulders." He moved smoothly into business, spreading his papers out on the coffee table in the living room, taking off his jacket, drinking from the tumbler of iced tea, and drawing Elly and her mother into his complex network of deals, mortgages, options, land values, and fair market prices. How much, Elly thought in despair, rests upon money!

Mama listened, nodding, until he had finished. "This hunting club that wants the land, what will they do with the house? And the farmyard?"

"Knock 'em down, I should think, Sonya. Be reasonable—what could they mean to a hunting club? Sure, they mean something to you, I'll grant you that, it's your home, but you know yourself how much work needs doing to bring that house up to par."

"Yes, work," Mama said bitterly. "Tear down, like war does. And it's a solid house, Lou, we've put a lot into it. It's got electricity now. And we fixed up the storeroom—there're four good bedrooms now, the parlor, and a kitchen. Why a big family could . . ."

"No central heating," Mr. McGuire pointed out. "One bathroom. Wood stove."

"It's right on the main road," Mama parried. "Sound barn. And my vegetable garden!"

"What are you trying to say, Sonya?" he exclaimed in frustration. "Surely you can't keep the place up with Leo's health and Phil away?"

"I keep forgetting about Phil," Mama said with a little apologetic laugh. "I suppose I can't," she said slowly, pleating her skirt with nervous fingers.

Elly found the courage to look at her mother's face, then she had to turn away from the pain she found there. It was her own pain she came to, the pain of Laura and the failure of *Twelfth Night*, the pain of her uncertainty about herself and the future, the buried pain that had been stirred up when Mr. McGuire came in and she was reminded that even in Franklin, her home, Jews were not the same as everyone else, and she would have to think about this, too, not push it aside. "Mama, what if we kept just the house and the yard around it and sold the rest? How would that be for you?"

Her mother looked grateful. "I don't know," she said slowly. "I do not like the idea to see men come and shoot on that land. Rich men. To take such good land from farming to be the playground for a few—and to see this. Can you understand me?" she pleaded.

"What do you mean?" Mr. McGuire asked. "Why, a place like that'd bring plenty of business to the town, plenty of jobs. You'd be surprised what it takes to keep a place like that up. Food and services."

Mama considered. "Yes, Lou, that's probably true, you'd know about such things. How much money?"

"What I have in mind—this isn't a firm offer, remember—is along the lines of twenty-five an acre. Prime price, believe me, but then you've got good land. Now that doesn't include any of the farm equipment—you can sell that at auction, pick up another couple hundred dollars."

"Seventy-five hundred dollars!" Mama said. "Such a lot of money!"

"Mama, it's not very much!" Elly exclaimed, surprised. What figure had she been imagining? "For all that land and all the work you put into it. It's a shame to give it up for so little!"

Mama was amused. "So tell me, what do you want? Can't you make up your mind . . ."

"It's true, I guess—I can't! I like this house, too . . ."

"I thought," Mama said sadly, "the land would be for you and Phil. A home. And money, too, if you needed. We have no mortgage on it, you could always mortgage for money. What kind of mortgage you could raise, Lou?"

He looked uncomfortable. "Not much, Sonya. Maybe

five hundred. No more. You don't run it as a farm, remember. Your little bit of garden, the few animals—they don't count for much. And with so many farmers losing their land—you're lucky the hunt club wants your place. Hell, they could find thousands of acres foreclosed, buy them cheaper from the bank."

"But we got what they want," Mama said heavily, each word dragged out of her. "So lucky us."

"Oh, Mama, I don't want to go back, truly I don't—only I don't want it sold, either!" Elly wanted to know it would always be there, that was it, like her childhood, so that she could reach out her hand and touch it.

"Well, we can't have it both ways," her mother reminded her. "If we could . . . ! Tell me, Lou, how much is this house we live in? Or won't the owner sell to Jews?"

Mr. McGuire blushed, coughed, and fiddled with his tie. "Look, Sonya, I don't make policy in this town. I'm only a businessman—what do you want from me?"

Mama suddenly looked very weary. "Decency, Lou, simple decency."

He coughed again. "I do my best, Sonya, it's a crummy world we live in and someone has to pick up the crumbs. Ha! Ha!"

"Spare me your cheap philosophy, Lou. I know it's not your fault, nothing is anyone's fault. Is this house for sale?"

"I think I could persuade Leaghan to sell it. Fifty-five hundred—in that vicinity. Helluva good idea, Sonya. You could live downstairs, rent out upstairs, pay your expenses—why not?"

Money, thought Elly, it's all money, money, and nothing more. Mama's beliefs were better than that! And now she was being asked to go against them.

Mama nodded. "Me, a landlady. A Tolstoyan landlady." She shuddered.

Pop came in then from the kitchen, bringing them the latest news. "Kaltenborn says the Germans are ready to hit Poland with all they've got. And the Russians will go for the Baltic states. Bastards!"

"Leo!" Mama said reproachfully.

"So think of a better name for them, my dear. What have you decided? Shall we go to Armageddon at the farm or in town? Tell me."

"It's very hard, Leo." And she explained Lou McGuire's proposals while the real estate man nodded in agreement and complimented her on her understanding. "I wish I'd never heard of any of this! Besides, I know the Kocinskis would like the land, but all they offer is ten dollars an acre on a mortgage, and if milk prices fall, then where are we? With nothing."

"Where you always wanted to be," Pop said.

"For me, yes. But not for the children. And not for you—not now. I don't know. I don't know."

In the silence they could hear the radio in the kitchen, playing music before the news came on again at ten o'clock. In another place, the clouds could have been bombers; not here. All was safe.

Elly looked at her parents with great pleasure. She seemed to have waked up from a long dream and found herself in a strange room with these adults who were her parents. And what good people they were! They didn't believe in money, money, and nothing else, and that was an enormous blessing, she realized, after listening to an hour of Mr. McGuire's talk of money.

Quinny with his brave plans for an auto dealership and his gentle yet persistent mockery of *her* plans; Aunt Anna with her laments over lost silver and china and her hopes pinned on carpets and bedroom sets—they were no different, really. But Mama and Pop were; they had given her something good to begin with, and she could see and be grateful for that, at least.

Of course, there was no turning away from the reality of money. "Mama, how much does Phil need for school? He deserves it . . ."

"Umm, I think of that. How smart he is!" Mama said, beaming. "What did you think, Lou, of his speech at the graduation?"

Mr. McGuire reddened. "Well, I'll tell you, Sonya, all I hope is his brains do him more good than some guys I've heard of—right here in this town. Wiped out in '29, brains and all."

Mama chuckled. "So you didn't like what he said about war and freedom? Ho, you wouldn't! He's not wrong, though."

"One war for Europe was enough, believe me!" Mr. McGuire said with some heat. "Let 'em stew in their own juice, if you ask me."

Elly jumped up, surprised at her own passion. "What do you know about it? You're not going to have to fight, anyway. Why are you afraid? You don't know how bad it is—you should hear what my uncle says . . ."

"Enough!" Pop said sharply. His eyes twinkled at her. "Fortunately, Lou, you stick to real estate, not to politics. Something we should be grateful for. So, let's hear the rest of this scheme, Sonya. You satisfied now, Elly?"

She wasn't sure. "I thought it would be easier—and that we'd be richer," she admitted.

Mama laughed. "You don't think so much money is riches?"

Elly shook her head. "I don't know what I expected—Pop, remember the first time I talked to you? Gosh, it seems such a long time ago! But it doesn't seem like an awful lot of money to me. I mean, by the time we pay for Phil's college . . ."

"And give to Anna and Michael some money," Mama cut in. "Not to mention putting a little aside for *your* college . . ."

"What about buying a house?" Elly asked. "The way I figure it, we've run out of money already!"

"The question is," Pop said, "do we want to own anything more and take on a mortgage now?"

Lou McGuire coughed. "The first question is: do you want to sell the farm."

"I try not to think of that," Mama said sadly. "But of course, you are right."

There was a long silence. A huge moth dove into the lamp and bumped its wings on the bulb, then whirled to hit the bright center again and again. Each time it was thwarted. Each time it came back, drawn irresistibly to the bright glow.

When Mama spoke again, it was to Elly that she looked. "How unhappy I was that you lived in your dream, yet am I not the same? This was my dream, and I didn't see it. Maybe we are not so different after all, eh? Have you awakened?"

"I don't know what you mean," Elly muttered. "I'm not dreaming—and I'm never going to wake up!"

Mama smiled. "What can I say? It is taking me more than forty years. Leo, what do we do?"

"Never have I said a single word to you about the farm," Pop said. "This is yours, Sonya. Only this—to everything there is a season. One of your favorite texts, right?"

Mama bit her lip. "You make it harder."

"Oh, Mama," Elly said, "those were good days. Only

they're over now." She wished she could convey a little of what she felt, could physically bring into the room great chunks out of the past, like some play enacted in the theatre of her mind. Instead, all she could do was speak and wait in the breathless heat for the movement of Mama's mind to carry all of them forward with it.

Mama stood up and wiped her face. "This is good enough," she said, half to herself. "So those days are over —maybe with the depression, God willing." She peered out into the summer night. "Lou, what do you recommend? As a friend now—do I sell to the club or to Henry? I know you'll get a bigger commission from the club, and you can't resist money, but try. So?"

"Jeez, it's hot here! Let *me* ask *you* a question, Sonya —what do you want to do next? Live over the store, stay here, buy in Woodmont? Plenty cooler there."

"You can keep your Woodmont," Mama said. "For Elly, it's Yankeetown or nothing. And you know where that leads!"

Elly knew. Silently, she bade farewell to Yankeetown. Without a pang.

The fan whirred, lifting the heat slightly and circulating it through the room.

"It's going to be different now," Elly said quietly. "Just the three of us. In another month it'll be like nothing ever happened, they'll all be gone, and Phil away . . ."

"Just like a wind that blew through . . ." Pop said, smiling.

"Exactly! Yet so much has changed, don't you think so?" Elly turned to her mother. "Mama, truly I don't care. Truly." And as she said it, she knew it was true.

Mama looked grateful. "Lou, this hunting club will really make so many jobs?"

"Sure. Building. Maintenance. Game management. There's going to be a dining room on weekends and summers. Good for the land, too, they'll keep the cover, dredge the stream. No cutting of wood."

Mama smiled. "Lou, even if I believed half, it would be too good."

Pop squeezed her hand. "Sonya, we had good years. I would not take one of them back. This is no time to talk of memories, there'll be plenty of time for that, but they are good memories, good days. If I could do more . . ."

Mama read the papers carefully, then she read them again and handed them to Pop to read. Elly wandered restlessly into the kitchen, where Uncle Michael and Aunt Anna sat in silence beside the radio, bleached of all pretension. She couldn't be afraid of her uncle when he was like this; he and her aunt were simply two people facing a life for which nothing had prepared them and having to accept the ruin of all they had called their past. "Hello," she said; they did not hear her. Their hands rested, almost touching, on the oilcloth covering the plain table. She wandered back into the living room.

"It's done," Mama said. "Now Lou takes it to the lawyer for the club, and then we see. Meanwhile, we hold an auction for the farm equipment—Lou says in two weeks maybe; he'll talk to the auctioneer in Newchester. Money for Phil—yes, it is good to think of that."

"What we did for the children, Sonya," Pop said, "was good. Now we must do something more."

"Something for me and you," Mama said, looking at him. "Especially for you." But she asked for a few days at the farm before the sale and the auction, and it was decided that they would return to the farm—"See, at least, a little of summer there"—then come back to the house, see the Blums off to St. Louis, and think about a final decision.

"There's much to think about," Pop said.

"Moving slowly is the best way," Lou McGuire agreed, now that he had the signatures on the option agreement. "You know I'll be in touch. Any questions, just call!"

After he left, Mama and Pop went into their room, talking softly together. The House blossomed with silence and isolation. Even the ticking of the clock was muted in the somnolent air.

Elly walked through the velvet night to meet Margot and Phil when they came out of the movies and tell them all the news. It was over. Nothing else mattered. She thought drowsily of the war and the farm, of losses and stars. The sky was speckled with them and the moon had risen above the hills. By the time of the next full moon, she would be sixteen. And living in town. She'd ask for a bicycle; that too would be the start of something new.

21

SST, SSST, SWISHED the tall grasses. *Auguseptember* was in the music of the birds. The cicadas chirred *hot hot* in air as crisp as toast with the heat.

Elly lay without stirring in her old room in her old bed and let the familiar sounds and scents flow over her. September 3rd. Her birthday. They had been at the farm for three days; the auction would be tomorrow, Labor Day, assuring a good crowd; on Tuesday they would pack up and leave the place forever.

Faint noises came from the kitchen. Mama. Strange. Ever since she had signed the papers, Mama was gayer—lighter, somehow. She sang while she worked, and the worried look had vanished from her face, which shone the way it used to before Pop's heart attack. Could she really be so happy giving up her dream? Was there something else? What?

Animal noises sounded from further away. Who would buy the horses? Maybe Muller on the next farm. Old man Kocinski would come for the chickens today. What a blessing! And the goats would go at auction. Who would want that funny pair, Weber and Fields? Only someone who liked goat's milk cheese. Not Elly!

Never again would she sleep in this room on a Sunday, watching the sky lighten and the leaf-shadows from the maple swim on the white wall by her bed. Nevermore. "Quoth the raven nevermore," she said, mocking her own dramatics, and Margot abruptly woke up.

"Happy birthday," she said.

Then they were silent. They had less and less to say to each other these days. Since Margot had accepted the move to St. Louis, she had been detaching herself, strand by strand, from everything in Franklin that had become familiar to her.

"Imagine," she said, "if I think only of this place and the one I have left behind, my head shall be filled up with memories before I am twenty, and there will be no more room for what is new."

Elly stretched lazily. Sixteen. Back to Franklin on Tuesday. School in a week. Lia back from Maine. She had written a letter to Elly in French and one to Margot in German liberally sprinkled with errors. Lia had not forgotten them.

"She is yours," Margot said. "I give her to you, how is that? For your birthday."

"Mmm. Not yours to give," Elly said, braiding her hair into a single plait down her back.

"The friendship is what I give," Margot explained. "How hot already! Can I eat your ice cream and cake in shorts, do you think? I mean, I do not interfere. No letters."

"Aw, come on," Elly muttered, embarrassed, remembering Laura. "I'm not like that any more.

Margot turned over and buried her face in the pillow. "I shall be down soon. Soon . . . soon . . ."

Elly lingered. She reached out for the books on the floor beside her bed, her journal and a volume of plays by George Bernard Shaw. What if she could persuade Mrs. Wilbur to do *Pygmalion* this year! And a talent scout would just happen to see her . . . ha! *Not bloody likely,* she whispered, in Eliza's cockney accents. When she was alone and daydreaming, how very good she was!

She wrote in her journal, "Sixteen today! What will happen this year? There is the war, of course, but that's rather exciting in a way. What an awful beast I am, to write that. Honesty is my only guide, all else is folly and self-delusion."

For the war had come; it was two days old, a baby of a war hurrying to grow bigger. Pop had received a thick letter from New York two days ago and was going to speak about it when the news broadcast had interrupted with the words they had been waiting for, yet found such a shock. "German troops and tanks crossed the Polish border at dawn German time . . . Hitler said . . . Benes of Czechoslovakia pledged . . . in accordance with treaty provisions, England and France have declared war on Germany . . . Russia to remain neutral . . . Non-Aggression Pact . . . Roosevelt declares . . . is reported that Warsaw is being bombed by planes of the German Air Force . . . Lindbergh . . . isolationists in Congress warn . . . American neutrality . . ."

And more, much more. News in the morning, news at six, at ten, at eleven, newspapers with screaming headlines, analyses, speeches; trips to Willimantic to buy magazines, *Life* and *Time* and *The Nation* and *The New Republic* strewn about; and talk, endless talk, Pop and Uncle Michael and Phil talking away all of yesterday, bringing out maps, arguing about troop strength, disagreeing on England and France. At least it was quiet now. The sun still rose, and the farm still rolled away around the house. The war was only words here. And Elly was hungry.

"Get up, sleepyhead!" She tugged on her cousin's pillow. "Tell me I look beautiful!" She had lost ten pounds. Ten more to go. She fitted her new dress over her flatter stomach and hips. "Like it? I love the color." Buttercup yellow. With the sixty dollars she had earned, she would buy a brand-new fall wardrobe, every bit of it in Newchester. Next week.

"For you a good color," Margot said, propping her head on her raised arm, "for me a disaster." Margot's new dress was white with blue flowers; she looked dazzling in it. Elly glumly made her bed and left her cousin to dress alone.

Fresh morning air flowed through the house from the open windows downstairs. The scent of grass and flowers was overpowering, a mix of the slightly sour odor of the zinnias and the sweetness of the meadow, which smelled like bread rising.

"Many happy returns," Mama said, wiping her hands and kissing Elly. "I did not think sometimes we would live through this year but . . ."

"We didn't, Mama," Elly said. "We died and were reborn." She twirled around in the dress. "Thank you, Mama, it fits perfectly, and it's beautiful."

"Wear it in good health. You've got more gifts by your plate."

Baba's parcel had come in the mail. Elly tore it open, scattering paper all around her, deaf to Mama's cluckings at her slovenliness. "Mama, look! A Russian blouse—the kind I always wanted!"

Mama gazed at it with affection. "Hand embroidery. I hope you will not wear this for gym and come to me to say, 'Oh, I forgot, Mama, what I had on, can you fix it, please?' This I could not fix."

"Oh, I'll have it forever, isn't it gorgeous!"

Then she saw the other gifts. "The smallest one first."

It was tiny but gaily-wrapped and tied with a green velvet ribbon that looked like the trimming on one of Aunt Anna's hats. "Mama, come look!"

Mama drew in her breath sharply as she came to lean on the table and stare at the tiny leather jewel box lined with green velvet that Elly held out to her. She picked it up carefully, turning it over to show Elly that it came from Florence. "Italy. Yes, they travelled much there—then. It is too good for a child. And you are so careless."

"Oh, Mama, don't spoil it, please! Isn't it the most beautiful thing? Was it Aunt Anna's do you think?"

"Well, of course! Where does she have money to buy such a thing here? Or ever again maybe? Be sure to thank all of them."

"Umm. Now, what to put in it?" She'd have to show it to Lia when the weaver returned.

There were two other parcels that had come in the mail. Both small and flat. Books? The one from Maine first. Two parts. A finely-woven woolen scarf in shades of burnt orange, gold, butternut. "Lia!" It was wrapped around a book. *Le Blé en Herbe par Colette*. "My second French book! Soon I'll have a regular library of them!" The slip of paper said, *Félicitations de ton anniversaire. Peux-tu lire ce livre? À septembre!* It was enough. And there was the other brown-wrapped package. Postmark blurred. Who? Where? Inside a wrapping of tissue paper. "Ah, look!" A small drawing in a frame. Pen-and-ink. A cluster of daisies against grass. "Laura!" She had remembered! Furiously, Elly scrabbled for a card. Nothing. A note. Lost among the ripped tissue paper. "A souvenir of Franklin. P.S. Owen did it. P.P.S. Someday it will be worth thousands!" No signature. "But she remembered!"

The screen door slammed. "Chores all done," Phil

said. "You've no idea how happy I'll be to leave that barn behind. Hey, little sister, you haven't opened *my* gift yet!"

Elly was breathless. Another package, this one wrapped in a gay red-and-white paper tied with a big red bow. Another book? "Can't wait to see!" A small leather-bound notebook and a fountain pen.

"Nice, eh?" Phil said. "Spotted it at Vaney's in Newchester and thought you'd like it. Real leather."

"Vaney's?" Elly kept stroking the soft leather. Vaney's sold jewelry, fine leather, and silver; never had she thought to own anything that came from Vaney's. "It's so soft!" And just the right size to slip in her purse. "Thank you, thank you, thank you. Oh, Phil, *quels cadeaux! Quel jour!*"

"It is only just begun," Mama reminded her, "so calm down. Later you may have more gifts—patience!"

"It's enough," Elly said, admiring the gifts once again. "And all of them perfect." Mama and Pop would give her a gift at her party, the way they always did. "Where is Pop?"

He had taken the radio into the parlor and was rocking and looking out the window, his hands folded over his stomach, while the radio announcer gave out the details of the German destruction of Poland. Uncle Michael perched stiffly on the edge of the pine armchair, head cocked, as he listened and whispered to himself in German. "Fires throughout Warsaw . . . destruction of railheads . . . refugees fleeing . . . Americans coming out by boat before the port facilities in the Polish corridor are destroyed . . . reliable reports of Russian troops massing on the eastern borders of Poland . . . reminiscent of earlier Polish partitions . . ."

"Good morning, Pop," Elly said, and kissed him.

"Ah! A special morning, eh? And for a special daughter. Too bad the news is not more cheerful." He turned the radio lower and looked Elly up and down. "Pretty dress. Pretty girl." He admired the gifts with her.

"You look so *happy*, Pop!" Elly exclaimed, surprised. Her father's face was tranquil and rested; he looked better than he had in a year.

He chuckled. "All's well that ends well," he said. "Tell me, you think Phil's going to do well at college? Columbia University! Who could have imagined such a thing? And you? Where will you go when it's time?"

Uncle Michael turned the radio off, unplugged it, and took it with him to his room. Elly and Pop looked at each other in silent merriment, not daring to laugh.

"I don't know, Pop," Elly answered. "Everything's so confused—isn't it wonderful?—but I guess I'll try for the Neighborhood Playhouse in New York." There! It had been said!

"You'll change your mind," her father assured her. "A smart girl like you. Acting, pah! No, no! For fun, maybe; a hobby. You'll go study English, something nice like that. Maybe teach even. God willing, I'll live to see such a thing—two children both college graduates."

Once she would have argued; now she would let nothing spoil her day. "Is that why you're so happy, Pop? Because of Phil?"

"It's a wonderful thing to see. Me, a foreigner, a storekeeper—and a son a university student, a scientist." And Pop smiled his slow, secret smile again.

Elly smiled back. Pop had his dreams, too. Phil wasn't even in college yet, and Pop was already seeing him as a scientist. She squeezed his hand. "Mom made the dress. Oh, Pop, are you glad we're leaving? The last Sunday." She pushed any regrets out of her mind.

"Don't remind your mother. She does not wish to spoil *your* day. Understand?"

At breakfast she watched her mother as if she were studying a stranger. Mama smiled and laid the food on the table with an almost holy reverence, but she kept turning her head to look out the big kitchen window to the line where the washed-out blue sky met the hump-back hills rimmed with dry pines.

Eating, Elly felt herself sliding out of her skin, moving into her mother's body, seeing through her mother's eyes, washing up with the accustomed movements of her mother's hands. She felt the sadness of yielding her place on earth and then, slowly, the overcoming joy of freeing herself of the burden of earth and possessions, even of will and desire, of casting herself entirely upon the love of her family and of a God who always listened. She was shaken with an extraordinary knowledge she could hardly hold.

She looked around the table. Phil and Margot were calmly eating buttered toast and murmuring to each other. They sensed nothing, nor did she speak. No longer must she tell all she knew, spit it out into the air half-formed. She could let it ripen inside herself.

"Mama, do you know I love you?" she said, clearing the table without being asked. "Now let's get ready for the party!"

"Sssh," Mama said. "Anna is still sleeping—she is completely worn out with this move of *hers*." She handed Elly a towel. "Help me finish with the dishes. Then go read your book, why don't you?"

"Stay out of your hair," Elly said. "O.K."

Phil offered to take her to town with him when he went to buy the papers, but no, she would stay here. The last Sunday on the farm. There was a lot to say good-by to. Forgetting about her new dress, she walked through the dazzling heat of the meadow to the woods and up the path to the beaver lodge. There it was, built up again on its sturdy base. Splashes and ripples in the still, shallow pool showed that the beavers were in residence, but she could not see them.

Below the pool the once flashing ribbon of water was a muddy trickle without fish. Eventually it would dry up; already a small tree had been gnawed to lie across it, and the dirt at the edge of the swampy area puckered where it was drying out. What would the hunt club choose? Beavers or fish? Well, it was no concern of hers. She could not even sit on a tree stump and open her book; mosquitoes loved the shallow water and buzzed around her head.

How much hotter the meadow was! The tall grasses, yellow and dry, crisped beneath her feet. Albert Kocinski was coming by tomorrow to cut them for hay. The dirt she sifted through her fingers crumbled dryly.

Then she lay down in the rustling grass, closing her eyes against the shattering blue overhead, and said a final good-by to the fields. Not to the sensation of lying under the sun in the grass and smelling the special, slightly sour, scent of earth and hay. That would remain even without the fields.

Brushing off her dress, she skirted around the far side of the meadow to the creek that marked the western boundary of their land. The rocks and pebbles in the bottom were visible above the thin trickle of golden brown water that glided like a snake over its crunchy bed. She slid down the crumbling bank, grabbing onto tree roots, and squatted down to take off her shoes before curling her toes and stepping across stones to the center, where the water lapped around her ankles. Further downstream, the creek bent away toward the Mullers' land, deepening and widening to a swimming hole where the water was shaded by willows and alders.

They had gone there yesterday with a picnic lunch, Margot and Phil, herself and Quinny, who had hitched a ride out to be with her and give her a birthday gift—a small pottery bowl he proudly told her he had bought from Lia because he knew Elly liked such things. Today he would be working with his father over in Newchester on an emergency job paying double time, which he could not turn down, replacing doors and windows on a burned-out house.

No matter. She had said good-by to him, too. She'd see him again in town, of course. And like him. But not the same way. After swimming, they had been lying side by side on the blanket spread over the tussocky ground, wonderfully at home in their suntanned bodies, which were drying under the hot sun, shielded only by bathing suits. Phil and Margot had swum downstream to sit on the huge rock that humped up in the center of the creek. She could barely glimpse them through the willows, talking earnestly, their heads close together, their feet touching as they sat in the same postures, hands clasping their ankles, foreheads resting on their drawn-up knees. Phil liked Margot . . . how much . . . did she like him . . . she listened to him . . . how different they were . . . would they ever see Margot again . . . ?

And then Quinny was close to her, his arm on hers, and he was on top of her all at once, kissing her so hard it hurt, his body tensing and his legs pinning her down. Instinctively, she turned her head away and tried to slide out; he grabbed her wrists. "I'm not going to hurt you . . . just a real kiss, y'know what I mean. A real kiss after all this time. C'mon, Miss Prim." She shook her head violently from side to side. Said nothing. Her heart beat faster. Felt his heart keep pace. His rough face against hers. Not boy's face; man's face. Hard body. Man's body. Didn't want it. Not him. Never him! Not real kisses, not his tongue inside her mouth, rooting around inside her. Not his hand fumbling at her bathing suit straps, up her thighs. Not yet. Not now. *I'm not ready yet!* Oh, why had he spoiled the day?

She had closed herself up as tightly as she could, resisting, lips locked together, face turned away, legs flailing. And he cursed her! Sat up, ran, jumped into the water, swam away from her, dove underwater again and again, wouldn't look at her, wouldn't talk to her. How was it her fault? What he wanted—why should she want it simply because he did? Not now. Not yet. Lunch had been awkward, that marvelous picnic lunch spread out on the blanket, and when he left, they both knew it was good-by, even though he reminded her of their date for the movies next week.

Now she didn't walk downstream as far as the pool but turned back to where she had left her shoes. No, she wouldn't go to the movies with him; what was the use? If that was what he wanted . . . ! Once again the image of Rob and Laura together flashed before her in the glittering sunlight. How *could* she? Someday there would be love, *had* to be love, and love was . . . well, different, not this mechanical pressure of body against body. Not Quinny. Poor Quinny!

"Then I'll wait," she announced to the meadow, and stumped back to the barn, stopping to dry her feet on the grass and put on her shoes. Good-by to the garden, half-harvested, going to weeds. She skipped the chicken house. It plain stank in the heat, no matter that Albert Kocinski had freshly whitewashed it; good riddance!

The barn was last because of the horses. The goats were all right; strong-smelling, true, yet good enough animals. Hard to feel much affection for them, even though, when she was younger, they had followed her all around the barnyard, bells clinking on their collars, and let her stroke their backs. The cats were only barn cats, much of a muchness in their fluffy kittenhood and plump cathood, mewling and rubbing against her legs, keeping the barn clear of mice and rats and running like greased lightning to jockey for the best position at milking time. Good-by cats, she said, patting them; maybe Mama would let her take one with them when they left.

She fed the horses each a carrot with some oats, patted their noses and called them by name, listened to them nicker and whinny, then led them out into the upper meadow, which was partially shaded by a grove of butternut trees. They leaped and bounded, happy to be out of the barn, and in a minute had bent their heads to the grass. Once she had loved them more than people, but that had been a long time ago, and this year she had shamefully neglected them. And now they would go. "So be it."

Coming down from the meadow to the kitchen yard, she saw Margot leaning against the weathered fence, staring at the distant hills veiled in a yellow heat haze.

"Do you know," she said, "we are all the time here since January and never went up closer to those mountains? I do not even know their name."

"The Berkshires. They're only foothills."

"The Berkshires," Margot repeated. "Thank you." She paused. "I came to look for you. Lunchtime."

"Have I really been gone all morning? And never even opened my book! Look at it—Lia sent it to me. In French!"

The house was deliciously cool. "Will you look at yourself?" Mama asked, vexed. "Honestly, Elly, aren't you too old to make such a mess of yourself? Where have you been? Go wash your feet and put on fresh socks —and bring me a hairbrush while you're at it."

She fussed, but she helped, brushing Elly's hair until it shone, then deftly twisting it back and pinning it in a smooth coil at the nape of her neck. "See! *Now* you look like a lady!"

"At last, I look just the way I want to, at long last," Elly told herself in the mirror, admiring the dress again and the way its crisp yellow set off her tanned skin, admiring her hair tucked and pinned like a young lady's, admiring her thinner self.

Then she curled upon the sofa in the parlor with her new book and the French dictionary, falling in love at once with Vinca, the heroine, and lost to all the preparations around her until Mama shook her by the shoulder.

"Surely, you don't want to be late for your own party? Here, carry this down!" It was the cake, frosted in white and decorated with yellow piping.

"Mama, you're wonderful to take the time to make this when you've got so much else to do!" And Elly hugged her mother.

"This year is the last—sixteen is the absolute end."
and-white checked cloth and the cake rising in the
How bright the old picnic table looked with the red-
center!

Phil had turned the crank to make fresh peach ice cream. "You'll never taste anything better," he assured Margot and a dubious Aunt Anna.

A belt of shadow lay across the field from the oak tree as they took their places. Pop waited until everyone was silent, then held up his hand. "Our last Sunday here.

Possibly our last celebration together—who knows? May we meet again for many happy times, for birthdays and weddings and births! The future we do not know. But for the present we are all here, we are alive, we have survived, and I think that is enough to be thankful for in this crazy world."

Immediately, Uncle Michael began to talk of the war as they ate a picnic dinner of cold meat and salad. "You will see that Russia comes in . . ."

"Poland is the linchpin of the East," Pop said thoughtfully. "Without Poland . . ."

"Linchpin? What is that?" Uncle Michael asked.

"Leo, you never can tell," Mama said.

"Sonya, sometimes you sound like a fool! Look at the map instead of consulting only your wishes! I tell you, it is all over in the East. Now it is a question of the Maginot Line. Will it hold? And the spirit of the French . . . I wonder at that."

"You had better wonder at your President and what he will do," Uncle Michael said severely, like a schoolmaster.

"Will we never be finished with talking about the war?" Aunt Anna asked from under her wide-brimmed straw hat. "Today is a party day, there is a certain spirit here . . ."

"Oh, I don't mind, it's all fascinating," Elly said. When *would* they stop? The sun slowly moved westward, and long fingers of light striped the lawn.

"Fascinating is not the word I would use," Uncle Michael said ponderously, turning his head to take Elly into the conversation. "Nevertheless, I can remember 1914, when we were so eager to run off to war, like children to the circus. So I do not condemn, mind you. However . . ."

Margot looked up and giggled. "Yes, Vatti," she said, "yes yes yes yes." She caught Elly's eye, and the laughter spread. Then she leaned across the table and said in a stage whisper, "Would you believe that my dear father has said I may wear a touch of lipstick when school begins? In the new *Vogue* there is a marvelous color . . ."

Phil was teasing Mama. "No more pacifism, then, if your dear Roosevelt takes us to war?"

"Shame on you! I speak of the moral authority such a man has."

Phil chortled, tipping back in his chair. "Mama, you're such a child!"

"The time for moral authority," said Uncle Michael, "is past."

"And the time for talking about the war is also past," Aunt Anna insisted. "Tell me, Elly, you like our little gift? We have so little, it is not possible to do as I would wish to make a thank you . . ."

"Everything of yours is in such good taste," Elly said, thinking with pleasure of that tiny jewel box taken from her aunt's own treasures. Impulsively, she added, "And your English is so much better."

Aunt Anna dimpled. "With this war, now we will not return. I pretended—it is no longer possible. So, St. Louis, here we come! That is correct English, no?"

"Which reminds me," Pop said. "Will we have a small farewell performance from you, Elly? Some speech?"

"Oh, we're not going any place, Pop, are we? You've not said a word. Honestly, with all this mystery, it's like the week before Christmas around here. And the auction's tomorrow! I can keep my furniture, can't I?"

Mama's eyes sparkled. "Surprise!" she whispered. "In a minute. More cake, anyone? More lemonade? Take another piece, go on. Who knows when we shall all be together again?"

Uncle Michael opened his case, took out a cigarette, tapped it on the table edge as he always did, fumbled for his lighter, spun the wheel once, twice, then the flame flared up, and he bent his head to it, inhaling deeply as the cigarette caught.

"I asked for a bicycle," Elly whispered behind her hand.

"A bicycle! So costly, no?" Margot asked.

"It'll be wonderful in Franklin—what fun!" Elly said.

"I will never have a bicycle," mourned Margot. "Not even in Berlin. Mutti was afraid."

"Silence, silence!" Mama called, her smile dimpling in her sunburnt face. Stray wisps of hair escaped from her bun to blow idly in the slight breeze out of the pine woods. Gray hair, Elly noticed sadly. "You wanted a bicycle, I believe."

"Wanted? I *crave* one, passionately!"

"So dramatic," Aunt Anna murmured.

"So spoiled," Uncle Michael insisted, stamping away from the table to look across the slope of land to the ragged woods rimming the road.

"Well, never mind," Pop said. "A bicycle is not what you're getting, and for one good reason. We are not moving to Franklin."

Elly sat for several very long minutes letting the news register. It didn't make any sense. "What do you mean?" They had rented the downstairs flat for another month, hadn't they? "Are we going to buy another farm?" she asked in bewilderment. Maybe it would be closer to town. "Oh, Mama, you wouldn't! How could we begin all over again?" As she talked, she grew more and more agitated, trying to piece together clues and hints, shrinking from the immense labor of building up another farm, unable to understand what had happened to tumble her dreams to pieces. "Another farm?" she repeated. "A smaller farm?" Her hands shook and pieces of birthday cake scattered on the grass.

"Be sensible," Mama said, "would we have an auction if we needed all the equipment again? No, I think I am finished with farming forever. And maybe it is a good thing, eh?"

"I had from New York a letter," Pop said, "two days ago—remember?—and then there was the news about the war and so on . . . we decided to wait for your birthday to give you a special present we thought maybe you would like. I think we were wrong to keep this secret, make it a surprise."

"Yes," said Mama, "you are right, Leo. Elly is not a child any longer to keep secrets from." She leaned back in her chair and squinted into the sun. "Remember all these times of going to New York? I was surprised myself to see how often this year I am going!"

"How should I remember?" Elly grumbled. "I wasn't with you. I never get to go any place." The fork in her hand was steady again, but she had lost her taste for any more food.

Mama smiled and kept talking, ignoring her complaints. "We met there—waiting at the Immigrant Aid Society—an old friend of your father from many years back, right, Leo? Herman Gerstner." Pop nodded, drumming his fingers on the table.

Mama poured more lemonade for them, the ice clinking in the glasses. "This Gerstner owns a bakery, so we talked much of small businesses and the ending of this depression, please God. We took dinner at their place more than once." Mama smiled at the memory. "Fine people. Good people. To make a long story short, this Gerstner and his wife wish to live away from New York, she has hay fever and he has asthma, and he likes fishing and so on. They are not so dazzled by New York as you are, my pet! So we have agreed to this, to make a trade, that they will have the grocery with living above—poor Cummings family!" Mama said, catching her breath, "—and we shall have his shop with the flat above, and it will be much easier on Leo as there are already bakers working, and I shall make some of my own things and we will manage. Why not? It is a fine shop with good trade—rich people, doctors' wives . . ."

Elly heard no more. "New York! We're going to live in New York? I'm dreaming, oh, tell me I'm dreaming! Am I dreaming, Pop?" She squeezed his arm.

"Not New York exactly," Pop said. "Watch it there, I'll be black-and-blue. Brooklyn. On Flatbush Avenue, right near the park and botanic gardens, so Sonya will not be so shut away from growing things. So for what do you need a bicycle in Brooklyn next to a subway station? Instead, we can buy all new furniture for your room."

Elly had forgotten about the bicycle. "Why didn't you tell me? Phil, did you know? Is it near Columbia? What's it like? Tell me everything!"

"So be quiet!" Phil said, grinning. "I'm an utter innocent—after all, it's not *my* birthday."

"A nice place," Pop said. "Now, don't you go expecting anything rich. That it's not! A few tables for coffee and lunch besides the bakery, a good trade, like Sonya says. It's a living, at least." Elly could tell, however, that he was deeply pleased.

"So *that's* why you were so happy this morning!"

"This is marvelous," Margot said. "I shall come to pay a visit to you when I learn to be a couturière." She was lapping up the last of the ice cream in her bowl, her red tongue going in and out, her blue eyes peeping over the rim, and Phil was staring at her with complete absorption. "You will not go away to school then—or not so very far away, am I right?"

"Ah, I don't mind," he said. "Living at home'll be cheaper, this year at least. Then . . . we'll see. I'll study on the subway. I can help out, too, you know in the bakery. We'll work it out. It's all the same to me." He never took his eyes off Margot.

"Fifty dollars a week free and clear is all I ask," Pop said. "And no more heart attacks. A brisk walk in the park, the newspapers, the radio, once in a while the movies—eh, Sonya, when have *you* last gone?"

"Yes," Elly went on, "I'll be able to go to the theatre all the time, won't I? What will it be like . . . oh, I can't imagine. I don't want to think about anything else. I'm so happy!"

The dark green hills rose gently from the pale green and straw-colored fields. A few puffs of clouds marked the blue sky, dotted with chicken hawks bobbing like leaves above the updrafts.

She would remember this scene, every bit of it, forever! That book Mrs. Wilbur had given her—*Of Lena Geyer*—came into her mind, with its visions of New York and opera and the glory of art. She wanted to be alone to digest the news. To leave Franklin—and all at once she saw what that meant—to leave Mrs. Wilbur. To leave Lia! Maybe she wouldn't even have a chance to see them, to tell them. To leave Lia! She walked up the hill from the oak tree past the house, taking the path to the barn and the upper meadow. Her face burned when she thought of the book and scarf Lia had sent. They were going to work together all winter on the French! No more.

The horses grazed peacefully in the field, lifting up their heads as she walked past, then bending them once more to the grass. All gone. The whole old way of life. Like one of those cloud puffs in the sky.

"Well," said Phil, "you've got what you wanted," and she jumped. He and Margot had come up behind her, shading their eyes against the sun blazing from the west before it settled behind the hills for the night. "Pleased?"

She nodded. "Umm. In a way. Only . . ." She held out both hands, open. "I used to think there were really happy endings—just like in the movies. But there aren't, you know."

"I know, I know!" he said. "Congratulations for finding out!"

"Well, now I've got to get used to that idea. It just goes on and on. Do you know what I mean?"

"Oh, make sense," he grumbled.

"I think I understand," Margot said. "A little. Already I jump over St. Louis and think of something more. But what?"

Elly nodded happily. "But what? Oh, I do feel good, you know!" She pointed to the table set out under the trees. "Look at them—still sitting there."

"All talking at once," Margot said, "and no doubt, of the war."

"How small and far away they look," Elly said. "How very far—just like the war. Who could believe it on such a day? Phil, doesn't it seem as if we're as remote as the stars?"

"Hah! Don't you know what a madhouse we'll have tomorrow? Margot, you've never seen an auction! Some remote! Some star!"

Elly ran a little way down the slope toward the house. "Oh, tomorrow," she said. "Tomorrow!" It could be a hundred years away. Today was today. "I'll be right back," she called to Margot and Phil, but they didn't hear her as they walked across the big meadow to the woods, following the path she had taken that morning.

She would go back to the table and her family. She would go up to her room and pack. She would write to Lia and, yes, to Laura, too. She would open the little leather bound notebook and begin a fresh journal. But not just yet. Right now she wanted to stop for a long minute and stand quite alone in a familiar field against a familiar sky, feeling in herself the end of something and the faint, confused stirrings of a new life about to begin.

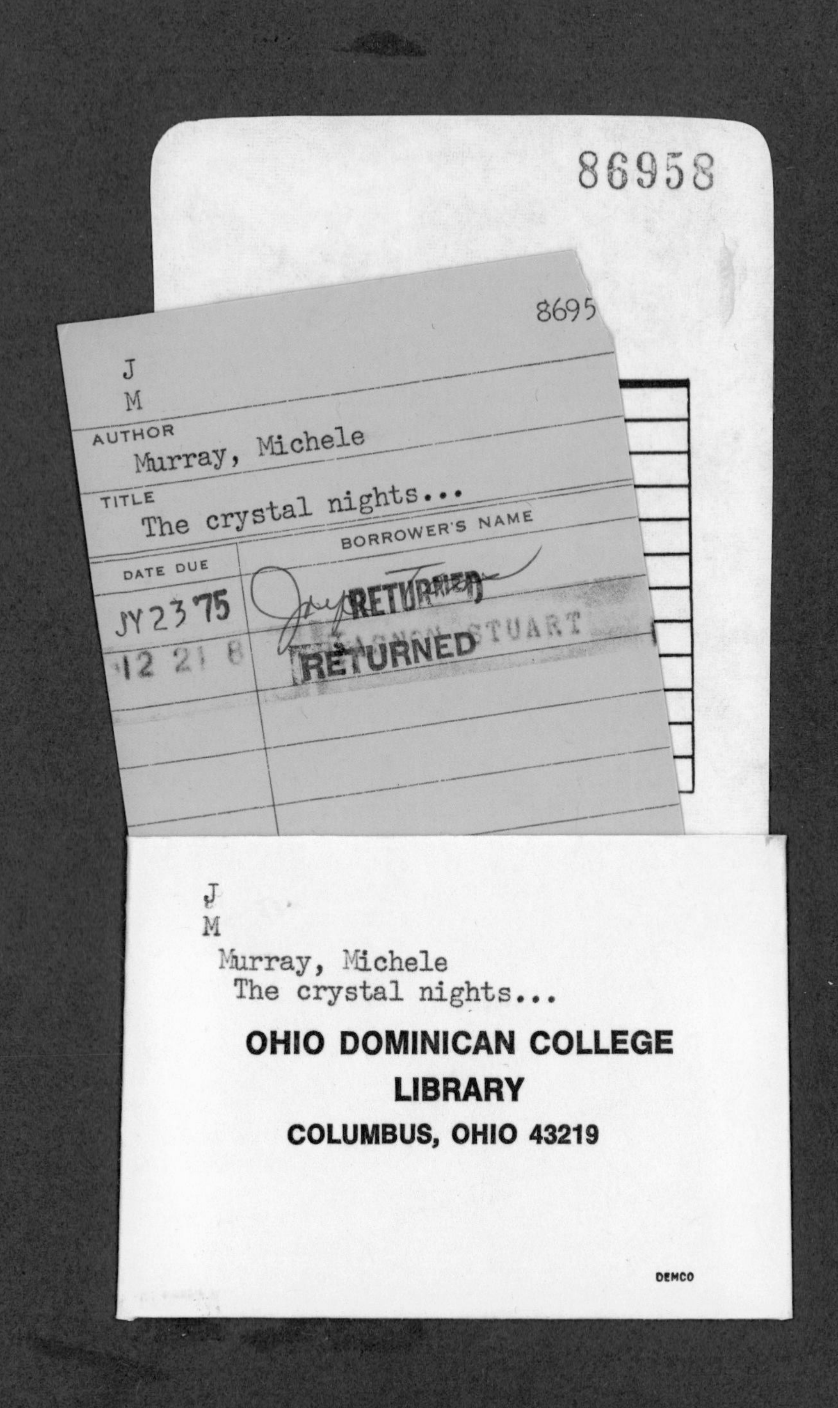